WEDDING SEASON

Book Five in the *Beach Reading* Series

"…the author creates one heck of a suspenseful page turner, featuring the characters already endeared to those of us who read the earlier books in the series. (While reading them all in order is not a must, as Abramson provides sufficient detail for 'newbies' to catch up on what they need to know, I do indeed recommend reading them all, as this is absolutely the best gay mystery series to come along in at least a decade!) As always, the writing takes you to the Castro instantly, and you can almost smell the sourdough bread!"

Bob Lind, *Echo Magazine*

"Abramson can tie more complicated knots and entangling nets than a 19th-Century sailor, his catch prolific and entertaining… 'Beach' is a state of mind, and Beach Reading can be done as enjoyably under an electric throw by the fireside as slathered in SP 40 by the lapping waves."

E.B. Boatner, *Lavender Magazine*

"Back in the 1970s, in the age of Harvey Milk and the singer Sylvester, a young man named Mark Abramson moved from his native [Minnesota] to San Francisco. There he became part of a generation of gay men who populated Castro Street and changed gay life forever, joining people such as John Preston, Randy Shilts and Al Parker (all of whom he befriended).

"Mark Abramson's love for San Francisco is most evident in his "Beach Reading" series; a gay valentine to the City by the Bay that promises to be the best book series of its kind since Armistead Maupin's *Tales of the City.*"

Jesse Monteagudo, *AfterElton.com*

WEDDING SEASON

Wedding Season

BOOK 5
IN THE
BEACH READING SERIES

Mark Abramson

Lethe Press
Maple Shade, NJ

Book Design by Toby Johnson
Cover Photograph by Chris Knight, Left Coast Scenes
Lighting by Doug Salin and Celso Dulay
Cover Model: Daniel Atwood
Author Photograph: David Bruner   www.davidkbruner.com

> *With special thanks to Giovanni De Grande for*
> *translating the rantings of Rosa Rivera into Italian.*

Mark Abramson
San Francisco
April 6, 2011

Published as a trade paperback original
by Lethe Press, 118 Heritage Avenue, Maple Shade, NJ 08052.
First U.S. edition, May 1, 2011
ISBN 1-59021-143-X   ISBN-13 978-1-59021-143-4

Library of Congress Cataloging-in-Publication Data
Abramson, Mark, 1952-
Wedding season / Mark Abramson. -- 1st U.S. ed.
    p. cm. -- (Beach reading series ; bk. 5)
ISBN-13: 978-1-59021-143-4
ISBN-10: 1-59021-143-X
    1.   Snow, Tim (Fictitious character)--Fiction. 2.   Gay men-
-California--San Francisco--Fiction. 3.   Family secrets--Fiction.
4. Castro (San Francisco, Calif.)--Fiction. I. Title.
    PS3601.B758W43 2011
    813'.6--dc22
                                    2011016032

Chapter 1

*C*hurch bells clanged and organ music thundered like the waves of a crashing sea. Tim Snow had looked forward to this day, his Aunt Ruth's wedding to Sam Connor. The ceremony would start any moment. He looked around and saw dozens of familiar, smiling faces seated at the Castro Theatre. Only… the Castro lacked a center aisle for the bride to enter on her father's arm and stroll out with her new husband and a beaming smile. And the entire room was far too bright to be a theater; the sun sent yellow shafts of light through stained glass windows onto the faces of women in flowered hats and men in suits and ties.

Tim stood at the altar beside Sam and his son Adam, the handsome fashion model from Chicago. The music changed and the organist reset the stop to sound a one-note trumpet fanfare. Now Tim wondered if they were in Grace Cathedral. It would suit Sam's style to be married at the top of Nob Hill, but Aunt Ruth would take a lot of convincing for anything so fancy.

A lone bridesmaid appeared, limped a few steps up the aisle and staggered. She grabbed the arm of a pew to right herself but reeled and fell. A middle-aged man in a blue suit tried to help her up, but she spat at him and pushed him away. Tim recognized his mother, blind drunk, but he was as helpless as anyone else to do anything about it. She dropped her bouquet and crawled toward the altar, drooling like a rabid dog. Her foot caught on the flowers, tore them apart and left a trail of crushed petals down the aisle. Tim's face turned red with

rage. Everyone must wonder why this pathetic woman was here.
Someone would figure out that the bride, Ruth Taylor, only had one
sister and since Ruth was Tim's aunt that could only mean that this
drunken woman must be… Tim would never admit it! He would
deny that he knew her, that he'd ever laid eyes on her!

Now he turned his anger toward Aunt Ruth, who hadn't yet
appeared. She should have known better. Why hadn't she warned
Tim that his mother was invited? She should have known that her
drunken sister would make a fool of herself and ruin Ruth and Sam's
big day —.

"—Hey! Wake up, Tim. Are you okay, babe?" Nick was
looking down at him, shaking him.

Tim murmured, "Yeah, yeah…"

They both lay back down and Tim felt Nick wrap one
strong arm around him, as warm and comforting as ever, and
soon they were fast asleep again.

Now Tim watched the wedding scene from above. The organ
music still played, but his mother was gone and it was peaceful
again. Waves lapped at a nearby shore and Tim could hear seagulls
and a distant foghorn. Maybe this was Adam's wedding to
Alexandra, but there was no ocean in Chicago. The organ's notes
turned into the sound of the sea again and faded away this time.
Now the congregation was dressed in pastels. Men and women wore
big flowered hats. Now he understood. Some of the men were in
drag.

It was a wedding alright, but it was at Arts restaurant on
Castro Street. The place was ten times bigger in Tim's dream than in
reality. Phil was playing the piano, naked, and there was no massive
pipe organ if you didn't count the one between Phil's legs. He wasn't
completely naked, either. He had on that silly bow tie and collar he
wore on special occasions with starched cuffs and silver cufflinks
and probably black patent leather shoes, although Tim couldn't see
Phil's feet. Tim moaned again —

— and felt Nick touching him, shaking him until he came
to.

"Huh?" Tim blinked. "Where am I? What's going on?"

"You're right here safe beside me, Snowman. You were just having another dream."

Tim was used to wild dreams, a common side effect of the HIV drugs he took every day. He didn't mind the dreams, as long as the drugs kept working, keeping his viral load undetectable and his T-cells were over 500 at last count. Most people had lots worse things than dreams to worry about; Tim knew there were lots worse things than HIV, too.

"What time is it?"

"It's almost seven thirty, time to get up. I was awake, anyway. It's time for us to pack up and head home pretty soon. You were mumbling about a wedding and then you mentioned Phil and something about an earthquake. I thought I'd better try to wake you 'cause you don't usually talk in your sleep. Are you sure you're okay?"

"Thanks." Tim sat up and rubbed his eyes. "Yeah… I'm okay… just a little headache. It wasn't such a bad dream except the part when my mother was shit-faced and ruining Aunt Ruth's wedding. I don't remember any earthquake. The whole thing was so weird and then I wasn't sure who was getting married. It might have been someone else. There were all these drag queens at Arts in big hats like Easter bonnets and lots of other people. I knew most of them."

"Do you want to go for a run on the beach? It might clear your head and we could work up an appetite for breakfast before we head back to the city."

"Head back…? What beach? Is that the ocean I hear? I thought I was listening to a pipe organ. Where are we?"

Nick lifted the palm of his hand to Tim's forehead. "It doesn't feel like you have a fever, but maybe you're a little warm. We're in a cabin south of Carmel. We were driving back up the coast from L.A., just taking our time and you said you wanted to stop here and spend our last night on the road. Don't you remember? We were planning to be back in San Francisco by this afternoon or this evening, but it doesn't matter to me. If you're not feeling well, we can stay here longer… at least until you feel better."

"Oh, sure I remember. I'm feeling okay now. Don't worry. It was just a dream."

"So… you were dreaming about a wedding, huh? Do you think it might have been *our* wedding? Yours and mine?

"Sam and Aunt Ruth were getting married," Tim said, ignoring Nick's attempt to get closer to him. "At first I thought it was in the Castro Theatre, but then I realized it was broad daylight and it would have been dark in there. Then it seemed like it was in some huge, cavernous place like Grace Cathedral or maybe St. Mary's or that big white one in Minneapolis just north of Loring Park."

"I think I detect a change of subject." Nick pulled away. "I was talking about you and me—"

"I remember last night and the night before and that place we pulled over in the car above the ocean and watched the sunset… You know, Nick, sometimes I think you and I do honeymoons so well that we should just stick to what we're good at. Why do we need to talk about getting married?"

"You remember all that, do you?" Nick slid in closer again and put one arm around Tim's shoulders. "Maybe we should go for a run."

"Yes, I remember now and I know a better way to work up an appetite than running." Tim pushed Nick back down on the bed. He kicked off the covers and climbed on top of him, straddling his chest. Then he leaned in close to nuzzle his neck and kiss him on the mouth. "Does it make me a top if I sit on it?"

"I'm not into labels, Snowman… just don't stop."

By the time they opened the door of the cabin the sun was high in the sky. They pulled on shorts and went for a barefoot run on the sandy beach and then took a shower together and finished packing. Check-out time was posted at 10AM but there was no one else around when they were ready to go. Tim dropped their room key through the mail slot of the locked office door. Maybe the proprietors were away on an errand.

They pulled over once to put the top up on the Thunderbird because a bank of white fog was piling in over the city. By the time they got home it would be cold enough to light the fireplace in Tim's living room on Hancock Street. Nick took a turn behind the wheel as they headed up California's Highway 1 toward Pacifica. Nick was happier than he'd been in a long time and he knew better than to press Tim again about any further commitments. Tim was right. They were very good at honeymoons. Weddings could wait.

Chapter 2

Ruth pulled a scarf over her head before she started the car. She felt dowdy in it, but no one would see her. She simply had to call Rene and beg him to fit her in while she was in the city. As she pulled out of Sam's driveway she felt not only dowdy but anxious and overwhelmed. All the way back to San Francisco from Hillsborough, she couldn't help wondering if she'd made a wrong decision, simply taken a wrong turn somewhere in her life or not been paying close enough attention to the signs all around her. She adored Sam. He was the best thing to come along since... She couldn't even remember the last best thing.

Sam was kind and gentle and handsome, a real silver fox, and they made each other laugh. He was crazy about her and he'd asked her to marry him and when it came right down to it... yes... she loved him very much. On top of that, although she hated to admit it, he was by far the wealthiest man she'd ever dated. She certainly wasn't after his money, but... oh... Why on earth did things have to be so confusing?

As soon as she set foot inside her apartment on Collingwood Street in the Castro district, Ruth felt better. Her cat Bartholomew gave her an angry glare and yowled at her for having been away so long. "What is it boy? Hasn't Teresa been feeding you enough?" She reached down to stroke the usually affectionate feline until he arched his back and let her

14

pick him up. "Oof, you're heavy!" She cradled him in both arms all the way to the kitchen and he finally started to purr again.

That was another thing; Sam wasn't much of a *cat person*. He wasn't exactly allergic to them, but whenever he stayed overnight with Ruth, he and Bartholomew kept a polite distance from each other. Sam had also made the mistake of mentioning her apartment in the past tense. It was over dinner just the other night. She'd tried making salmon the way Arturo taught her—hot skillet, not too much oil, not too long on either side—and it came out moist and perfect. She was so proud of herself when she savored the first flakey bite and then Sam had said something about how this apartment *used to be* so convenient for her when she worked at Arts, as if she didn't work there at all any more.

Her schedule at the restaurant was minimal these days, but the apartment was another matter. She couldn't imagine giving up this place. This was where her nephew Tim lived for years. This was where she'd spent her first few weeks in San Francisco the summer she decided to pack up her life in Minnesota and move out here. "But I have such wonderful memories here," she'd told Sam that evening over salmon. "You can't expect me to give all that up when we get married."

Ruth sat down on the edge of her bed and kicked off her shoes, remembering their conversation. "Don't you think someone else might need the apartment?" Sam tried to appeal to her thoughtful side, what he called her 'care about the world' nature.

"It's not as if there's any shortage of apartments in San Francisco these days, Sam. I see vacancy signs on every other block in the Castro. If and when Arturo and Artie ever needed that apartment, they would tell me. Besides, haven't you and I created some nice memories of our own here, Sam?" That was when Ruth reached across the table and ran the tip of her index finger up the side of his neck and around his earlobe. She still knew how to change the subject and make a man come around. "Eat your salmon, darling, and we'll have dessert later."

Now that she was home again, Ruth scrounged through her closet for something to wear to work. Between Sam's place and hers she didn't know where anything was these days. She had clothes everywhere. She'd neglected to do laundry before she left the city on Monday or during the time she was at Sam's house. Delia, the cook and head housekeeper, would have been happy to wash out a few things for her, but Ruth wouldn't hear of it.

That was another thing; where would she fit in with Delia after Ruth and Sam got married? Delia was the mother of Sam's only son Adam and she'd been running that big old house all these years, planning the menus, doing the shopping and most of the cooking. She was in charge of the rest of the household staff too, the other maids who came in to help serve whenever Sam had guests and to keep the place spotless. Delia was happily married to Sam's gardener, Frank, but it still seemed like a sticky situation. Ruth had agreed to marry Sam, but he'd said she would be "queen of the manor" and Ruth wasn't sure about the domestic arrangements. Besides, she'd told him there were already enough queens in her life, what with working in a gay bar and restaurant on Castro Street. She didn't want to be the queen of anything!

Ruth loathed confrontations of any kind. The only thing she didn't like about bartending was when normally pleasant people drank too much and got into a tiff about something. She hated it even more when she had an argument with someone she cared about. She almost never argued with Tim, but there was such a close tie between them they could practically read each other's minds.

Having an argument with Sam was equally foreign to Ruth, but there'd been tensions this week and it all boiled down to a wedding, what should be a happy occasion, and the problem wasn't even *their* wedding. Sam insisted that Ruth come to Chicago for the wedding of his son Adam to Alexandra, a beautiful woman he'd met in his modeling career. Once Sam got something stuck in his head, he could obsess about it until it drove Ruth crazy. As good as she was at changing the subject, Sam was set on this plan and he kept bringing it up.

Chicago was a long ways off, but there were elaborate wedding plans underway already. Sam insisted that since Frank was escorting Delia to the wedding, it would perfectly natural for Ruth to be there, too. The ceremony was to be held in a big African-American church and Ruth was sure she'd feel out of place with the parents of both the bride and groom there. The reception would be grand, too. Ruth didn't want to impose. All these thoughts were spinning through her brain as she got dressed for work. If Ruth and Sam were going to argue about Adam and Alexandra's wedding, she dreaded the day when they started making serious plans about their own!

Artie had the bar nearly set up for the dinner shift before Ruth got there. He'd been tending bar for nearly as many years as he'd been entertaining in drag. Both of them came naturally to him, but there was more money in tending bar these days and it was more comfortable in boy-clothes. Hell, as co-owner with his husband Arturo, Artie could wear whatever he wanted. He could tell something was bothering Ruth as soon as she arrived at Arts restaurant. "What is it, Ruth? Is Sam having cold feet about getting hitched? Or is it you that's having second thoughts?"

"It's not that so much, Artie," Ruth started cutting limes for the Saturday dinner shift. There were only a handful of early customers at the front end of the bar and a few at tables. One couple was lingering over dessert and apparently talking business after a late lunch at a window table. Artie stood at the end of the bar near the kitchen sipping a cup of coffee, waiting for it to get busy enough to come behind the bar and help out.

"Sam and I have hardly talked about our wedding plans. We've started to once or twice, but we haven't even set a date.

What's the hurry?" Ruth knew if it were just her and Sam there wouldn't be any problems at all. "We want to keep it simple, just a few close friends and immediate family. Tim and Nick, of course, and we want you and Arturo to be there, along with Jane and Ben and the kids, naturally… the neighbors on Collingwood." Even that list sounded like too many when she named them off out loud.

"Arturo and I were hoping you and Sam might get married here at the restaurant," Artie said. "He wants to cater the whole nine yards and have an open bar for your guests. I even talked him into closing for the whole day and we'll really do it up. Nick could decorate the place with potted trees and flowering plants and do some big arrangements, not to mention your bridal bouquet. We wanted to make it our wedding gift to you both. Arturo will be so disappointed."

"My goodness, it sounds like you and Arturo put more thought into our wedding plans than we have." Ruth hoped to nip this discussion in the bud, but she didn't want to appear ungrateful. "That's awfully sweet of everyone, Artie, but like I said, we haven't even set a date yet and I don't know when we will. Sam is out of town again. We were thinking of Christmastime at one point, but…"

"Oh, a Christmas wedding would be perfect! I'd love to decorate the place all in red and white and green!" Artie beamed. "If you don't want to have the ceremony itself here, you've got to at least let us throw a party in your honor."

"Oh… Artie! I just don't know…" Ruth felt herself starting to clam up and hold everything inside, even when it might do her good to talk about it. This just didn't seem like the time or place. Maybe she could sit down with Tim sometime, or have a nice visit with her upstairs neighbor Teresa one of these days. Ruth missed having more women friends to talk things over. All these gay men in her life were charming, but they were more interested in the latest gossip on Castro Street or South of Market than in having a good heart-to-heart.

As far as her wedding to Sam was concerned, an elopement or a quiet little ceremony down at City Hall sounded like just the ticket. There were so many people's feelings to be considered all of a sudden. "Maybe a party afterward would be nice, Artie. I just don't know when. There's so much to straighten out, first. We'll have to wait and see…" Her nephew Tim approached the waiters' station with an order for two dry martinis. "What do you think, Tim? Artie wants to throw a party here for Sam and me when we get married."

"I think that's a great idea, Aunt Ruth. In fact, I think you've almost got to." Tim started to remember his dream again. "Unless you're planning to have it at Grace Cathedral or the Castro Theatre, your friends would be crushed if they didn't get to help you celebrate!"

"The Castro Theatre?" Ruth laughed. "That's hardly what we had in mind. We're thinking small and simple and intimate. After all, it's a second marriage for both of us. The only thing we've decided on is that his grandchildren should be involved. Sarah is the perfect age to be a flower girl and little Samuel Timothy Larson could be an adorable ring bearer, although he's still awfully small. That's all the more reason to wait until he grows some more. It all sounds too formal to me, but I'd love to see those two kids dressed up for the photographs at the foot of the staircase at Sam's house… or maybe in the rose garden. Getting married in the rose garden would mean waiting for just the perfect time of year, but what's the hurry anyway? Maybe next June, a year from this summer…"

"I just have one stipulation, if I may…" Tim was serious all of a sudden.

"What is it?"

"I know it might sound silly, but I had this really weird dream the other morning just before Nick and I came back to town and… ," he trailed off.

"I'm well aware of your dreams, Tim," Ruth encouraged him to finish his thoughts. She knew how often his dreams held more meaning than Tim could understand. They'd even helped her solve his ex-boyfriend Jason's murder. Ruth's mother, Tim's grandmother, had been known for her dreams, too, although in those days people didn't like to listen to that kind of talk. "What was your dream about, dear? What did you want to stipulate about my marriage to Sam?"

"It's not about your marriage." Tim clicked the end of his pen with his thumb. "It's about the ceremony… what I mean is… Aunt Ruth… you don't intend to invite my mother, do you? I know she's your only sister, but she was in my dream and it was a disaster."

"You were having a dream about my wedding?" Ruth asked. "My, my!"

"I'm not sure. It was somebody's wedding. It could have been yours and Sam's. Nick got worried and shook me and woke me up before it ended. It might not have been yours, I suppose, but my mother was there and she was stinking drunk and she ruined everything."

"I've hardly thought about your mother lately. Yes, she's my only sister, so I try to keep in touch. There's a small part of me that still believes in miracles. I know how poorly your parents treated you, but I try not to give up on people. I wrote her a letter quite a while ago. She doesn't have e-mail."

"What did you write her about?"

Ruth thought for a moment. "Let me see… I must have mentioned Sam. I may have said that your health was good and that you'd inherited Jason's house on Hancock Street. Of course I did. That's why I told her she could write me at your old address from now on, not that she ever sent a letter there before. Anyway, I haven't ever heard back from her."

"Good!" Tim walked away, satisfied with her answer and his tray of drinks, and Jake approached the bar to order a pair of Ramos fizzes for the couple in the window still going over some contracts.

Ruth separated an egg and dropped the white into the blender. "Oh, Artie… it's all too much. You know what Tim said to me the other day? He said we should just skip the wedding and go on the honeymoon."

Artie laughed. "He would! He and Nick must have had a nice trip down the coast and back. He's been smiling ever since he came back to work. That boy has had his share of honeymoons over the years and no one has ever managed to slip a ring on his finger."

Jake said, "No, the rings they wear are always somewhat lower on the anatomy… and I don't mean he's gotten anything pierced, Ruth. Don't worry; he would have told me or at least asked for my advice about it."

Ruth wasn't sure what Jake meant by 'somewhat lower,' so she just smiled and flipped the switch on the blender, cutting off any further conversation for a moment. She no sooner finished Jake's drink order than a party of eight walked in the door and the phone started ringing. "Artie, I think I need you now. Get the telephone, would you? I'll greet the newcomers." Ruth headed toward the front end of the bar and the stools were soon filled with customers. Artie was grinning from ear to ear when he hung up the phone.

"Who was that, Artie?" Ruth asked. "Good news?"

"You'll never guess who's coming in for dinner tomorrow night! Oh, my God! You're not working, are you? I need you, Ruth. I'll have to redo the whole schedule."

"No, you don't have me down for a double; I think Scott's working, though."

"Well, I need you to work and everyone had better be on their best behavior, that's all I've got to say. I'll call Scott and tell him to get a haircut by tomorrow afternoon."

"Who's coming in for dinner, Artie?"

"Rosa Rivera, that's who!" Artie shouted, but Ruth looked blank. "Don't you watch television, Ruth? She's all the rage. She has that show called *Let's Make it Happen* on cable access. I can't believe you don't know her, Ruth! And I can't believe she's coming here to Arts! The publicity will be fabulous! I should call the gay papers, at least. I'll have to get a fabulous arrangement for behind the bar and fresh flowers on all the tables. Wait 'til I tell Arturo!"

Tim headed toward the front where more new customers were looking over the menu and Ruth got his attention. "Tim… have you ever heard of this Rosa Riviera person?"

"Oh sure, she's a camp. She's got some kind of TV show, but I've only watched bits and pieces. I think it's on late at night. Last Halloween a bunch of guys on Castro Street went dressed in drag as her."

"Tim says he knows Rosa Riviera, Artie," Ruth tried to sound encouraging.

"It's Rivera, not Riviera and of course he knows her. Everyone does!" Artie was jotting down notes on a piece of paper. Next he relayed the big news to Jake, who'd have to work the brunch shift tomorrow instead of dinner. Tim and James would work the dinner shift with Ruth and Scott behind the bar and Phil at the piano. As liberal as he was, Artie didn't want Rosa Rivera's first impression of Arts to be their heavily tattooed and pierced waiter, Jake. "You know… Rosa Rivera is fast outgrowing her cable access show. She's even had spots on the KRON weekend morning show between Jan Wahl and Henry Tannenbaum."

"Wow, that's hitting the big time!" Jake snorted and Artie glared at him.

"I don't watch a lot of television. What does she do, exactly?" Ruth asked.

"You name it! Cooking, fashion, arts and crafts… remember back when Martha Stewart was in prison? If only Rosa had been around then, she could have stepped right in and filled her shoes. And she does it all with such a cosmopolitan flair. She's going places, you mark my words! I've never seen her in person, but I watch when they repeat her show late at night sometimes when I get home from work."

"How exciting, Artie," Ruth tried to feign some enthusiasm, although she had never heard of this woman.

"Tim, you're going to have to wait on her table," Artie said.

"I'm not even on the schedule for dinner tomorrow, Artie," Tim complained. "I'm supposed to work Sunday brunch with Jake, like always."

"Sorry, you'll have to switch. Jake and Patrick can do brunch and you and James can work dinner. I wish we had more ethnic employees to show off besides James. Ruth, you simply must be here to work with Scott behind the bar."

"That's fine with me, Artie. Sam's going away on business again anyway, so I was already planning to stay in the city this week. I don't have any other obligations." She stopped to think as soon as the words were out of her mouth. She'd planned to get her hair done, if Rene could squeeze her in sometime. She also had a ton of laundry to do, and some letters to write. There was nothing she had to do on Sunday evening, though, and she was starting to get curious about this woman that Artie was so enamored with. "Is Rivera a Spanish name?"

"I think she's Italian. She has the most darling accent. Well, you'll meet her tomorrow and we can find out. I'll take the night off from behind the bar so I can act as host. I don't know what I should wear! I'll be a nervous wreck, I'm sure."

"You'll be fine, Artie."

"Ruth, can you watch the bar by yourself for a minute? I've got to run back to the office and redo the schedule and make a few phone calls. It's going to cost me a fortune to get the flowers I want on such short notice. Maybe I can reach Nick to help me."

"He's at my place, Artie," Tim said.

"Good. Then I've got to go see what Arturo has planned for the specials tomorrow night. They'd better be fabulous! Oh, I've got a million things to do and I'm sure I won't sleep a wink tonight. Gawd, I wish she'd given us more notice. I can't believe Rosa Rivera is going to be *here* tomorrow in person!"

Chapter 3

Tim crept up the stairs on Hancock Street and slipped his key into the lock. He didn't want to wake Nick, so rather than turning on the tap in the kitchen he grabbed a bottle of water to wash down the pills he'd already laid out. "How was work, Snowman?" Nick yawned. He'd fallen asleep with the television volume turned low, but he was awake now. The light from the screen played across Nick's bare chest and shoulders. Now that Tim was home, he was happy to keep him company, if nothing more. The musical guests on *Saturday Night Live* were beginning their second number, which signaled that it was nearly the end of the program.

"It was okay… fairly busy." Tim slipped out of his shoes and unbuckled his belt. "I didn't mean to wake you. Sorry. Have you been asleep long?"

"It's okay. Not long. I lasted through most of the evening news. There wasn't much news, really, but it's supposed to be warmer weather tomorrow and through most of the week."

"I think I'll take a quick shower. I feel kinda sticky."

"Oh, it's Scissor Sisters. They're supposed to be gay, or at least some of them are. A friend of mine went to see them perform at the Warfield last time they were in town and he raved about them."

"Do you mean one of your employees?"

"No…" Nick reached for the remote to turn up the volume. "I have some friends outside of work, you know, but this one also happens to be a client." Nick didn't mean to sound bitchy, but he was still groggy and Tim was talking while he wanted to hear the TV.

Tim didn't know why he was questioning Nick. It wasn't that he didn't trust him. Tim felt better in the shower, letting his tensions run down the drain with the soapy water. Still, it was strange to think of Nick having friends Tim didn't know about after all this time. He had friends with whom he discussed pop music groups? He never talked about music with Tim, but then Tim didn't pay much attention to the latest fads in music or movie stars or politics or celebrity gossip. Nick was always more aware of what went on in the world than he was.

At least Tim was never bored when Nick was around. They were spending 'quality time' together these days, as the pop-psychologists on the TV talk shows might say, not that Tim wasted time watching talk shows, either. Tim spent most of his days off during the mid-week up at Nick's house overlooking the Russian River. And Nick timed his drive down from Monte Rio on Friday nights to arrive in San Francisco when Tim was getting off work at Arts. They might stop for a drink at one of the Castro bars afterward, but they were usually eager to go back to Tim's house on Hancock Street and climb into bed. Some nights they pretended it was their first time and some nights they did it on the kitchen table or in the bathtub or the living room in front of the fireplace. Some nights it even felt like their first time, but not lately… not since they'd been back from L.A. Nick usually stayed until Monday morning, but that cut it close for his work, since he did the bank deposits from the nursery on Mondays. Fortunately, most of the traffic was heading into the city at the hour when Nick headed out over the Golden Gate Bridge.

Tim was about to turn off the shower when he saw Nick standing at the toilet. "Wow, you must have been holding that for a while. Been drinking beer?" Tim reached for a towel.

"Don't turn the water off, babe. I was coming in to join you."

Tim stepped out of the shower and gave Nick a quick kiss. "I'll meet you in bed, okay?" Tim knew that a lot of guys envied him. Nick was a great looking guy. He was fun and smart and sexy and successful, and he was good to Tim. They were crazy about each other, but every once in a while a small part of Tim missed the old days, the lonely days, the exciting days when he had no one to answer to.

"Don't fall asleep before I get there."

Sometimes Tim just wanted to go out and trash around and sometimes he just wanted to be alone. It seemed like a stupid thing to complain about and Tim wasn't really complaining. He was just frustrated by the sameness of his life these days. There was comfort in coming home to find Nick asleep in his bed, but sometimes Tim just wanted to curl up and crash. Tonight he was tired and now Nick was wide awake. Tim almost hoped that if Nick wanted sex tonight, they could hurry up and get it over with and get some sleep.

Their car trip to L.A. was fun, but it felt like a sexual marathon. It had been great, Tim had to admit, but enough was enough. They'd spent hours in the car talking about plans for the house on Hancock that he'd inherited from Jason. Some projects Tim could do by himself, even if they took months. They would add to the value of the place if he ever wanted to sell it, though Tim couldn't imagine that day would ever come.

Property values were something Nick would consider more than Tim would. Nick could picture Tim selling the house someday to move up north to the Russian River where they would live happily ever after in marital bliss among the rustic redwoods. Nick was all about growing old together. Tim didn't like the idea of getting old at all.

Nick must have changed the channel after *Saturday Night Live*. There was a movie on now, but it was one Tim had already seen. He flipped through the channels past a lot of infomercials and landed on a station playing music. He didn't care. Now Nick was singing in the shower and Tim was fighting sleep. His mind floated off in a dozen directions, the evening at work at Arts, his Aunt Ruth's upcoming marriage to Sam, his recent dream about a wedding, customers at the restaurant discussing politics, whether the Giants would win another World Series next year and whether the 49-ers would ever get to play in another Superbowl or complaining about their lousy neighbors planting trees or building another story onto their houses to block what little view they had left.

Tim was half asleep when Nick got out of the shower. "I couldn't hear what you said, Babe. The water was running."

"I didn't say anything. Maybe I was talking in my sleep. I was thinking how everyone on Castro Street is planning my Aunt Ruth and Sam's wedding."

Nick appeared in the bedroom doorway naked, rubbing a towel through his long blond hair, so he still didn't hear. "What's that, Snowman?"

Tim thought he should tone down his exaggeration. More people on Castro Street were actually planning what they needed to pick up at Walgreens or Cliff's or planning whether or not to go see some old movie star who was appearing *live and in person* at the Castro Theatre next Friday night. Or they were thinking about the sexy stranger they saw bending over to tie his shoe at the ATM outside the Bank of America and hoping he would be at the same bar they were going to that evening. "I said it seems like everyone at work is talking about Ruth and Sam's wedding."

"Oh, right… Have they set a date yet?" Nick pulled back the covers and slid into bed.

"No, I don't think so."

"I've been thinking about cutting my hair. What do you…?"

"No!" Tim was wide awake now. He threw his arms around Nick and pressed his face against his chest, taking in the slick clean smell of his skin. "You can't cut your hair. I love your hair." Tim reached for a strand and held it to his lips. The moon must be in some weird sign tonight, Tim thought, even though he didn't take much stock in such things. One minute he was half asleep and wanted Nick to leave him alone and the next minute he was obsessing about something as silly as the length of Nick's hair. Hair would grow out again.

"What's all this about?" Nick wrapped his arms around him. "I should threaten to cut off my hair more often."

"Your hair is perfect just the way it is. You remind me of the covers of those trashy romance novels at Walgreens, stripped to the waist and rescuing the fair maiden from the clutches of evil."

Nick grinned and slapped Tim's ass. "Alright, then. I won't cut it. But what are you doing reading trashy romance novels?"

"I don't read them. I just look at the covers when I'm shopping for cards or wrapping paper. Those guys are way too straight."

"Well, that's a relief!"

"I did read a bunch of gay novels a while ago that Arturo loaned me."

"Like what?"

"I thought I told you... books by Felice Picano, Armistead Maupin, John Preston, some David Sedaris. Arturo had them packed in a big box on Collingwood and he loaned them to me before I moved over here. I'd stick one in my backpack every time I went to Baker Beach or Land's End or over to Black Sand in Marin. I finally finished them all."

"Look out for John Preston. He'll give you kinky ideas."

"Oh, yeah? How would you know?"

"I read *Mister Benson* back in college."

"And what might happen when I get those ideas?"

"We'll have to spiff up Jason's old playroom, that's what. His sling is still down there in the basement, isn't it?"

"It should be. I loaned it to Jake for his birthday party, but he brought it back. I can't imagine us *playing* in the basement with the pitter-patter of Sarah and her little brother Samuel's feet over our heads."

"We could move it upstairs and make the spare room into a combination playroom, guest room, office…"

"There's a lot of other stuff to do around here too. Are you still planning to take out that sickly old redwood tree in the back yard? It's getting worse. It would improve the view of downtown."

"I can get some of my guys to do it. Okay, first the tree and then the playroom. I thought you wanted to refinish the floors too."

"One of these days…" Tim said. Nick's grandparents had lived in this apartment for years with the hardwood oak floors covered by wall-to-wall carpeting. They rented the upper floor of the duplex from Jason's lover Karl, who left it to him several years before Jason was murdered and subsequently left the house to Tim. The kitchen and bathroom had layers of ancient linoleum, but the same oak flooring ran throughout both levels. Jason had refinished the floors on the downstairs flat years ago. Nick had also suggested new decks off the back of both units and stripping the paint off the mantle of the fireplace. "Yup… one of these days," Tim repeated.

"You better get to sleep," Nick snuggled closer and readjusted his weight. "You have to work Sunday brunch and I have a long drive ahead of me."

"Right… Sunday brunch." Tim had forgotten about Rosa Rivera and the change in plans at work. "But you don't usually work on Sundays, Nick. What's up?"

"I'm short staffed, remember? Jenny's on vacation and there's a big wedding at one of the wineries this week. We're not only doing the flowers, they're renting a truck load of trees and erecting a tent for the reception."

"Yeah, I guess I forgot. Come to think of it, I'm not working tomorrow morning. Artie changed the schedule at the last minute. Have you ever heard of Rosa Rivera?"

"Sure, she's like the poor man's Martha Stewart. I've seen her on TV a couple of times. '*Let's make it happen!*' You've seen her, no?"

"Make *what* happen?"

"That's her motto or her theme or whatever… '*Let's make it happen!*' You mean you've never seen her show? What about her? What made you think of Rosa Rivera?"

"I've never watched a whole episode, but I know who she is. She's coming to the restaurant for dinner tomorrow and Artie acts like there's royalty in town or something. Didn't he call you about the flowers?"

"I had my cell turned off."

"Well, he's changed the schedule so Aunt Ruth will work behind the bar with Scott and he wants me to wait on Rosa Rivera's table. He's got James coming in, too. I guess he wants to show her how diverse we are with our one black waiter."

Nick's only response was steady breathing. He was sound asleep. Tim slid his hand up the arm that was wrapped around him and pulled Nick's hand to his lips to kiss each finger in turn. He reached for his pills on the bedside table, swallowed them down with a slug of bottled water and wished both Nick and himself a night of sweet dreams.

Chapter 4

Tim reached across the bed, but Nick was already gone. Damn! He'd been dreaming about Nick, or someone who looked like him, for the past hour. Maybe the dream only lasted a few minutes. It was hard to tell with dreams. *Seven minutes.* That stuck in Tim's head. In seven minutes he might go crazy if he didn't do something. Why didn't he and Nick get it on last night? He was about to explode!

Tim didn't have to work the brunch shift today. He could pop in a porn CD or one of the old VHS tapes from Jason's collection. Pornography pre-AIDS was hotter than most of the stuff they made these days. It was exciting to watch guys doing the things you weren't *supposed* to do anymore. Barebacking was innocent then and it was still fun to watch. Tim couldn't spread any diseases just by watching. He could get off in seven minutes and then get on with his day, vacuum the apartment, clean the windows, hit the gym or paint the kitchen.

Tim looked out the west windows at the fog, still thick and hovering over the city. He rolled onto his side, punched the pillow and had a third idea. He could go somewhere. He could throw on some clothes, grab the car keys and take a drive. There had to be someplace in San Francisco where a guy could find some quick relief on a Sunday morning. There must be other guys in the same predicament out there in the hills surrounding Eureka Valley. Couldn't they help each other out? Seven minutes was still stuck in Tim's head… or seven inches… or was it just the number seven? A lucky number.

If this were a medical condition, he would see a doctor. No, Tim had to take care of it on his own… or with the help of a sexy stranger who had the same needs this morning. It should be as simple as getting a haircut or having his teeth cleaned.

Nick was gone until Friday, so he was no help. Nick wouldn't have to know about this. Nick should be past the Golden Gate Bridge by now. He might have crossed the Marin County line into Sonoma. Tim remembered the drive-in movie on the county line. He and Jason stopped there once outside the fence one clear night on their way home from the river. They smoked a joint, put the top up and the seats down in Jason's old Thunderbird while a straight porno movie flickered across the screen. They almost got caught. That was hot, but the thought of it only made Tim's present situation worse.

If he had a boil he could see a dermatologist to have it lanced. The throbbing would stop once that fluid was out of there. Then Tim would be able to get on with his day, stop at Cliff's and pick up paint samples. He wanted to paint the kitchen first. The wallpaper Nick's grandparents had when they lived here was faded and starting to peel. He wanted to strip the linoleum from the oak floors. Jason would have finished that project by now. Nick offered to help Tim do it, but Tim thought it was a rainy-day job and there was no rain this time of year.

He could drive up to Buena Vista Park in less than seven minutes—fog or no fog—and be home again in half an hour. That was Tim's last thought before he fell back into a deep sleep and a dream that was so vivid that he could have sworn it was real.

In Tim's dream, he lit a joint before he pulled out of the driveway. He took a second hit before he turned left to 19th Street and he was high before he turned right onto Castro. When he drove past Arts he was so stoned that he forgot he was only dreaming. He'd been this stoned for real a few times, so stoned that he *thought* he was dreaming, but this time it was the other way around. It didn't much matter to Tim. It was the same sensation either way. A guy in front of Cliff's Hardware waved and smiled. He was either an Arts customer or someone who recognized Tim from the gym. Tim lifted two fingers off the steering wheel to return the greeting. He turned left onto 14th Street. Jason used to drive this way to visit a friend on Roosevelt Way. Tim went along once, but that guy had long ago moved away… or died. Tim knew he was stoned when he had trouble parallel parking on Upper Terrace.

A man yelled, "Morning!" He was another one of those people Tim recognized, but wasn't sure where from. The man had to be in his fifties or sixties, tattooed, muscular… white T-shirt, Levis, boots. He was sexy, one of those guys Tim wanted to be when he reached that age if he lived long enough, the kind of handsome that a really handsome man always is, no matter his age… well-preserved, the kind of man who takes care of his body. He was almost at Tim's car now. The man's pale blue eyes radiated wisdom and kindness, but hadn't he had those same eyes since he was a boy?

"How's it going?" Tim nodded and lifted two fingers again. No reason not to be friendly.

"Lots of horny guys, but not much action, mostly window-shopping, not trying anything on... I've got to get to church." The man had a motorcycle parked across the street. He unlocked his helmet from the chain and pulled it over his head. "Seeya, Tim."

He knew his name! Maybe he was a friend of Jason's who also recognized the car. Tim hoped he wasn't a friend of Nick's. There were no secrets in the Castro.

Even in Tim's dream, the morning had turned warmer in the seven minutes since he left the house. The sun was making the fog dissipate and the quiet was serene, so high above the city. Tiny birds chirped and squirrels rustled through the trees, but Tim heard little else. A slight breeze whispered through the eucalyptus trees above him.

The park had been re-landscaped in the past year or two, part of Obama's stimulus package, Tim imagined. Most of the old cruising grounds of crumbling pathways, gnarled undergrowth and hidden cul-de-sacs had been torn out. New paved paths and wooden boardwalks—everything sterile and handicapped-accessible—spanned the southern hillside of prim new seedlings, neatly spaced rows of groundcover planted into soil that was soaked with decades of histories, gallons of spilled seed and rich stories.

Nick would know the names of all the plants, of everything that grew here. Tim recognized lilies and irises, nasturtiums that grew like weeds and California poppies blooming golden everywhere. It was a more logical choice of state flower than Minnesota's. Tim had never even seen a lady's slipper in the wild, only in the greenhouses.

Now Tim knew for sure that he was dreaming. The park was the way it was… before the new landscaping. The old dirt paths were still there; the crumbling earth, the tree roots worn from men's asses in Levi's sitting on them, creating make-shift benches. Used condoms littered the ground. Branches provided enough privacy for a tryst with a stranger... or three or four. The old park had been landscaped by nature and thousands of footsteps of men who had trolled these paths for decades.

Tim remembered a night when fog filtered through the undergrowth. It made him think of the forest in *Sleeping Beauty* and he wished a prince would hack his way through the brambles to find Tim in the castle at the top of the hill and wake him with a kiss. The park still had a storybook feel in the morning, or Tim was stoned, even in this dream. That could be it.

He'd heard stories, no doubt from Jason, of nights when the road to the top was still open and lined with cars. Every night after the bars closed, cars and campers and pickup trucks with mattresses in the back filled the parking lot. They partied for days and nights, weekends and weekdays, as long as their drugs held out. Wild stories! Nowadays, you were more apt to see new mothers pushing strollers under the same trees where men in leather used to hang their slings.

Tim grabbed his car keys and headed up the hillside, stepping in poison oak and glad he was wearing boots and long pants. He saw another man on the path who looked sexy until he got closer and Tim caught a whiff of a pungent smell. Cologne? After-shave? Maybe only soap, but it went straight up Tim's nose. How could anyone get near him unless they had a bad cold? Stupid.

The next man he saw was on a path above him... interesting, from a distance... shirtless, handsome, well-built—great chest. He wore mirrored sunglasses, so Tim couldn't get a look at the eyes. Sometimes the eyes were important. Or not. Even in a dream, his seven minutes were up a long time ago. It felt like an hour since he'd started the car in his driveway on Hancock Street.

The guy saw Tim too and started down the hillside toward him. Then Tim noticed the black sandals and red socks that must have been a Christmas present... in high school. Didn't this fool own a full-length mirror? He was obviously a gym fanatic, but he must spend all his time on his upper body and completely ignore his pasty little legs. Even that might be okay, but Tim couldn't get past red socks in leather sandals.

Then Tim saw the third guy and he felt like Goldilocks. This one was *just* right... dark and handsome with hard nipples that poked through thick black chest hair under a mesh white tank-top. Tim loved Nick's blond Nordic look, but variety *was* the spice of life and this was only a dream, after all. Tim couldn't feel guilty about a dream. Olive skin and thick black eyelashes made him look... Mediterranean? Tim was guessing.

"Sup?" The guy spoke to Tim. "Lookin' for trouble?"

Tim only smiled. Did the guy have an accent? That was always a turn-on. The two of them ducked into a nearby cul-de-sac of gnarled branches overgrown with wild ivy where they shared a seven-minute adventure. The guy offered Tim a handkerchief afterward, but Tim had his own, so the man said his thanks and walked away. Tim stepped out of the damp shade and sat down on a sunny log to catch his breath in the afterglow. Branches above him framed a picture of distant rooftops and ships on the bay. The morning sun cast angular shadows across the valleys. Tim wondered how a place so beautiful could exist in the heart of the city. But how could a city even be as beautiful as San Francisco? Even the fire-trucks' wailing sirens were so far they sounded like a memory.

Tim should have left by now, but it was too late. The swarthy young man came back and sat down on the log beside him. "Ready for round two?" he asked. "You're the hottest guy here today, man..."

This was supposed to be anonymous, wasn't it? The accent wasn't as sexy, now that Tim was finished. "Thanks... no... I've got to go. I was just chilling out." Tim attempted a smile. "Did you just get here? Maybe you need to look around some more."

"Maybe you're right. My name's Bruno." He extended his hand.

The formality of shaking hands seemed strange after the intimacy of sex. Tim thought about Nick and felt guilty. He fumbled with his bottle of water, dropped it, picked it up again and reached out his hand to return the greeting, barely whispering, "I'm... Tim... hi..." He almost made up a name. Something was wrong with anonymous sex that wasn't.

"Seeya later, Tim." Bruno lifted his shirt to wipe his forehead and in so doing he exposed his chest. Then he peeled the shirt off over his head, laced it through a belt loop and walked away.

"Wow!" Now Tim wanted to reconsider the offer of "round two," but Bruno was following a young redhead who had just walked by. Tim headed toward the Thunderbird, but he heard noises coming from an alcove below him. Three muscular men, one on his knees, the blond in the middle was getting the lion's share of attention. Tim could only see the back of his neck and his denim shirt draped over one bare shoulder. Their movements were smooth enough to have been choreographed.

Tim imagined they'd met at the gym that morning and then came up here after their workouts in order to more fully appreciate each other's bodies. It beat getting kicked out of the sauna by someone who wasn't getting any and didn't want anyone else to either.

They moved to the left and Tim saw that the blond had a pony tail just like Nick's. One of the others pulled it loose with his fingers and the blond shook his head to let it fall. No one else had hair like that besides Nick! Tim jumped, lost his footing and started to slide. He tried to grab hold of a branch, but it snapped off and the racket was enough that the men stopped what they were doing. Tim rolled over and over as he fell, like Alice down the rabbit's hole, and landed at the feet of the three big men. "Hi…"

"What have we here?" The blond asked. He looked nothing like Nick, which made Tim smile until he laughed. All three of them were fully hard and standing over him, unperturbed by the interruption, except for maybe the laughing part. Tim wanted to say something more, but they weren't here for conversation. Tim wished he could take a picture of this. He wished Bruno hadn't come along first. He wished he hadn't fallen, hadn't laughed, and hadn't made such a fool of himself.

Now the moment was gone. "Sorry, I…" Tim stood up, brushed himself off and found his way back to his car. They were out of his league, anyway, and they couldn't have thought he was laughing *at* them. They were right out of a porn movie. Tim drove down the hill and found a parking spot in front of Walgreens. Within seven minutes he was looking at paint samples in the back of Cliff's. Tim's mind was back on what he wanted to do with his day, vacuum the apartment, clean the windows, or paint the kitchen. After seeing those three men in the park, he wanted to hit the gym more than ever. Then he noticed a really cute guy in white painters' pants that were spattered with more colors than the rainbow flag outside on the corner of Market and Castro Streets.

The painter noticed Tim, too… gave him a big smile and was just about to say something to him when Tim woke up.

Chapter 5

Tim half expected to find a wet puddle of white overflowing his navel when he awoke, but he hadn't had a wet dream in years. Even when they were wildly sexual, the most vivid dreams he'd had since childhood, Tim's psychic dreams—part of that so-called "gift" he'd inherited from his grandmother—even when they were crisp and clear and bright, they were obviously never intended for his pleasure. That was one more reason Tim resented them. If he had to be cursed with dreams he didn't want, couldn't he at least have a wet dream now and then? And now he had a headache too.

Tim nearly forgot about Rosa Rivera coming to Arts this evening. He usually worked the brunch shift on Sundays, but today he'd have to go start work at about the time he was usually leaving. Without Nick to wake up to, this didn't feel like a Sunday at all, but as long as he had the day free, he might as well get something done.

Tim chugged down his pills with a cup of coffee and a big bite out of a bagel that he finished on his way down the stairs. He walked over to Cliff's to look at paint samples for the kitchen. Even if he did nothing more than look, it was a step in the right direction

The same guy in the painters' pants from Tim's dream was at the hardware store. Tim didn't notice him at first. His back was turned, but Tim recognized the spattering of colors on the fabric of the pants leg. Then the guy turned around and... sure enough, it *was* the same guy. Tim couldn't help but stare, which the guy took for cruising and grinned. Tim jumped, startled that the man was real, and gave him a big foolish "aw, shucks" grin in return.

Tim loved cruising, even when he never expected anything to come of it. At its essence, it was just two guys acknowledging each other, an energy exchange in which each of them was lifted a little higher, both of them had their day brightened. Still, if his dreams were this real nowadays, Tim's psychic gift must be getting stronger. And he imagined that having wide-awake sex with this guy might be fun too.

It wasn't that Tim wasn't satisfied with Nick. He knew how lucky he was to have found him, how lucky the two of them were to have found each other, but every once in a while he missed being single. Maybe he missed the thrill of the hunt. Tim would never jeopardize his relationship with Nick and he'd never hurt anyone's feelings intentionally. It was just that he'd woken up horny this morning and with Nick not around the old patterns returned to mind. After all, he'd been single a lot more years than he had been in a relationship.

Tim spent the next hour scraping the crumbling old linoleum off the kitchen floor, but it wasn't very gratifying. It was taking forever. Tim finally gave up, showered, found a clean shirt and pressed a crease into his slacks to wear to work. He knew Artie would want him to look his best to wait on Rosa Rivera.

Tim gasped when he entered the restaurant. It hadn't been so filled with flowers since Jason's memorial gathering a couple of years ago. He felt a split-second pang of déjà-vu and the heart-dropping sense of loss over Jason's murder, even after all this time. Then he thought of being held tight in Nick's arms and he snapped out of it. "Wow, Artie, you've really outdone yourself! It looks like the first floor of Macy's at Easter time!"

"It better look good. These flowers cost me a fortune and I couldn't get hold of Nick, so I had to pay retail for everything."

"He had his cell phone turned off. You should have called over there on my land-line and yelled at him over the answering machine."

"Well, it's too late now. Ooooh, I'm a nervous wreck! Rosa Rivera will be here in an hour or so!" Artie kept saying the same things over and over. "I wonder what she's like in person. I wonder what she'll order. Out of all the restaurants in town, I can't imagine why she even *heard* about this one. What does she want?"

Ruth tried to calm Artie's fears as best she could. "Maybe she's an old fan of yours from when you were at Finocchios. She's probably coming here to get your autograph."

"I knew every time there was a celebrity in my audience at Finocchios and they came there to see Artie Glamóur! They weren't coming to see *this* tired old thing!" he wailed.

"Maybe she wasn't a celebrity back then."

"Oooh… I hope she never saw my old act. She'll expect someone else entirely, someone years younger and lots thinner! How bad do I look? Be honest with me. I must have gained five pounds since breakfast."

"You look fine, Artie!" Ruth insisted. Artie had on a black long-sleeved shirt, black slacks and black patent leather shoes. He was wearing more jewelry than would ever be considered masculine, but the only color he sported was a red tea-rose boutonnière in his lapel.

"I just wonder what she wants. I wonder what she'll order. I wonder what she drinks." Artie was so nervous he was driving everyone else crazy. "James, are those flowers drooping already? Make sure they have water in them!"

"I'm not even supposed to be here," James said. "Don't yell at me. Where's Patrick, anyway?"

"He worked brunch. He had to leave early to catch a flight to Palm Springs," Artie said as Jake walked in the door and Artie turned on him, "What are *you* doing here? I gave you the night off."

"I forgot my book. I'll bet it fell out of my backpack in the kitchen." Jake walked slowly toward the kitchen doors as he took a good look around. "Besides, I wanted to see how the plans were shaping up for the grand arrival of her majesty. You've put out even more flower arrangements since brunch, haven't you, Artie?"

But Artie ignored him. "Tim! That knife has a fingerprint and I can see water spots on that wine glass. Change it right away, please. Ruth, there's dust on that Jack Daniels bottle."

Arturo was usually the more stable one in their relationship, but even he was getting nervous about cooking dinner for this woman. Artie's anxiety was rubbing off on him too. He stood in the doorway to the kitchen and listened to Artie bark orders at their employees until he couldn't take any more. "I've never even heard of this Italian broad!"

"You should all watch her TV show," Artie said to no one in particular as the doors to the kitchen swung shut behind Arturo. "The other night she took a wooden table that looked like it came from a garage sale and when she was done with it, you could have sworn it was on loan from the DeYoung museum. Then she designed a whole party buffet around it. She's brilliant! Oh, I've learned some amazing things from her, like how to get beet juice out of white chiffon."

"I've never even seen you wear white," Ruth said over her shoulder as she continued to dust the liquor bottles with a bar towel.

"And I thought you hated beets!" Tim said.

"I bought some pickled beets for Arturo. He likes them. Then I dropped the jar in the kitchen sink at home and it splattered all over the place. The juice came out of the fabric, thanks to Rosa Rivera's little tip, but there's still a stain on the ceramic tile. I should ask her about that."

"What was her secret tip for the fabric?" Tim asked.

"I'm not telling," Artie pouted. "None of you deserve to know. All you do is make fun of her... and me! If you start watching her show sometimes, maybe you'll catch that episode in reruns."

"Nobody is making fun of *you*, Artie…" Scott said. "Maybe *her*, but not you. Would you like a cocktail? It might help settle your nerves."

"Just a tall glass of club soda with a squeeze of lime, Scott. That haircut looks good on you. You should keep it like that."

"Thanks, Artie…" Scott always wore his red hair short and he thought it had been a waste of money to get an unnecessary haircut just to humor Artie, but he didn't argue.

Artie stared out at the passersby on Castro Street for a few minutes. He took a sip from his glass and then turned back toward the bar. "Ruth, dear…" he whispered, "put a splash of vodka on top of this, would you? Not too much… well… more than *that*!"

"What's Patrick doing in Palm Springs?" Ruth asked.

Jake watched Ruth top off the glass with vodka and answered her question before Artie had the chance. "Haven't you heard? Patrick is going back to the Betty Ford clinic."

"No… I hadn't. I'm so sorry!"

"It's only for a reunion," Artie said. "Jake… shame on you! That's how rumors get started, you know… and if you're going to be here when Rosa Rivera arrives, take some of that jewelry out of your face!"

"I'll be out of your hair in a minute, Artie. Patrick told me there was a very famous closet case in his group at Betty Ford and he thinks he can get some more dirt on him this time. Maybe he can even *out* him!"

"Who is it?" Tim asked. "Is it someone we know? An actor? I know… I'll bet it's another one of those *family values* politicians. Maybe Patrick can seduce him if he's not too ugly."

"Patrick couldn't tell me his name," Jake said.

"They're sworn to strict rules about confidentiality," Artie turned back to Ruth and smiled, "just a touch more vodka on top, dear."

"But he *did* say…" Jake paused for suspense, "… that it's someone we used to see on television all the time."

"Is he a soap opera star?" Tim asked.

"No… better yet…" Jake was enjoying this. It might turn into a fun evening to stick around and watch and besides, Artie couldn't really yell at him if he was off-duty. "He's a very well-known… very closeted… very homophobic… Republican!"

"I knew it!" Tim shouted. "Aren't they all?"

James agreed. "The ones that are always foaming at the mouth against gays are usually the deepest in the closet."

"I'll say!" Tim agreed.

"Until they come out,' Jake said, "and then, instead of foaming they're drooling over all they've missed!"

"*Ciao*, everyone!" All eyes turned toward the door as a vision of buxom flesh in sparkling layered fabrics swept into the room. It was Rosa Rivera, live and in person and there was nothing subtle about her appearance or her entrance. "*Che carino*! What a sweet little place. *Questo va benissimo!*" she said loudly and then added, under her breath, "This will be perfect for the plan I have in mind…"

Chapter 6

Rosa Rivera's outfit showed off her breasts to their maximum effect. They obviously had major support from some marvel of engineering that she wore under her clothing. When Ruth saw the beauty mark on Rosa's cheek she wanted to dampen a handkerchief to wipe her face as she'd done to Tim and Dianne when they were little. She had to control herself to keep from spitting on a cocktail napkin.

"Rosa Rivera!" Artie rushed forward and kissed her hand. "I'm Artie. Welcome to Arts. Thank you so much for coming. It's such an honor to meet you!"

"*Grazie mille*, Artie… I am charmed to meet you and what a lovely diamond! *Molto bello…*"

"This old ring?" Artie blushed.

Jake said to Tim, just barely out of earshot. "Look at those heels! I don't know how she does it. They must be six inch stilettos! And her make-up reminds me of Tammy Faye Bakker… may she rest in peace."

James crossed himself at the mention of Tammy Faye, then chipped in. "Man… I'll betcha that woman could show cleavage in a turtleneck!"

"Do you think they're real?" Tim asked.

"Don't be silly!" Jake scoffed. "They don't move a whisper. I've seen drag queens with tits that looked more real than those! I'm gonna get closer so I can hear what they're saying..."

"May we offer you a cocktail?" Artie asked. "Miss Rivera, this is Ruth Taylor. She'll get you whatever you'd like to drink and I'll have just a tiny splash of vodka in this one, Ruth, please..."

"Campari and soda, if you don't mind. Not too strong, not too much ice and with a twist of lemon, please. What a sweet little uniform... Ruth, is it? Did Artie pick that out for you?"

Ruth had her back turned to reach for the Campari bottle and it was lucky that Rosa couldn't see the look on her face. Uniform, indeed!

"That's not a uniform," Artie laughed. He could only imagine what Ruth must be thinking. "Now, Rosa... may I call you 'Rosa?'... Didn't you have a reservation for two? Who's joining you?"

"My assistant is parking the car. Ah... here he comes now! Bruno! I'd like you to meet Artie. He's one of the owners of this charming little place. *Bada a ciò che fai e non mettermi in imbarazzo!*"

"How do you do, Artie..."

Tim couldn't believe his eyes! It was the same Bruno he'd met in his dream in Buena Vista Park this morning, but now the dark hairy chest was covered in a gray suit, an ivory shirt and a green silk tie. Bruno turned toward Tim, but his gaze was fixed on Phil who was just sitting down at the piano.

Artie seated the two of them at a window table that wasn't even in Tim's section, but signaled for him to come over. Other customers were staring now. Tim wondered whether they were fans of Rosa's television show or if they were checking out her sexy escort. Bruno did look stunningly handsome in his suit and Tim could only wonder if he was as hairy in real life as he was in the dream.

"I'd like you both to meet your waiter, our wonderful Tim Snow." Tim managed a polite smile and nod of the head, but they didn't notice him. Between Artie's fawning over Rosa and her attempts at flattery in return, Tim might as well have been invisible. Rosa may have glanced in his direction, but it was hard to tell under the thick mascara on her false eyelashes. When Bruno wasn't busy checking out Phil, his eyes were locked on his menu.

Tim's instinct was to be insulted that Bruno ignored him after they'd had sex with each other that very morning, but it was only a dream, after all. When he reminded himself that Bruno had never seen him before, Tim was relieved, but still a little hurt. He supposed some people came to restaurants for other reasons than to check out the waiter, but this was Castro Street. Bruno could have at least taken a break from staring at Phil to flirt with Tim a little.

The restaurant was busy! Tim didn't normally work Sunday nights, so he wasn't sure what was normal. He guessed that some of the crowd was made up of Rosa's fans and others were just curious. Artie must have told everyone he knew that she was coming.

After dinner she asked to see the kitchen, so Artie took her back to meet Arturo while Bruno disappeared onto the sidewalk to smoke a cigarette.

"You don't like her, do you?" Tim asked his Aunt Ruth across the bar.

"I would never say anything nasty about a successful and independent woman with a television career and her own business." Ruth unloaded a tray of dirty glasses onto the sink behind the bar. "It would sound like I was jealous and I certainly am not…"

"What did she do to piss you off?"

"She made a point of complimenting me on my 'uniform!' Does this look like a *uniform* to you? Tell me. I bought this dress at Neiman Marcus. It was on sale, but still; it's Neiman Marcus. I usually wear slacks and a blouse to work in, but Artie insisted that I wear a dress tonight and she thought it was a uniform and that Artie had picked out for me. Hmmph. Why don't *you* like her, Tim?"

"I never said I didn't like her. Did I? She just seems conniving to me. I don't know what she wants, but she's not just here for drinks and a free dinner. Artie sure is crazy about her though, so I don't want to say anything negative... not yet, anyway."

Artie and Rosa returned from the kitchen and sat down at a pair of open stools at the front end of the bar where Scott was working. Arturo came out a few seconds later and asked Ruth for a stiff shot of bourbon. She poured him a double, which he swallowed in a single gulp before he went back through the swinging doors to the kitchen without another word.

"Where is Bruno?" Ruth asked James when he came up to the waiters' station.

"He's out in front having a cigarette. All those Europeans smoke, don't they? He followed Phil out to the sidewalk when he went on his break."

"I'll bet she doesn't know about apples," Ruth said to Tim as they listened to Artie pretend to know French while speaking to an Italian about crepes and foie gras. What was worse, Artie hung on every word that fell from her overly-painted lips and pretended to understand them all too.

"What do you mean about apples, Aunt Ruth?"

"Oh, nothing... just that she knows all about shad roe and pheasant and which clams are in season, but I'll bet she doesn't know what apples make the best pie or which ones you want cold and crisp from the refrigerator or which ones are the best during football season to put on a stick and dip in warm caramel with chopped nuts. Just look at her carrying on."

"Okay, you talked me into it," Tim said. "I don't like her either and I'm sure Arturo doesn't. I wonder what she did to piss him off. Did you see him chug that shot? What was it?"

"Bourbon."

"Oh-oh. That's not a good sign. He gave up bourbon a while ago."

Tim went into the kitchen to fetch one of his last dinner orders, but Arturo had his back to him, so Tim didn't ask any questions. It would all come out in good time. This crew was like a family—dysfunctional at times, but secrets didn't stay secret for long.

When Tim got back to the bar, things were slowing down. Rosa's laugh had died down a couple of decibels and she was slipping back into the outer layer of her ensemble, finishing her drink and getting ready to leave. Phil hadn't returned to the piano yet, but Tim didn't see anyone on the sidewalk. "Where's Bruno now?" he asked his aunt. "Did he go to retrieve the car for the grand dame?"

Ruth didn't hear him, but Tim noticed Bruno and Phil coming out of the men's room together, just as Rosa started looking around for her wayward assistant. Tim was glad his first encounter with Bruno was only a precognitive dream. It was obvious that Bruno had another interest at Arts. Tim turned back to totaling his checks while he wondered whether Bruno knew that Phil was a hustler.

"Artie, I'll talk to you soon." Rosa turned back to wave at the entire restaurant in a royal farewell as she sang out, "*Arrivederci*, everyone! Let's make it happen!"

Tim had nearly forgotten about Bruno and Phil when he felt a pinch through the fabric of his slacks that made him jump. It was Bruno. "Nice ass, Tim. Seeya!"

Chapter 7

Tim usually spent his nights off from Arts up at Nick's place on the Russian River, but this week he stayed in the city to work on his kitchen. He'd barely opened one eye on Wednesday morning when he heard a chainsaw outside. He thought he was dreaming, but when he opened the other eye the noise was as real as his hangover. The clock on his dresser said 9:02 AM. Beside it was a stack of new porn CDs, still in their cellophane wrappers. Now Tim remembered the winning streak he'd had with his raffle tickets at The Edge last night—a benefit for the AIDS Emergency Fund. Every time he won another prize he bought another round of drinks for the guys on either side of him and a shot for the bartender. It was good public relations when you worked in the Castro. Tim figured there ought to be a way to take it off his taxes; being a homeowner was expensive.

The chainsaw was real and it was nearby. Tim stepped into a pair of jockey shorts on the floor and pulled them up while he shuffled to the kitchen window. He saw a crew of workmen, some on ladders and some standing around under the redwood tree in his back yard. Nick said he'd get rid of the diseased tree for him, but Tim hadn't expected it to happen so fast. The root rot had taken years to come on with the uppermost branches turning brown and then yellow. Nick called it "heart rot" as only Nick would, giving an almost human aspect to most living green things. He told Tim he suspected that it started when the next-door neighbor's house had a leak in their basement plumbing.

Tim stepped out onto the deck, still half-naked in only his jockey shorts, and yelled, "Hey! What's going on here?"

"We work for Mr. Musgrove," one of the workers answered. He looked like a college kid, husky, tanned and very cute. "He told us you wanted this sick tree out of here."

"I did, but…" Tim still couldn't believe this. "I *do*. But I didn't expect it to happen today! Where the hell *is* Nick? I mean Mr. Musgrove?" Tim was sure the only time he'd put those two words together before was when he was first introduced to Nick's father. "Didn't he come with you?"

"No sir. We were supposed to start a job in Marin County this morning, but they cancelled, so Mr. Musgrove told us to come here instead. He gave us your address and directions to find the place. This won't take long. We're good. You'll see."

The chainsaws started up again before Tim could say any more. He closed his back door and the kitchen windows he'd left open overnight. He did want the tree out of there. It needed to be removed; that would make his view of the lights of the downtown skyline even better, but this was morning! He hoped Jane and the kids downstairs were already awake. No one could sleep through this noise.

Just then the doorbell rang. Tim reached for a pair of old sweatpants and, hopping from foot to foot, pulling on the pants, stumbled to the front window. He looked down. "Aunt Ruth! Come up if you can stand the noise."

When Ruth got to the top of the stairs she started giggling and pointing at him. "What were you thinking when you got dressed this morning?"

"I didn't exactly 'get dressed' this morning. The chainsaw woke me and I just grabbed whatever…" Tim turned toward the mirror, lifted the elastic waistband and looked down his crotch. "Geez, I must have these on backward. Want coffee? I set the timer before I went to bed last night. I can smell it. It's ready."

"Maybe not," Ruth shouted as the chainsaws kicked back into high gear. "I can't even hear myself think. What's going on?"

"Nick sent some workmen to take down that sick old redwood tree. I was planning to get rid of it anyway, but I would have put if off for months."

Ruth held her fingers over her ears and shouted, "Let's get out of here! Can I take you out to breakfast?"

"Can I go like this?" Tim looked down and remembered he was wearing nothing but his sweat pants. He had his fingers over his ears, too.

"That's entirely up to you, dear, but you might want to put on some clothes."

"Nudity is all the rage in the Castro these days," he shouted. "I've seen naked guys sitting in the plaza outside Orphan Andy's lots of times."

"Let's eat indoors, then. And I think most restaurants require shirts and shoes, even here in the Castro."

"I haven't even showered yet." Tim sniffed his armpit, removed a finger from one of his ears and held his nose with it instead. "I want to hear all about Sunday night… especially about Rosa Rivera. Did Artie tell you what she wanted?

"I can't *hear* you!"

"You go on ahead and I'll be quick, I promise. You wanna try to grab us a booth at Orphan Andy's? I'll take a quick shower and be there in fifteen minutes… well, maybe twenty, okay?"

"Take your time," Ruth yelled and nodded. "I need to make a stop at Walgreens anyway."

Even with the shower running, Tim could hear the chainsaw. He hoped none of his neighbors were upset. If he'd known in advance, he could have warned them. He let the hot water pour through his hair and down his back for just a minute after he rinsed off. Then he jumped into some clean clothes without getting fully dry and tossed his dirty sweats in the general direction of the hamper. This afternoon might be a good time to do laundry… or not. Tim could always procrastinate.

Ruth was sitting in the window when Tim arrived at Orphan Andy's. "Nice! This is even better than a booth. I'll bet you have good parking karma too. So… what's up? Are you and Sam still getting married or has he started beating you again?"

"Don't even joke about a thing like that… it's so far from the realm of possibility and you know it!"

"What is it, then? Doesn't he still want to marry you?"

"Of course he does. Do you know what you're going to order?"

"Woody knows what I want… two, two, and two."

"What?"

"Two eggs, two hotcakes, two sausages… or you could have bacon instead." Woody is a part-time nudist too, aren't you, Woody?"

Ruth turned, leery of being introduced to a naked man, but their waiter was pouring coffee at the counter and hadn't heard Tim. And Woody was wearing a kilt today, to Ruth's relief. "Maybe I'll order an omelet, but I suppose they're huge here."

"Do you still want to marry Sam?"

"Of course. It's just that things are so complicated. I want the best of both worlds, you know? I don't want to give up my little apartment and my job and everybody at Arts and you and—"

"Give up *me*?" Tim sat up straight. "What does he intend to do, spirit you away to some exotic foreign country? What's wrong with the house in Hillsborough? I thought things were going fine between you two."

"Things *are* going fine. That's my point. Things are fine the way they are. Why change anything? He thinks I'm going to give up San Francisco entirely, give up my apartment and find another home for Bart. Now he thinks he's allergic to cats, he says…"

"Well, if worse came to worst… Bartholomew could come to live with his Uncle Tim on Hancock Street." Tim said the words without an ounce of conviction.

"Nevermind. Maybe Bart can become an outdoor cat."

"I think you've just got cold feet. There's something to be said for marriage, isn't there? Isn't that why we gays are fighting for it so hard? I never cared one way or another, but I love to see the right-wing nuts go into hysterics about it and in your case it's totally legal and there's a lot to be said for marrying into money!"

"I don't need Sam's money—" Ruth was interrupted when Woody arrived to take their order. Now Ruth wondered what he might be wearing under his kilt, so she didn't dare to look at him. She realized she'd been about to raise her voice, so when Woody left and she started in again, she lowered it a notch. "I don't need Sam's money. I have my own money. And besides, he has children and grandchildren to think of… with more on the way. That's another thing; he wants me to come to Chicago for Adam and Alexandra's wedding."

"So? Why not?"

"Delia and Frank will be there. They're going early, in fact. And Alexandra's parents, of course…"

"And you're afraid of being the only white woman at the wedding… is that it?"

"No, that's not it!" The other waiter refilled their coffee cups and Ruth lowered her voice again. "I'm more concerned about being the only white woman in that big old house in Hillsborough."

"What? You don't get along with Delia? Since when?"

Four young men got up from a booth to leave. One held the door open for the others while a 1940 streetcar clanged its bells and started off its run to Fisherman's Wharf by making the curve through Jane Warner plaza. Woody brought their food and Ruth unfolded her napkin. "Listen to those fog horns, will you? We're blocks from the water, but they sound so close."

"Don't change the subject. Did you and Delia get into a cat-fight or something?"

Ruth chewed slowly and shook her head. "Delia is wonderful to me… to Sam, to Frank, to her son, to everyone. That's the problem. She runs that house so beautifully, where do I fit in? It was one thing when I was a guest, but after we're married, I don't know. They don't need me. She and Sam have so much history together. They have a child together—"

"Adam is no child," Tim interrupted, "and neither are you."

"They'll soon have grandchildren together!"

"So what? Adam and Alexandra are crazy about you. Everyone loves you, Aunt Ruth. Have you talked to Sam about any of this?"

"I tried to, but it felt like it was going to turn into an argument and I don't want that, so I dropped it and changed the subject."

"Aunt Ruth…" Tim took a sip of his coffee and waited until he was sure she was listening. "Did you want my advice or were you just looking for an ear to bend? I mean, if you just want to vent, you can say so. I'm willing to listen and keep my mouth shut. I know I can always count on you to do the same for me, but…"

"Do you *have* any advice for me?"

"Stop shying away from that argument. You and Sam are always so lovey-dovey I'll bet neither of you has ever raised your voice."

"Tim, you know me better than anyone. Considering my background with Dan, you can understand why I hate to argue."

"Now, don't bring Uncle Dan into this. Sam Conner is nothing like him and you know it! Sam deserves better than any such comparison."

"I know he does." Ruth smiled.

"So talk it out with him. If you end up having an argument, at least it will clear the air. You'll both know exactly where you stand. He didn't fall in love with you because he could boss you around!"

Ruth's visual focus was on her fingernails, trying to open a little foil packet of jam, but she was listening. "I suppose you're right. She caught her reflection in the window and instinctively touched her hair. She was a good-looking woman for her age, as long as she had her brilliant hairdresser Rene to cover the gray and she didn't let her figure get any larger than petite. She gave up on opening the jam and wished she'd ordered fruit instead of a big heavy breakfast.

"Then you get to have the fun part, you know... making up again."

"Sam and I have never had so much as a disagreement over what to eat for dinner."

"Why would you? You can order whatever you want from the waiter at Fleur de Lys."

Ruth laughed. "Yes, it's true... I'm a very lucky woman."

"Just wait until the time is right. Get his shoes off. Better yet, get his pants off. Get him in a good mood and then ask him where you stand. Tell him how you feel. Don't be in any hurry. Wait until just the right moment... and then let me know how it goes."

Ruth shook her head and smiled at her nephew. "You're too much."

"Now, what about Rosa Rivera? What did Artie tell you? What did she want with him? What's going on?"

"It wasn't Artie that she wanted, but the restaurant."

"Speak of the devil. Look, there she is!"

Ruth glanced down at this morning's *Chronicle*. The Datebook section had a quarter-page article and photograph of Rosa beaming at the camera. The caption read: *"Rosa Rivera—local rising star makes it happen again."*

"Not there," Tim said. "Look outside. There she is live and in person!"

"Oh my." Ruth covered her mouth. Rosa and a camera crew were getting out of a van parked in the Chevron station. She beamed at the handful of people sitting at the outdoor tables as if they were there just to see her. The camera crew set up a few shots of Rosa among the potted trees with the giant rainbow flag billowing on the other side of Castro Street in the background. "Tim… what if she sees us?"

"So what? Do you really think she'd recognize you *out of uniform*? She wouldn't remember me. She barely looked up at me the whole time I was serving them. Tell me what she wanted at the restaurant."

"Well, you know that coffee table book she did on Holidays and Celebrations?" Their waiter arrived to clear the next table and asked if everything was alright. "I'd love another cup of coffee, Woody, whenever you get a chance. And do you mind if I have a look at this newspaper?"

"Someone left it there," the waiter said. "You can have it if you want."

"Never mind the *Chronicle*," Tim placed the palm of his hand across Rosa's picture. "You can read it when you get home. What did she want at Arts?"

"I was trying to tell you… she's planning another book to go with her new season of TV shows. This one is all about San Francisco weddings—neighborhood by neighborhood. She's doing a big Italian wedding in North Beach and a Chinese wedding in Chinatown. She's found a Samoan couple getting married out in South San Francisco. I hear they have some wonderful rituals, not to mention the food."

"Yum."

"Artie told her that Sam and I might be getting married in a Hillsborough mansion and you should have seen her eyes light up. I could have killed him!"

"Did you say anything?" Tim asked.

"I gave him such a nasty look I didn't have to. He told her Hillsborough was well outside the city limits and that '*Bay Area Weddings*' doesn't have the same kind of ring to it that '*San Francisco Weddings*' does. She's hoping this project will get her nation-wide exposure. That woman won't be satisfied with cable access for long. Channel 4 is not her final destination, either, you can mark my words."

"That's all well and good, but you still haven't told me what she wants with Arts."

"Well, naturally, she wants to include a gay wedding. Artie asked her why she didn't just go to MCC or any gay-friendly church, but she wants to do it in a gay restaurant on Castro Street. She'll also have more latitude than she would in a church. She'll transform the whole place and give Stanlee Gatti some competition. You can imagine how Arturo feels. He didn't care for her at all!"

"Why not?"

"You saw how she is. Arturo's old-fashioned. He likes me, but he's not all that crazy about women in general, especially not when they're loud and pushy."

"Arturo adores you, Aunt Ruth, but you're no average woman."

Ruth laughed. "Well, Arturo's first impression wasn't good. She was sticking her fingers into everything, tasting his sauces, pushing the new dishwasher out of her way. It'll be fun to watch them work together on this project. Poor Arturo…"

"Do you think it will come to that?" Tim asked. "Is this idea of using Arts a done deal?"

"You know Artie," Ruth said with a sly grin. "He can always get his way. He just has to pretend Arturo's the boss. It works the same way with a lot of straight couples, you know."

"Fascinating." Tim was thinking how he might be able to use that psychology on Nick if he ever needed to.

"You've known them both a lot longer than I have, Tim. I'm surprised you never noticed."

"Who does Rosa have in mind for the gay couple? Anyone we know?"

"Artie suggested all sorts of people. You know… like Tony and Jeff, my neighbors that moved into Ben and Jane's old place. They're young and good looking and they'd photograph well.

"You mean they're both butch, right? I'm sure Rosa wants gay guys who don't look too gay. Do Jeff and Tony *want* to get married?"

"I don't know, but they might be willing to for the sake of a good party and being on television and all the gifts. I think the winners get a free cruise or something... some kind of trip. Your name came up, of course. You and Nick would be Artie's first choice."

"Oh-oh! Nick would like nothing better, but he's *serious* about it. I don't think he'd want to do it on a television show," Tim thought about it for a moment. "He'd better not try to trick me into something. He knows how I feel. I'm like you. I don't want change. Things are fine with me, just the way they are. We don't need the gifts, either."

"Don't forget about your complimentary copy of the coffee table book that goes along with the series." Ruth was being sarcastic now. "It'll be chock full of photographs and recipes and all sorts of helpful wedding tips!"

"Artie can forget about it. I wouldn't mind if Nick and I had more time to spend together, but I like my freedom. I don't want to get married. I'm all for the fight against Proposition 8, but mostly because it pisses off the right-wing conservatives. Whenever Nick brings up having a ceremony, I change the subject."

"Have you had an *argument* about it yet?" Ruth asked with a satisfied smile.

Chapter 8

Tim intended to go home after breakfast and get back to work on the kitchen floor, but the noise of chainsaws was still deafening, so he kept walking, right past his house, and ended up in Dolores Park. Tim thought it wasn't warm enough to take off his shirt and lie in the sun, but a few die-hards near the uppermost corner were unfurling blankets and squeezing cold tubes of expensive sun-tanning products across their bare flesh.

Ruth headed home after breakfast, too, but stopped at Buffalo Whole Foods at the corner of 19th Street. She was daydreaming over a basket of figs when she felt a tap on her shoulder. "May I buy the pretty lady a drink?"

"Artie... you startled me!"

"What are you up to?"

"Nothing... I just had breakfast with Tim and I'm heading home... nothing at all. You?"

"I was going to walk over to the restaurant, lock myself in the office and finish up some paperwork, but you could be an angel and help me procrastinate. Besides, how often does a gentleman offer to buy you a drink on *this* street?"

"It's too early for alcohol. Maybe I could force down another cup of coffee." Ruth smiled and took his arm as they crossed Castro Street toward Arts.

"How's Tim this morning?"

"He's fine, but they're taking down that sickly old redwood tree in his back yard and the noise is horrible."

"Who are *they*? Not Tim and Nick, I hope."

"No, Nick sent some of his workmen down from the nursery.

"Good. That must be a dangerous job… such a big old tree… and I can't imagine Nick chopping anything down, as much as he likes to grow things. I'd expect him to try nursing it back to health the way he did Tim after his accident."

"I think that old tree was beyond help, some kind of root rot, but maybe that's why Nick sent his people to do it when he wasn't around. He couldn't bear to watch them cut it down. I'm sure it will be a good thing in the long run. There'll be more sunlight for new things to grow."

"And that'll give Nick and Tim another project."

Ruth thought about Nick and Tim planting new things together and it made her feel old. As hard as she tried to ignore the fact, tomorrow was her birthday. Even though most people assumed she was younger, Ruth's driver's license insisted that she was pushing 60. Her life was more than half over while Tim's life with Nick was in its infancy, or so she hoped. Her relationship with Sam was no longer new, but that was just as well. She didn't have the patience for growing pains anymore.

"And how are you doing these days, Ruth?"

"Fine," Ruth answered Artie's question as if it were only small talk. He had the coffee machine brewing behind the bar and Ruth sat down on a barstool, but her mind was a million miles away. She was glad she'd been able to talk to Tim about some of her thoughts, but she still wasn't happy. Maybe she would have to talk things out with Sam—or 'argue' them out, as Tim suggested—and suffer whatever consequences came of it. Maybe she was only imagining that things were as bad as she thought. She wasn't even sure whether Sam really was upset with her. But how could Sam go out of town on business when tomorrow was her birthday? Tim hadn't mentioned it either and he had to know when it was. It seemed like she was the only person on earth who knew when her birthday was except for the DMV. Ruth never liked a big fuss, but it was nice to be remembered. Was it possible that Sam didn't even know the date? She knew when *his* birthday was, but she'd gone through his wallet once while he was in the shower in order to be certain.

Ruth wasn't sure whether Sam was acting cool toward her because of her not wanting to go to Adam's wedding or maybe his feelings toward her had dwindled when she dropped hints about not pressuring her into their marriage plans. It wasn't like him to forget her birthday, though. That could be a deal-breaker. He must know... or did he? Tim was busy these days, too. Certainly he would remember to call her at some point tomorrow.

"Are you sure?" Artie interrupted her train of thought and set his own steaming mug of coffee at the space next to hers before he came around the bar to join her.

"Sure of what, Artie?"

"Are you sure you're fine?" Artie clarified his question. "You seem a little down in the dumps these days, that's all. If everything's okay at Tim's house, then I guess there's a problem with Sam? Or is it something else that's bothering you? I hope you're not having a problem with anyone here at Arts."

"What makes you think that?"

"Don't try to bullshit me, Ruth. You may think I'm just a silly old drag queen, but—"

"Artie, I never!"

"I know you weren't too crazy about Rosa Rivera's visit the other night, either. This isn't about her, is it?"

"Artie, where do you get such ideas?" Ruth tried to sound defiant, as if he could read her mind and she should do something to stop him. It never worked, but she tried. Her face must be an open book. But Rosa Rivera hadn't entered her thoughts in a good fifteen minutes, so Artie was barking up the wrong tree on that account.

"Nobody else liked her either, if that makes you feel any better. She's quite the character, I must admit, but in spite of the way she comes across in person, that woman is very popular with the public and she's going places. Mark my words, when her new wedding series on TV makes it big and the souvenir wedding book comes out, it could really put us on the map."

"You're so funny, Artie... I was just telling Tim this morning to 'mark *my* words' and now I don't even remember what we were talking about. Well, I hope you're right about Rosa."

"I'm always right. Why doubt me now?" Artie asked with grin. "Rosa Rivera will be famous nation-wide within a year and we can say we knew her when. Just think, if you can get one second of air-time on her special, people will flock to Arts, just so they can buy a drink from Ruth Taylor and they'll leave huge tips so that you'll never forget them. You'll get postcards from your own fans from around the world! The tourists will take more pictures in front of Arts than at Coit Tower and the Golden Gate Bridge combined. They're always taking pictures in front of Harvey Milk's old camera store up the block. Maybe we can get a plaque in the sidewalk too."

"And I suppose if you got to appear on the show, it would be very good exposure for Artie Glamóur."

"Hmph! Well... maybe you don't need the money, but the rest of the employees could use the extra tips if we had more business. I'm just looking out for everyone else's well-being."

"Business is already pretty good these days, isn't it?"

"You're only here working on the weekends. We could use some help the rest of the time. Sometimes we don't ring up enough sales to make it worth turning on the lights."

"I didn't know that..." Ruth tried to act sympathetic, even though she knew Artie exaggerated wildly.

"But enough about Arts and Rosa. Are you sure there's nothing troubling you, dear? Is there anything I can do to help?"

"I've already talked things out with Tim this morning. He thinks I need to talk things out with Sam. I don't know if it would do any good to go over it all again with you. I know you're a good listener Artie, but it's no big deal. It's just that Sam wants me to go with him to Adam's wedding and I'm not sure where I'm going to fit into things in Hillsborough, much less Chicago. Oh... I might be better off going home and cleaning my apartment. Sometimes just getting some chores done can make everything look rosier again. I need to dust, water the plants, run the vacuum around and I know there's some laundry to do."

"I have work to do, too, but I tell you what. Why don't you let me take you out for a nice lunch this week... just the two of us? How about tomorrow? If you're feeling better by then we'll call it a celebration and if you're down in the dumps, we'll get roaring drunk. We can tie on a beauty and drown our sorrows. How does that sound?"

"Lunch sounds nice, Artie." Ruth swallowed the last of her coffee. "Call me in the morning and tell me where. I don't have any other plans tomorrow at all."

Ruth hadn't imagined that her only birthday celebration would be lunch with her landlord and employer, but it was better than nothing. She stood up and turned toward the door before Artie could see the tear that was about to roll down her cheek.

Chapter 9

On Thursday morning Artie was still going over the list for Ruth's surprise party. He'd reached all of the guests except Teresa and she lived right across the hall from Arturo and him on the top floor of their building on Collingwood, but now he was back at the office in the restaurant. He'd called the Indian restaurant three times with details he'd forgotten earlier. He had to make sure everything would be perfect. It was nearly time for him to get dressed to head downtown when he got Teresa on the phone.

"A party for Ruthie? I'll be there with bells on! I already got her a card at Walgreens. It's the only place in the neighborhood you don't have to sort through a million pictures of naked men just to find a nice pretty birthday card." Teresa had lived in Arturo and Artie's building on Collingwood since her divorce from her high school sweetheart Lenny, now an out and proud member of San Francisco's gay "bear" community who preferred to use "Leonardo" ever since he'd met his new "hus-bear" Teddy... er... Theodore.

Teresa still slipped up sometimes. She was known for her love of a good cocktail but she was so good-natured that no one ever dared confront her about her drinking and she was a large enough woman to handle it well, usually.

"Now grab a pen and write down the address. I'm surprised you already knew it was her birthday."

"I have a calendar with everyone's birthday I know. It's on my computer. You know me; if I didn't have it written down someplace I wouldn't remember my own name." Teresa let out a laugh while she wrote down Artie's instructions. "Is Marcia coming? She can ride with me." Marcia was the male to female transsexual on the second floor across the hall from the young gay couple Jeff and Tony.

"Yes, everyone's coming, but it's a surprise so if you run into Ruth keep your big mouth shut and don't be late."

Teresa hung up the phone and started down the stairs with a bag of trash and a bag of empty bottles for the recycling bin. That was when she got a frightening shock. It looked like someone had left a pile of old clothes between the garbage cans. Maybe that meant the containers were full and she'd have to take hers back upstairs or risk Arturo's wrath if they got fined. Teresa opened the lid on the black container and was glad to see plenty of room inside.

What she wasn't glad to see was the pile of clothes. It moved. Teresa screamed and a disheveled middle-aged woman—who'd been sound asleep a minute ago—screamed too and ran up the stairs and out the front gate just as Marcia rushed out of her apartment on the second floor with her cell phone in her hand.

"What's going on down there? Teresa, are you alright?"

"There was a homeless woman back there! She was passed out between the trash cans. She scared the living daylights out of me!"

"I'll bet you scared her too. By the sounds of the screams, I thought someone was getting murdered. I already called 9-1-1. Well, I'm just getting dressed, so… if you're sure you're alright…"

"I'll be fine. Thanks, Marcia."

"Aren't you coming to Ruth's surprise party? You'd better hurry. I'll wait for you and we can take a cab together."

"No, I'm driving, gotta move my car anyway. You can ride with me."

By the time Teresa gathered her wits and climbed the stairs to the first floor, there was a police car parked outside the gate and what looked like a boy in uniform peering inside. "You alright ma'am? There some kinda trouble here? We got a call, but…"

"Yes, yes, I'm fine. Some homeless woman got in and she startled me; that's all. That sort of thing doesn't usually happen around here."

"Well, the gate isn't locked here, see?" The police officer pulled it open and Teresa realized the boy in uniform was actually a woman. "The latch looks froze up. You got any WD-40? That ought to do the trick."

"I think so. I'll have to look through the junk drawer. Do you want to come in to fill out your report or whatever? I wish you would. I don't know when I've had such a shock. Come on upstairs. I'm on the top floor."

"Nice place you got here. I like all the sunlight and the natural wood. Just look at that view you've got of the big rainbow flag and the Castro Theatre! You lived here long? It's *real* homey!"

"Thanks, I like it… since shortly after my divorce, I guess." She noticed the name on the brass tag on the policewoman's uniform and stuck out her hand. "My name's Teresa. It's good to know you're right on the spot, Officer Fuller."

"Call me Birdie, Ma'am," she smiled. "Everyone does except the assholes on the force that call me 'sir' behind my back, but hey… I've been called worse things."

"If you need me to sign anything, I'll be glad to. I'm sure Marcia would too. We're not used to having people sneak in here. Marcia used to be Malcolm, though. I don't know if she got her sex-change down on the paperwork yet, so for legal purposes…" Teresa was still shaken up and rambling nervously.

"Nah, don't worry about it. Let's just get that gate working so it doesn't happen again."

Teresa continued scrounging through the kitchen drawer. "Let's see... pliers, electrical tape, a dead flashlight... Here it is! WD-40! I'd invite you to join me for a drink, but I'm expected at a surprise birthday party for my downstairs neighbor, Ruth. I don't know what the hell to wear. Maybe you could join me another time. I make a mean Bloody Mary..."

"Thanks, but... um... I don't drink on the job. Let me have that can and I'll give your front gate a quick squirt. I'll be back in a second."

She dashed down the stairs two at a time and came back up the same way a couple of minutes later.

Teresa calmed down and thought about what had just transpired. "That poor old homeless woman must have snuck into the garbage nook for some rest. She was probably just as startled as I was. But we've never had anyone sneak in the building before. I'm sure she meant no harm, it's just that if she got in that easy, there's no telling who else could."

"The WD-40 should take care of the lock for the time being, but you ought to tell the landlord to have a look at it. The fog makes things rusty and the spring is old, too. It needs to be replaced. Who owns this building?"

"Arturo and Artie. They own Arts bar and restaurant on Castro Street. Artie used to be a big performer at Finocchios before they closed down a few years back."

"Artie Glamóur? I'll be damned! I haven't seen Artie in years. I worked the beat shift in North Beach when I first started on the force. Artie was a big celebrity back then. Sometimes we had some drinks and laughs after we both got off work. How's he doing?"

"Artie's fine. They both are. You should stop in and see him sometime. He's there behind the bar most nights."

"I'll do that. Is he still dressing up like a girl?"

"Now and then," Teresa laughed out loud. It seemed to her that Artie would have an easier time looking like a 'girl' than Birdie Fuller ever could. "Not nearly as often as he used to, I reckon…"

"It was real nice to meet you, Teresa," the policewoman stuck out her hand again. "Tell Artie hi from Birdie Fuller and tell Arturo to get that lock replaced. That gate should be okay for a while, but until they really get it fixed, be careful that it always latches shut behind you."

"Will do, Birdie. Thanks!"

Chapter 10

A rtie's instructions were for Ruth to meet him at noon at a little Indian restaurant on O'Farrell Street that he and Arturo had discovered recently. She drove round and round looking for parking in the streets where Union Square elegance butted up against Tenderloin squalor. In this part of town, a block in either direction could make a huge difference. Women in high heels carried shopping bags from Saks and Magnin's on Powell and the streets to the east, but a few yards west of the cable car tracks they lay crumpled on sidewalks begging for cigarettes and spare change. Ruth realized she'd driven past Rene's salon twice already, which reminded her that she needed her hair done, even as she was feeling sorry for the poor women outside the windows of her Prius who could never afford such a luxury.

Ruth finally found a lucky parking spot in the same block as the restaurant and entered an ornate high-ceilinged room filled with potted plants and exotic art. Artie had mentioned that the restaurant shared a lobby with a once-elegant old hotel. When he told her it was being remodeled and turned into something classy and expensive, it seemed to Ruth as if that could describe half of San Francisco.

She saw two people sitting at a bar on the opposite end of the lobby, but no sign of Artie. One of them looked

familiar, though. From the back he looked a lot like Sam and
he appeared to be having an intimate conversation with a
woman in a wide-brimmed red hat. Ruth thought this might
be a perfect place, in its present condition, for a married man
to take a "lady" for a few drinks and then check into a room
upstairs. In spite of the gentrification going on here, they
might still be renting rooms by the hour.

Ruth looked at a menu and then glanced over at the
couple again. It *was* Sam and now he was holding hands with
that woman! Ruth was furious to think that he'd lied about
going out of town, forgotten her birthday and now here he
was consorting with some overdressed floozy in a hotel lobby
on the edge of the Tenderloin! Tim had suggested that she and
Sam needed an argument. Well… now she had a good reason
for one!

Ruth hid behind a potted palm and dug through her purse
for her new cell phone. She had Sam's number programmed
into her old one, but Ruth was sure she remembered it. She
watched his back, but he didn't make a move to reach for
his phone. He must have turned it off so as not to interrupt
his little tryst. At the same time the voice message came on,
there was a crash from the kitchen, followed by an angry
chef cursing at someone. Ruth nearly dropped the phone, but
righted in time to leave a message:

"Sam, I can hardly believe what I am seeing. Even though
we had that little tiff, I still thought things were going well
between us. I can't understand why you'd go sneaking
around with another woman, especially on my birthday!"

The *other woman* let get of Sam's hand, turned on her
barstool and gazed across the room. It was Artie in full drag
and he'd spotted her. "There you are, Ruth! Come over here. I
was just showing Sam some of my old costume jewelry."

"Artie! Sam!" She dropped the phone back inside her
purse as Sam jumped up and rushed across the room to take
her in his arms.

"Did I surprise you, sweetheart?"

"I thought you were out of town, Sam. Oh, yes, I'm sure I have never been more surprised in my whole life."

"I *was* out of town. I flew back this morning. You didn't think I'd miss your birthday, did you?"

"How did you find out when it was?"

"How did I find out? Don't you remember? We talked about our birthdays on our first date, the night we had a bottle of champagne after dinner at Jardinière. Remember when we missed the Mozart but caught most of the Mahler? We joked about how if we were young and on our first date, we'd be asking each other's sign. You knew more about astrology than I did. I figured you must have been quite the free spirit in your college days, even at Stanford."

"Of course, Sam," Ruth tried to smile. "How could I have forgotten a single moment of out first date?"

"Is anything the matter, dear?"

"No… nothing. I'm just so happy to see you. What a lovely surprise to see you and Artie *both*. I never imagined Artie would be all dressed up like this yesterday… when you invited me to lunch. With you out of town, Sam, I thought it would just be the two of us, Artie and me and… I'm so very surprised, that's all."

Ruth wished with all her might that she could magically erase the past five minutes of her life. How was she going to explain the message she'd left on Sam's phone? She'd never distrusted him before.

"Artie and I planned everything," Sam said. "Just wait until you see the rest of your surprise."

A waiter opened a pair of tall doors into a formal dining room where there was an enormous table filled with happy faces. "Surprise! Happy Birthday Ruth!" The shouts burst forth as Sam and Artie led her through the open doors into a private dining room along with a wave of cheers and laughter and applause. "Surprise! Happy Birthday! Surprise!"

There were Tim and Nick and Arturo and even Ben and Jane and the children and Jeff and Tony, nearly all of Ruth's favorite people in San Francisco including some of her regular customers at Arts.

Ruth was overwhelmed. This reminded her of her first night back at Arts after returning from Minnesota when she'd packed up and moved to San Francisco. How did Artie and Sam ever manage to pull this off? And she thought everyone had forgotten her birthday.

As happy as she was at the sight of so many friendly faces, Ruth was also frantic about the call she'd made to Sam's cell phone. She wanted to cry. How could she have thought Artie in drag was a woman that Sam could be attracted to? If Sam were going to fool around with another woman, wouldn't he choose someone a bit daintier, more ladylike and delicately feminine, she thought to herself… someone more like me?

Artie in high heels was even taller than Sam and even though he had lost some weight due to his constant dieting, he was still heavier than Sam. Ruth tried to excuse her misjudgment because she'd only seen them seated at the bar together, not standing. Still, she should have known better. All those thoughts raced through her mind as they led her toward the seat of honor.

"Happy birthday, Miss Ruth!" It was her hairdresser, Rene. How she wished she'd made another appointment with him before today!

"Rene! Mai Ling! I must have driven past your salon at least twice trying to find my way here. You'll have to check your schedule and get me in to see you soon. I'll call tomorrow. I promise." Ruth turned and gasped as Nick's grandmother came toward her. "Amanda! What a wonderful surprise to see you here!"

"Happy birthday, Ruth." The elderly lady shook hands with the birthday girl before her grandson Nick led her to a chair. Tim was on Nick's left with Ruth and Sam across the table from them with Arturo and Artie on either side.

Tears flowed down Ruth's cheeks and she let them. She could blame her emotional outburst on all on the happiness she felt at her big surprise. After hugs and kisses around the room, everyone was seated, drinks were served and Ruth began to relax a little. Artie must have planned the menu and ordered for the entire group. Ruth was grateful to him for everything, but especially for not inviting his latest "find," Rosa Rivera.

The waiters spread huge platters of food from one end of the table to the other. Everything was served family style and everyone here felt like family. From the smell of savory curries, exotic herbs and spices and several foods Ruth didn't recognize, it was all delicious, even though she had no appetite. She had to figure out a way to extricate herself from that phone call she'd made, but she'd have to worry about that later. "Oh Sam… I was so sure you were out of town. I hadn't even heard from you. I just can't believe this."

"Artie and I have been planning this for some time… and Arturo, too. Jake and James are here and Patrick got back from Palm Springs just in time. Scott helped us get hold of some of the regular bar customers to invite… like Terry and Chris here. I hope he remembered all your favorites."

"I'm sure he did. It's so nice to see you all." She rubbed the palm of her hand against the breast pocket of Sam's suit where he always kept his cell phone, but there was no lump there. "Sam… where's your cell phone, dear?"

"I left it in the car. I didn't want to think about business during your party."

"How sweet of you."

Ruth glanced around the room and realized the only people missing were two of her neighbors from Collingwood Street, Teresa and Marcia. Then she looked up and saw them coming in the door.

"Sorry we're late!" Teresa yelled. "I had a terrible fright at home and then it was a bitch finding parking. Where the hell are we, the Tenderloin? Pardon my French. I didn't see the little ones here."

"That's okay," little Sarah, whom Tim referred to as the magic child, piped up. "I know a bitch is a mommy dog."

"It's not the Tenderloin; this is the 'Theatre District,' Teresa," Artie said and Teresa finally recognized him.

"Oh my Lord! Is that you, Artie?" She let out a roar of laughter. "I wondered who in the hell that broad was!" Teresa had apparently already forgotten there were children present. Tim wondered how she got through a day in the classroom without swearing.

"Happy birthday, Ruth!" Marcia shouted as she and Teresa took their seats. "I thought you looked familiar, Artie."

"Doesn't he?" Ruth asked. "He reminds me of a girl I knew in high school, but she was a bit of a tomboy. Artie's a lot more feminine." Ruth was relieved to have the attention diverted away from her. She'd have to come up with an excuse to 'borrow' Sam's cell phone later. She could say hers needed charging or it was acting up. She'd get his phone and erase the message before he had a chance to hear it.

"Thanks, I'm sure," Artie said. "I don't think 'tomboy' is a bad thing for a dyke, but golly, 'more feminine than a tomboy' doesn't exactly put me in the running for Mrs. America. I was hoping for something along the lines of Joan Collins… back in her *Dynasty* days. What happened at home?"

"Speaking of dykes," Teresa said, "That reminds me… the reason we're late is because I discovered a homeless woman sleeping between the garbage cans."

"How do you know the homeless woman was a dyke?" Tim asked. "Did she have an old shopping cart from Goodman's Lumber or was she wearing Birkenstocks?"

"No, the homeless woman wasn't a dyke," Teresa said. "Well, I don't know. She could have been, I suppose. The cop was a dyke."

"What cop?" Arturo asked. "Don't tell me you called the cops!"

"She didn't; I did," Marcia said. "I thought someone was being murdered downstairs. Between Teresa's screaming and that other woman's, they got all the dogs in the neighborhood barking all the way to the north side of Market Street. At least we found out we're well protected. She was there faster than I could hang up the phone."

"Your 9-1-1 call hadn't even gone through yet," Teresa said. "She heard me screaming from the corner. I never knew my voice could carry so far."

Tim looked at his Aunt Ruth across the table and they both rolled their eyes.

"What did the cops say?" Artie asked.

"There was just the one, and she said she knew you, Artie. Do you remember a gal named Birdie Fuller? She said you two went way back together."

"Birdie Fuller! Oh my yes! From North Beach, but I haven't seen her in years."

"Well, you will soon. She got transferred to the Castro. I told her all about you and Arturo and the restaurant and she said she'll stop in to see you,"

"Birdie Fuller! Well, good! The Castro hasn't had a good lesbian on the beat since that dear Jane Warner died. I'm so glad they named the new plaza after her. Do you remember Birdie, Arturo? We used to hang around back stage at Finocchios after my show. It'll be great to see her again"

"Oh yes…" Arturo said. "I remember Birdie Fuller. What a sweetheart. Who could forget? What else did she have to say?"

"She said you need to get the front gate fixed," Teresa said. "I had some WD-40 she squirted in the lock, but she says it'll just keep acting up until you get a new one."

"I'd been meaning to anyway," Arturo said. "We don't need people sleeping back there. Remember when that church in the Mission burned down a while back. Some homeless folks built a fire in the alley to keep themselves warm and it got out of control. I'll get the gate fixed."

Marcia told Artie how *fabulous* he looked and asked what possessed him to come to Ruth's birthday soirée in drag. Artie was always thrilled to have an audience so he launched into one of his *long* stories. Ruth relaxed a bit, started picking at her food and listened to Artie.

"… and that was the year we got back from Viet Nam. Arturo was still down in L.A. taking care of family business and I was tending bar on Polk Street. I got a room in a big old flat on Turk Street with a bunch of guys. We called it 'lower Nob Hill,' but that really *was* the Tenderloin. Anyway, I woke up one morning and wished I hadn't. I opened my bloodshot eyes and saw a dress on the floor and it wasn't mine!"

"Don't you hate when that happens?" Jake asked and everyone laughed, but Artie had the spotlight now.

"Then I saw a pair of red high heels beside my bed and this was years before Donna Sachet had blown into town. I saw a pair of pantyhose and a crumpled dress. Oh, children, let me tell you… it wasn't pretty! And in my bed was an even bigger mess!"

"Who was it, Artie?" several people asked at once.

To paraphrase the immortal words of Dianne Feinstein, 'the suspect was Dan White.' That was his real name— Dan White! He'd been a guest of one of my roommates at a Halloween party the night before. I don't remember how he ended up in my bed, but can you imagine living in San Francisco in those days with the name of Dan White? This was before *the* Dan White was so infamous, but the Danny White in my bed that morning was still around town long after November of '78!"

Arturo interrupted to explain to those under thirty that Dan White was also the name of George Moscone and Harvey Milk's assassin. Artie went on, "Poor Danny White. I got to know him—the gay one, I mean—after the party. I wonder whatever became of him. I suppose he fell to the plague in the 80s, but I'll never know for sure. I didn't see his picture in the *B.A.R.* obituaries and I've read them religiously all these years… I still do."

"He means AIDS," Arturo had designated himself to be Artie's translator.

"But Artie…" Ruth asked. "About this Halloween party… why was finding those clothes in your room a surprise? I thought you were already doing drag in Viet Nam."

"I already told you they weren't mine. Oh, I know how Arturo loves to tell those stories about Bob Hope and the USO, but that was just playing dress-up. I never did serious drag in the service. Not even that morning after the Halloween party, but I did try on those red high heels right quick and they fit me like a glove. Then I slipped into Danny White's dress and left him passed out in my bed. You should have seen that apartment. It was a disaster. I had to step over moaning bodies. It was like a battlefield the length of that entire hallway, but I found some lipstick and mascara someone had left in the bathroom, so I painted my face a little. Then I found a red wig on the floor… well, that queen had let it slip so far off her head she didn't even feel me snatch it."

Tim looked over at Nick and wondered what he was thinking about, but Nick appeared to be captivated by Artie's story, as did everyone else. Nick's grandmother Amanda was even taking notes.

"I gathered up a few accessories from among the wounded… a feather boa here, some bracelets there… you know. I made it to the kitchen, put on the coffee and whipped up about a gallon of Bloody Marys. I turned on the stereo and people started coming around. By the time the coffee was ready, I was on a roll, dancing, singing along to the record player, cracking jokes. Nobody touched the coffee unless they put some Irish whiskey in it first, but the party went on all day! I was having a fabulous time, my dears! I decided if doing drag was this much fun, I should put an act together. What wonders a pair of red high heels and a borrowed dress can do!"

"What an interesting story!" Amanda Musgrove looked at Artie in a new way, as if he might become a character in one of her mystery novels.

"That's quite a story, alright," Ruth said and realized that she and Amanda, the oldest heterosexual females in the room, were the only people who had remarked on it. Maybe the young gay men were interested too, but they didn't know what to say. She hoped that their quiet might be a sign of respect for their elders. Then a crew of waiters arrived with a cake and everyone sang Happy Birthday. After Ruth blew out the candles, they wheeled another table in. This one was piled with gift-wrapped packages.

"Those can't all be for me! This feels like Christmas morning. Maybe we should move back into the other room and open the gifts in there. I'm sure some of you wouldn't mind stretching your legs."

"Or getting a drink at the bar!" Artie said. "That darling bartender looks lonely."

"Before we move," Sam said, "there's one present I'd like you to open in front of everyone." He reached into his breast pocket—where his cell phone ought to be—and handed Ruth a white envelope.

"What on earth, Sam?"

"Maybe I'd better explain to all our friends. When Ruth agreed to marry me, she made me a very happy man, but I know that everyone in this room loves her too, enough so that she has misgivings about coming to live with me in Hillsborough full-time."

Ruth spread open an official-looking letter with a logo at the top that looked like some kind of business stationery. "What does this mean?"

"It's the lease to your apartment on Collingwood Street, paid in full for one year in advance. This way you know I'm not pressuring you into making any sudden changes. I'm just happy for every moment we get to spend together."

"Oh… Sam," Ruth hugged him.

"Get it while you can, honey," Teresa shouted. "Do you feel like a kept woman now, Ruthie?"

Everyone laughed and Sam put his arms around Ruth as she whispered, "That's thousands of dollars, Sam!"

"Shhhhhh," Sam pressed his finger to her lips and replaced it with a kiss. "I thought about what you said and you were absolutely right. Besides, it'll be nice to keep a little pied-à-terre in the city when we don't want to drive all the way back to Hillsborough. That's assuming I'm welcome to spend the night."

"You are more than welcome any time, silly."

"There's no excuse not to get that gate fixed now," Arturo said. "We can afford to have the building painted one of these days, too. It needs it."

Ruth heard her cell phone ring and pulled it out of her purse. She couldn't imagine who might be calling her. Almost everyone she knew in San Francisco was right here in this room. She felt a moment of panic, as if it must be bad news. "Ruth, is that you?"

"Yes, it's me, but I can barely hear you. Who's this?" Ruth didn't recognize the voice, but she blamed it on a poor connection. She assumed it must be someone else who remembered her birthday but she couldn't think of anyone who was missing. "Can you speak up? Otherwise, maybe I could step outside where I can hear you better." She tried to move but was penned in at the seat of honor.

"You goddamn sleazy, home-wrecking tramp!" It was a woman's voice, but it couldn't be anyone Ruth knew. "I'll bet you didn't expect to hear back from *me*, did you?"

"Who on earth is this?"

"Just shut up and listen. I got the message you left on his phone. So he's calling himself Sam these days, is he? Last time it was Steven. His real name is Stuart."

Ruth remembered the crash of dishes and the yelling in the kitchen earlier. She'd never actually heard Sam's voice mail come on, but she'd assumed she was leaving him a message. "If you want my lousy husband, I should let you have the son-of-a-bitch. It would serve you right, but now you know he's no catch! He's been cheating on me for years and now he's two-timing you, too. Hah! Where did he pick you up? At the track? Vegas? I hope you aren't another one of those cheap hookers he goes for. There's not enough penicillin in town for the likes of you gals."

"It was a wrong number!" Ruth grinned and felt an enormous burden being lifted. "I'm terribly sorry. Please try to calm down. It was only a wrong number. I'm sure everything will turn out just fine. Please! Don't be so upset! It was all a big mistake. I'm sorry! You must believe me!"

Ruth laughed out loud and dropped the phone back into her purse. If she and Sam were going to follow Tim's advice and have an argument, at least it wouldn't be about infidelity. She didn't have to feel pressured now, either. Sam made that clear with a year's lease on the Collingwood apartment. The only things left to argue about were Adam's wedding in Chicago and what to do about Adam's mother Delia and where Ruth fit into the household.

Ruth could twist herself into knots of worry at the drop of a hat, but today was her birthday and this was the first surprise birthday party she could ever remember. Here were nearly all the people that she knew and loved in the world. Why worry about a thing?

"Who was that?" Sam asked.

"A wrong number. Let's go into the other room and drink champagne and open my presents."

"But you said *you* were sorry. Why were *you* apologizing, if it was just a wrong number?"

"The poor woman was so distraught I felt sorry for her... her dog ran away... again."

Chapter 11

While Ruth was still opening birthday presents, Tim headed for the men's room at the Indian restaurant. He stood at the urinal and his head began to spin. Maybe he'd had too much wine with lunch. Had he stood up from the table too fast? He hoped he wasn't getting sick, but he felt so dizzy he had to place both hands on the porcelain to brace himself. He finished, zipped up and washed his hands, splashed cold water on his face and looked in the mirror. He thought he looked okay but the second he turned away from the mirror he caught a glimpse of his mother's face, as if she was standing right behind him. He turned all the way around—twice—and the vision was gone, but now he was even dizzier.

"What's up, handsome?" Nick was waiting right outside the door and grabbed him for a quick kiss. "Where're you going? You okay?"

"Yeah, just a little dizzy, that's all. What about you? Are you spending the night in the city or what?"

"I have to drive my grandmother back to Alameda when this wraps up, but then I could stop by your place… for a while, anyway. Are you going straight home?"

"Yeah, I'm going home." Tim thought he might go straight home to bed.

"Did those workmen do a good job on the tree? I can't wait to see how it looks with your downtown view exposed. Did they clean up their mess?" Nick licked his lips and nuzzled Tim's neck and earlobe. "Don't you want me to stop by, Snowman?"

"Sure… I guess it would be okay," Tim yawned to feign disinterest, but Nick had already turned to rejoin the party. Tim realized that it had never occurred to Nick *not* to stop by Tim's place afterward. Nick was always so damned sure of himself it was intimidating, but that was part of what made him so perfect; he was Tim's opposite in that way and in so many others. Tim hadn't been sure that Nick would be able to come down for the party at all, much less bring his grandmother along, but he knew his Aunt Ruth was thrilled to see them both.

Tim tried to think how many days it had been since he and Nick last had sex. How many days had it been since the dream about Buena Vista Park and that guy Bruno—Rosa Rivera's assistant? How long had it been since Tim complained to himself about Nick being around so much? Now all it took was a quick kiss and a grin and some grab-ass in the hallway of a straight restaurant in the Tenderloin and Tim couldn't imagine ever wanting to be with anyone else.

The dizzy spell had passed now. Tim took a deep breath, rounded the corner and found Nick standing in the doorway. They both watched Aunt Ruth open some silly little gag gifts and Tim teased, "I'm not working tonight, so... can you stay over or not? If you can, I'll run home and air out the bedroom, get rid of last night's trick towels, change the sheets… you know."

"You do that," Nick smiled and slapped Tim on the ass again.

The first thing Tim did when he got home was take another long hot shower. With Nick coming by, Tim could think of little else but getting naked with him. He was angry at himself for his mood swings and thankful that Nick never seemed to notice. Nick was almost always *in the mood* or at least in a cheerful mood. Tim envied him that.

Tim turned off the shower knobs, dried himself off, pulled a bath towel around his waist and stepped into the kitchen. There was nothing much for dinner later, but he could call out for delivery or microwave something. The kitchen floor was a mess of linoleum chips with bits of the old hardwood floor showing through. Why had he thought he could do this project himself? It was a huge job! Tim tried to sweep the worst of the mess into the corner before Nick arrived. He looked out the window where the old redwood tree had been. Nick was right. The downtown panorama was spectacular, although the afternoon fog was coming in with a vengeance. Nick had better hurry up if he wanted to see the view.

Tim thought he heard someone whistling "happy birthday to you…" When he reached his bedroom he was startled to see Nick, bare-chested, perched on the side of the bed unlacing his shoes. "Hey! When did you sneak in?"

"I rang the bell, but you didn't answer, so I used my key. I figured you must be in the shower. Come here!" Nick was all hands.

"I though you wanted to look at the view."

"I like this view just fine." Nick pulled Tim down onto the bed with him.

"But the fog is coming in and it'll be gone soon." Tim dropped the towel and let Nick roll on top of him, pinning him down with his body and working the muscle of his tongue between Tim's lips and teeth. Tim reached down to unbuckle Nick's belt and when he could breathe again, he panted a moment before he spoke. "Get undressed… and I mean it… come and look at the view before all that's left is the top of the pyramid building."

"Oh, okay!"

Tim tugged at the cuffs of Nick's pants until they slid all the way off and Nick headed toward the kitchen in his socks and jockey shorts. "Hey, what's this?" Tim asked, but Nick was already gone. A piece of fabric stuck out of Nick's pants' pocket, a splash of faded pink and pale yellow. Tim gave it a tug and held a woman's handkerchief in his hand. It was so sheer he could almost see through it and now Tim was dizzy again, much worse than before. Tim was awake, but he was suddenly far, far away…

Tim Snow was a little boy again. This vision was as clear as any of his psychic dreams. His family was on a picnic… a sticky-hot summer afternoon… tall trees everywhere… maybe outside of the city. No, it was Minnehaha Falls. His Aunt Ruth and Uncle Dan were unpacking their car and his cousin Dianne was whining about the heat. Uncle Dan and Tim's dad each opened a beer and Aunt Ruth hoisted something heavy out of the trunk… a big thermos jug with a spigot on the side.

"Are you ready for some nice cold lemonade, sweetheart?" She was already quenching people's thirsts back then.

He could hear her voice now. *"Are you ready for another round of Margaritas, boys?"* But that was a question she would ask at Arts. Time was jumbled and Tim's thoughts were a spinning kaleidoscope that stopped spinning again and landed at this summertime picnic in Minnesota, years ago.

"The boys can have their beer. I made lemonade for the rest of us." Aunt Ruth meant that the lemonade was for the women and kids, but Tim's mother had her own thermos. Was it because it was her birthday that no one questioned her having her own *special* lemonade? Tim's grandmother wasn't there. Now he remembered. This was the summer after she died. Tim's mother and Aunt Ruth were still too sad to talk about it. Tim had tried to tell his mother about how vivid his dreams had become since his grandmother's death, but she didn't want to hear it. He couldn't remember if he tried to talk to his dad about anything. Doubtful.

Tim had emptied his piggy bank to buy a handkerchief for her birthday. It was white with red and yellow flowers. He spent the day of her birthday, the day of the picnic, waiting for just the right time to give it to her. A summer storm cut short their plans and he forgot about the handkerchief until they were on the way home. Hailstones bounced off the windshield. Tornado sirens wailed their warnings from the south. When they got inside the house Tim climbed out of his wet clothes and remembered the gift he had for his mother's birthday. He carried it into the living room, but she was already passed out on the couch, so he left it on the embroidered pillow where it would catch her drool.

Tim held this handkerchief from Nick's pocket up to his nose. He didn't recognize the smell. He knew his Aunt Ruth's scent and he thought he'd know Nick's grandmother's. He heard his Aunt Ruth's voice again. *"If people notice your scent when you walk into the room, it's too strong. It should be so subtle that they only notice something missing when you leave."*

"It'll be beautiful at night when all the lights come on downtown," Nick yelled from the kitchen. "Hey, what happened? Whatcha doin'? I thought you were right behind me. Come in here!"

Tim, still naked, grasped the door frame and took a few faltering steps, still holding the handkerchief. "Where did this come from?"

"Oh… that? I found it on the edge of your driveway just now. I thought it must be Jane's from downstairs, so I picked it up. You'll see her before I do."

"This isn't Jane's. Look how worn it is. It looks like it's been put through the wash a thousand times; the colors are faded and the edges are tattered."

"Well, it's a little too flowery for any of the guys on my work crew, don't ya think? Do you think your Aunt Ruth dropped it?" Nick wasn't paying attention to the handkerchief. He pointed out the window again. "This is great with the tree out of there! What did I tell you? Now all you need is the new deck off the kitchen so we can sit outside and enjoy the view."

"Yeah, you were right again," Tim stared out at the thickening fog, but his mind was many miles and years away.

Nick walked his fingertips across Tim's shoulders, then flattened his hand and let it slide down Tim's back, pulling him closer. "Come on. Let's go to bed."

There was no better lover than Nick, as far as Tim was concerned, but he still had cravings sometimes. Nick always talked like he'd be satisfied to settle down and make it just the two of them once and for all, but Tim feel trapped at that kind of talk. Tim might even be happy with Nick's fantasy of monogamy, if only he'd stop talking about it! The "BIG IT" involved marriage, whether it was legal in California or not, and a lifelong commitment, moving in together; it was all just too scary!

Tim told his Aunt Ruth to talk out her feelings with Sam. Maybe he should take his own advice. The trouble was; talking was the thing he wanted to avoid. He would just have to try. They sat at the kitchen table now, an hour or so later, still naked after their lovemaking, and watched the dark sky. The fog had long since obliterated Tim's new view of downtown San Francisco from the northern windows. They ate leftover pasta Tim had reheated with garlic bread and a salad with a cheap bottle of red wine from Trader Joe's. "I meant to tell you…" they both said at the same time.

"You owe me a beer!" Tim said.

"What?"

"We always used to say that when two people said the same thing together at the same time; 'You owe me a beer,' but the one who says it first wins."

"Oh…" Nick looked slightly dazed.

"Sorry… maybe it was a Minnesota thing."

"No, I know what you mean. I've heard that before; I just forgot about it."

"Whatever… you go first. What did you want to tell me?"

"Oh… you'll never guess who I saw when we left the party."

"Martha Stewart!" Tim took a wild guess and laughed as he stretched out his leg under the table, slid his toe up Nick's bare leg and rested his foot in his crotch."

"Ooooof! Careful!" Nick readjusted his position and tore off another hunk of garlic bread. "No, but you're on the right track. Rosa Rivera."

"No kidding! I'm surprised Artie didn't invite her to Aunt Ruth's party. Where did you see her?"

"In the Tenderloin. My grandmother asked me to drive up and down some of those streets until we found a certain little corner store. It had to have a green awning. She's working on a new mystery and she needed to find it and figure out which direction the one-way streets ran on either side."

"Huh?" Now Tim looked lost.

"She's always been like that. She gets obsessed with details. Anyway, we ended up driving by Glide Memorial and there was Rosa. She was standing out in front with Reverend Cecil Williams and a camera crew. It must be one of the locations for her wedding season shows she's been advertising."

"She has?"

"You're the one who told me about them."

"Well, I knew she was *doing* them, but I didn't know she was *advertising* them already. I've never seen her show."

"It's on tonight. We could watch it later. But what was it *you* meant to tell me earlier?"

"Oh that..." Tim let his voice trail off. He didn't really want to talk about all *that*.

"What?" Nick reached down to grab onto Tim's bare foot, still resting between his legs under the table. By working his thumbs along the sole, he knew just where to drive Tim crazy. "Ve have vays to make you talk..." Nick tried to conjure up a German accent like on one of those late-night re-runs of *Hogan's Heroes* on TV-land.

"The other day after you left to go back up north, I was..."

"I'm listening."

"Let's go back to bed. I'll tell you in there, okay?"

"Now you're talking!" Nick let go of Tim's foot and stacked their dinner dishes to soak in the sink for the time being.

Once they were both in bed, Tim closed his eyes and tried to remember. "I was so horny that morning! I was having these amazing dreams and I thought you were right here beside me like this, but when I woke up and reached for you I remembered you'd already left for work. I was still half-asleep, I guess, and I kept thinking I only had seven minutes, for some reason."

"Seven minutes for what?" Nick repositioned himself so they were facing each other in bed. He picked up Tim's other foot and started the same deep-tissue massage.

"Aaaaaw, that feels so good!"

"Don't change the subject or I'll stop. What did you mean about seven minutes?"

"I don't know. It was just that I had a lot of things I wanted to do that day, like get to work on the kitchen floor, but you know how sometimes when a person has sex on the brain it seems like you can't get anything else accomplished until you take care of it?"

"I know," Nick shook out his hands for a second before he went back to work on Tim's feet. "I have my five-fingered friends here and when one wears out, thank God I'm ambidextrous enough to use the other one. So what did you do, Snowman? I'm still not sure what you meant about those seven minutes."

"I just thought I'd allow myself seven minutes, that's all. I thought about… you know… popping in a video… or even just taking a cold shower, but instead I fell back to sleep and I had this dream that was so real!"

"Yeah?" Nick knew all about how Tim's dreams could mean something out of the ordinary. He didn't fully understand how they worked, but he loved Tim enough to simply accept the fact. "What happened in your dream?"

"I drove up to Buena Vista Park and there was this one guy with these crazy red socks in black leather sandals and another guy who smelled like he'd bathed in sweet cologne and there was Rosa Rivera's assistant, that guy Bruno…"

"Had you even met Bruno yet?"

"No, that's just it… I'd never even seen him before, but I dreamed about him…"

"Oh wow, Tim! That's like something out of the Twilight Zone. Do-do-do-do, do-do-do-do…"

"Shut up… I know… it gives me goose-bumps… but then in my dream I saw you from behind and—"

"Me? What would I be doing in Buena Vista Park on a Monday morning? You thought I'd leave your nice warm comfortable bed… not to mention these sexy feet… to go beat the bushes in the park and try to avoid stepping in dog shit or some homeless encampment looking for sex with some smelly guy in red socks?"

"No, it wasn't you; he just looked like you from the back. He had hair like yours and he was getting it on with these two other guys like they'd all just come from the gym or something. They were in a clearing in the bushes and I slipped and fell down… like through a hole."

"Like Alice?"

"Exactly! Down the rabbit's hole… that's just what I thought, too." It was uncanny when Nick made remarks like that. They'd gone together to see the Johnny Depp version of Alice in Wonderland in 3-D back when it played at the Castro Theatre, but still… Tim felt like Nick could read his mind. "I landed flat on my back right between the three of them."

"Sounds pretty hot. I almost wish it *had* been me instead of some other blond guy. Maybe we should go up to that spot sometime and see what kind of trouble we can get into."

"But all I could do was laugh! And besides… it was the old Buena Vista Park in my dream, the way it was before they re-landscaped the south side.

"Aw, Snowman, you and your dreams!" Nick let go of Tim's feet, leaned forward and kissed him. "That dream doesn't sound so bad, except for the guy with the smelly socks."

"The smelly guy wasn't the same one that had the red socks," Tim started to explain, but decided to drop it. "What time is it, anyway? When does Rosa Rivera come on?"

"It should have already started. Haven't you figured how to work your Tivo yet?"

"I'm still figuring out my cell phone."

"You're hopeless. Where's the remote?"

"It's on the bed stand. Here…" Tim handed it to Nick, who flipped through the channels with one hand and put his other arm around Tim.

"Let's make it happen!" Rosa Rivera beamed into the TV camera. She had apparently just returned from a commercial. "Here we are outside the Victoria Pastry Company in the heart of my own little North Beach neighborhood. We'll be going inside in *un breve momento* to see how they make their delicious wedding cakes. *Bellissimo!"*

Nick looked over at Tim, who was already fading.

"And don't forget our big gay wedding at Arts Restaurant on Castro Street later on in this series. If you and your same-sex sweetheart want to be considered, you have until Gay Pride Sunday to enter. Just stop by Arts or go to my web-site for an application."

Nick set down the remote and rummaged through the bedside table's drawer for a pen.

Chapter 12

Tim had nightmares every night that week. He wanted to blame the bad dreams on his HIV medication, but he was used to those dreams; they were vivid, not ugly. These dreams about his mother were horrible. The only good thing about them was that they evaporated as soon as he woke up. There might be a few seconds of anxiety when he first opened his eyes, but then he barely remembered them until the next time.

He'd rarely thought about his mother in years, much less dreamed about her. It must have been the handkerchief Nick found in the driveway that started all this. Tim tried not to think about what it meant and managed to repress those thoughts until Thursday morning when he tossed his dirty laundry into the washer and there it was again. He thought about throwing it in the trash or burning it in the fireplace, but he dropped it into the bin with a load of towels and added a little extra detergent for good measure. When it came out of the dryer, Tim folded it up and shoved it to the back of his sock drawer. At least it didn't smell anymore.

Nick drove down again on Friday night and they had two good nights together after Tim came home from work. Nick liked stopping in at Arts on those evenings. Sometimes he had dinner at the bar and visited with Ruth and Artie or Scott. Sometimes he stopped at the Midnight Sun and watched music videos for as long as it took him to drink a beer. Most weekends he brought his briefcase filled with paperwork to fill the hours until Tim finished work at the restaurant.

Sunday morning Tim woke up screaming. It was only 5AM. Nick shook him gently at first, then harder. "Wake up! Tim! Come on, Snowman, you're having a nightmare… it's okay. You're safe now. You're here with me, babe."

"It's not my fault. It's not my fault! She was already on the floor when I came home. I tried to help her get up, but she wouldn't move. It's not my fault! I didn't do anything!"

"Wake up!" Nick yelled this time and held him closer.

Tim had tears in his eyes when they blinked open. "My mother…" he started to say as Nick rocked him in his arms. "Every time she gets drunk my dad blames me for doing something to make her wanna go and do it again and then… then she gets mad at me and I didn't… I don't know what else I'm supposed to…" Tim's mind was coming back into his head. He was here now. Nick was holding him and everything would be okay.

"It's alright, babe. It was just a dream. I've got you…"

"Wow! I was only about ten years old! You know she wasn't always like that." Even though he was here now, part of him lingered in the limbo of half-sleep.

"There were times when she was sober. We baked ginger cookies at Christmas. The whole house smelled good, not like booze. Sometimes she took me with her to the store and bought me candy and she always said, 'Don't tell your Daddy.' She was nice to me sometimes…"

"It's okay now, Snowman."

Tim tried to focus on Nick's face, pulled himself closer and kissed Nick full on the lips. Then he turned his pillow over to feel the cold side, pressed his face into it and fell back into a restful sleep this time. Nick thought about waking him to say goodbye, but Tim was sleeping like a baby by then. He left a note instead, saying he'd be back in a few hours after his meeting with a client in Marin County.

Ruth had a few early customers at her end of the bar as soon as Arts opened for Sunday brunch. Sam had to leave town again the day after her birthday party, so she'd spent the rest of the week in the city, which turned out to be more stressful than she could have imagined. At least on the weekend she was back to the normalcy of her routine at Arts.

Artie adored Ruth, as did everyone, but she wasn't herself lately. He could usually get her to confide in him, but not this time. He noticed that she put on a good face for her customers, but even some of them were aware that something was wrong with her. She'd mentioned that Sam was out of town again, so Artie figured that must be part of the problem.

Artie wasn't doing so well either and he usually loved this time of year, late spring in the Castro, when the ornamental plum trees down Collingwood and up 19th were loaded with bushels of pink blossoms. There was more morning fog than usual and it felt like there'd been an eerie full moon over the Castro for the past few nights. Artie wasn't usually one to take much stock in that sort of thing. He'd dealt with the public, whether on stage at Finocchios or here behind the bar, long enough not to let a bad day throw off his pace, but there seemed to be a string of bad days lately. Maybe he had a hangover. Then Artie got just the surprise he needed. Ruth had her back to the door and didn't even notice when Birdie Fuller walked into Arts for the first time.

"Artie Glamoúr!" Birdie yelled. She recognized Artie right away, even though it had been ages and she'd rarely seen him fully dressed in men's clothes.

"Birdie!" Artie came around the bar to give her a hug. "How's my favorite dyke on the force?" Artie was thrilled to see his old friend and happy for the distraction. "What are you drinking, sweetheart?"

"Nah… nothin'… I'm *working*, Artie… maybe a quick cup of coffee. How the hell are you? It's been way too long. I just found out the other day where I could find you again." Birdie sat down on a bar stool for a quick visit. She could be here legitimately under the pretense of following up on the gate incident, but mostly she just wanted to see Artie. "You're looking great, man. You've gained some weight, haven't you?"

"You bitch!" Artie screamed. "I've lost weight compared to where I was. I really packed on the pounds when I left Finocchios, but I've been slimming back down lately. I'm planning a secret comeback, but don't tell anyone." Artie explained to his old pal about Rosa Rivera's big plans and how he hoped to fit into them. This visit from Birdie was just what Artie needed to lift his spirits and remind him of the good old days.

The restaurant was quickly filling up with the usual brunch crowd and Birdie was about to head out, since Artie was getting too busy making drinks to talk with her. Then the phone rang.

"Arts! Artie speaking!"

"Artie, it's Teresa. Have you seen that police woman Birdie Fuller down there?"

"She's right here, Teresa." He caught Birdie's eye and mouthed Teresa's name while gesturing in the direction of Collingwood. Ruth thought for a moment that he was pointing toward her, so she stopped what she was doing. Teresa talked so fast into the phone that Artie couldn't make out half of what she said. "Hold on, Teresa. Here, Birdie... you talk to her."

Then Marcia came running in the door and it was obvious that something drastic had happened. Her hair was a mess and she didn't have on a speck of makeup. No one had ever seen her in broad daylight looking like something the cat dragged in. "Oh no... now what?" Artie asked under his breath to no one in particular. He could see a trace of the boy named Malcolm that Marcia used to be, especially along the jaw line.

Arturo stepped out of the men's room, drying his hands on a paper towel, headed toward the kitchen. Marcia saw him before Artie did and the next time Ruth looked up, all three of them were engrossed in rapid-fire conversation at the far end of the bar. Birdie Fuller set the phone down on the bar and joined them for a few seconds before she raced out the door. Ruth put the telephone back on its cradle and asked, "Is something wrong?"

"That homeless woman is back," Marcia said, "... the same one Teresa saw the other day by the trash cans. She was in the building again! Teresa found her down in the laundry room this time."

"What was she doing?" Ruth asked.

"Laundry, I guess," Marcia said sarcastically. "How would I know? She was passed out on the floor in the corner."

"I had that gate fixed the very next day," Arturo said as if someone were blaming him. "You know I did. You all got new keys. Someone must have left it open. Are the boys home?"

"Jeff is," Marcia said. "We both heard Teresa scream and came running. Tony's driving the streetcar on the F-Line on Sundays."

"What happened to that poor woman?" Ruth asked.

"Poor woman?" Marcia's jaw dropped. "What do you mean? This is the second time she's scared us half to death! She came to when Teresa screamed and then she staggered out of there as fast as she could."

"Oh my..." Ruth shook her head.

Then Marcia remembered something else. "That reminds me, Ruth. Your door was standing wide open. I thought you must have come out when you heard Teresa screaming too, but then I wondered where you were. I forgot you were working today. That woman must have broken into your apartment. You've been robbed!"

Ruth grabbed her purse and keys from behind the bar and squeezed past Artie. "I'll be back just as soon as I can, Artie. I'm sorry to leave you alone."

Tim was bringing out the entrees for a party of twelve celebrating someone's job promotion. He was running back and forth from the kitchen and hadn't noticed what was going on at the bar until he needed drinks and there was no bartender. He'd been in a daze lately too. It was always easier for Tim to zone out than to deal with anything difficult in his life. That was probably why he liked to smoke pot. "Artie? What's going on? Could you get me some drinks please?"

"I'm coming." Artie stepped back behind the bar.

"Three Bloody Marys, one Screwdriver, two Ramos fizzes, one Irish coffee no sugar and a Mimosa, please."

"Coming right up." Artie separated raw eggs. The whites went into the blender and the yolks got saved in a Tupperware bowl for Arturo to use in his Hollandaise sauce.

"Where's my Aunt Ruth?"

"Teresa found that homeless woman back in the building again and Ruth's door was standing wide open, so she ran home to check on things."

"Do you think that's safe? What if someone broke into her apartment and they're still in there?"

"Birdie Fuller is over there now. She's armed. And, besides, they said the homeless woman ran out the door as soon as Teresa saw her."

Ruth knew there was no one in her apartment as she gently unlocked the door. She wondered if Teresa had closed it or Marcia did… or maybe Birdie Fuller. Ruth knew that her 'guest' wouldn't have taken the time to close the apartment door when she ran from the laundry room to flee the building. Now Ruth would have to go out and try to find her before there was any more trouble. She looked around at the mess on her living room floor, a ragged coat, a suitcase with one latch broken and a pile of tattered clothing. That reminded her to check the laundry room across the hall. She felt the damp clothes in the dryer and dropped more quarters into the slot before she went back out to the street.

Ruth turned left at 19th Street past Rikki Streicher Field, her eyes scanning every bush, every doorway, every parked car with anything strewn across the back seat. Where could someone hide in broad daylight on a Sunday noon-time in the Castro? People were out walking their dogs or driving by, looking for a parking space on their way to church or brunch or the bars. Ruth's mind raced trying to imagine where someone who was scared might go to hide. At least Tim was at work, where she should be. Artie would just have to get by without her for a while.

And where was Sam when she needed him? Another business trip—nearly two weeks this time—and each time he called she had to pretend everything was normal. Was he in Seattle today? Ruth couldn't remember. She had too many other things on her mind.

A truck flew by on Diamond Street. Ruth caught the words *GLASS & SASH* on the side, but the paint was so worn she thought it said sushi. Or was Sam back in San Diego? It didn't matter. Near panic, Ruth felt stoned. Ridiculous. She hadn't smoked pot since that first day she arrived at Tim's old apartment—her apartment now. The subject of marijuana had never come up with Sam… one more thing she didn't know about him. What did Sam think about it? Or alcoholics? Sam seemed to be a moderate drinker. He was moderate in most things. Ruth appreciated that.

But she'd agreed to marry him and there were so many things he didn't know. And things she didn't know. Where *was* he when she needed him? Ruth hadn't even told Artie what was going on. She knew he suspected something, but he was so wrapped up in Rosa Rivera these days he hardly noticed Ruth's problems. And Tim was the last person she could tell.

She turned left up 18th Street to Hattie, right on Market to Church Street and all the way around Dolores Park. Again, there was no hiding place. Ruth walked up Hancock to Tim's house, stood in the driveway and stared at the view. The redwood tree was gone. What a huge difference! But despite the view and the fact that it was dying anyway, despite knowing that time passes and things she had long taken for granted had to change, Ruth missed that tree. She missed a lot of things she hadn't thought about for a long time.

"Aunt Ruth!" It was little Sarah, the magic child, yelling from the kitchen window. "I'll be right out!" Ruth rummaged through her purse for a handkerchief and caught a single tear on her cheek as the back door slammed and the little girl ran toward her. "Hi, Aunt Ruth!"

"Sarah, you're getting so big I can hardly lift you." Ruth planted a kiss on her cheek before she set her back down again.

"Are you looking for Uncle Tim? I think he's at work today."

"Yes, I know he is. I was just having a look at where the old tree used to be…"

"Sarah? Where are you?" a voice called out.

"It's Mommy," Sarah said to Ruth. "I'm out here in the driveway, Mommy."

"I told you not to leave the house without me, didn't I?"

"It's okay, Mommy. Aunt Ruth is here," Sarah shouted to her mother and then whispered to Ruth. "She's afraid of the scary lady."

"What scary lady?"

"A scary old lady was looking in the window. Last time Daddy chased her away, but this time Mommy saw her first and Mommy doesn't like it when—"

"Hello, Ruth." Jane rounded the back corner of the house and came toward them down the driveway. "You get right back in that house, little girl!"

"But there's nobody out here except Aunt Ruth and me."

"Don't argue with me, young lady! You know I told you not to go outside without me."

"Bye-bye, Aunt Ruth," Sarah ran back down the driveway toward the back door, waving. She wasn't scared of any old lady.

"Bye-bye, Sarah."

"Are you looking for Tim? He's at work today, isn't he? I'm sure I heard him on the stairs earlier. Nick's truck was in the driveway last night, but he must have left early this morning."

"I was just… I wanted to see the view with the old tree gone, but now that you mention it, I ought to be at work myself. They'll wonder what happened to me."

Her apartment was empty when Ruth got home from work that evening. She gathered the clean clothes from the dryer, folded them and carried them to the living room. Most of the blouses still had stains on them and she hesitated before she put them back in the broken-down suitcase on the floor in the corner.

Ruth went to the kitchen next. She did a careful inventory of the liquor and dumped much of it down the drain. Some things she rarely used anyway—cooking sherry, spiced rum she'd bought for a Christmas dessert, a half-empty bottle of bourbon. Where did that come from? Maybe Tim had left it behind when he moved out. Could she have moved it with her all the way from Minnesota? No, and it didn't matter anyway. She lined up the rest of the bottles on the counter, the full ones—the good stuff—plus all the wine. She packed it into boxes with newspaper in between so the bottles wouldn't break. If she couldn't find a good enough hiding place she would bring it upstairs and ask one of the neighbors to keep it for the time being. Teresa had a full bar already, but she could store it for her.

Ruth was half asleep in her rocking chair when she heard a key in the door. By the time she could stand up and step into the hallway she heard a thud and looked down at the miserable wreck of a human being on the floor.

"Oh, Betty, what am I going to do with you?"

"Waaaahhh?"

"Come on… let's get you in here on the couch." Ruth lifted her sister by the shoulders. "Whew, you stink! I said you could stay here, Betty, but you've got to behave. Tim isn't going to want to see you like this, you know."

Ruth knew it was unlikely that Tim would ever agree to see his mother anyway, after what she had done to him. Ruth went on talking, even though her sister was dead to the world. "And you can't go around frightening people. You scared Teresa half to death and I heard you were over on Hancock Street looking in the windows when Tim wasn't even home. I

don't know how long you intend to stay in San Francisco, but
we need to have a serious talk about the rules around here…"

Chapter 13

" *but there's an old saying that if you don't like the weather in San Francisco, just hold on for twenty minutes and it's bound to change...*" Steve the weatherman on the Channel 2 was wrapping up his final report. It was nearly 9 AM so the morning news out of Oakland was over anyway. Tim reached for the remote and switched off the TV set. Next up was Doctor Oz and Tim didn't want to watch that. If he wasn't a friend of Dorothy's and he didn't have a wicked witch on the show, Tim wasn't interested. Besides, Aunt Ruth had always said that daytime TV would rot your brain.

Tim had spent the cool foggy mornings this week with the classical station on the radio. He'd finished scraping up old linoleum from his kitchen floor. Nick would come down this weekend with a belt sander for the next phase of the project, but today the fog was clearing. Tim had been cooped up in the house too long and he was stiff from being in a cramped position on the floor. He missed the gym lately too. Working out gave him a different kind of stiffness that he liked and he could always stretch it out in the steam room afterward.

But Tim missed the sunshine even more. He jogged over to Dolores Park and scanned the half-naked bodies getting a healthy glow for the weekend. A couple of them had just arrived and Tim tried not to stare as they undressed. With

Nick up north, it was hard not to let his mind go there. He tried harder to think about Nick. Yeah, that new kitchen floor would make a big difference. Nick had plans for a new deck off Tim's kitchen and one off the Larson's apartment downstairs.

Tim ran in place at the corner of 20th and noticed a swarthy guy he'd seen at the gym. How could anyone forget that body? He was changing out of his Levis into a miniscule pair of black swim trunks by pretending to cover himself with a towel, like the hunky surfers changing into their wet-suits at Ocean Beach. Tim tried to think about Nick some more, but Dolores Park was a porn star convention this morning. Tim saw porn stars on Castro Street nearly every day, but they were usually wearing more than a Speedo. He often saw naked people on Castro too, but they were rarely the porn stars, unfortunately. According to an article he'd read in SF Weekly, most of the naked guys on Castro Street were straight. Go figure.

Yeah, Nick really was a great guy! Tim was so lucky to have found him, to know him, to have him in his life. Tim hadn't even thought about any of his old boyfriends in a long time. Corey Donatelli sent a card last Christmas, a picture of him holding a Golden Retriever puppy with the White House in the background. Or was it the Capitol? Tim had never been to Washington D.C., even though Corey had invited him to come and visit. Corey had his hair cut short in the picture. It made him look older. He *was* older, which Tim thought made him look even more hot.

Yeah, Nick was such a great guy. Tim alone would never have gotten around to building a new deck or refinishing the hardwood floors or taking out that old dying redwood tree and exposing the view. Tim stopped running and sat down on the bench at the top of the park. He looked out at the view of downtown and wished he had a joint; it was a perfect day to get stoned.

Now he saw a guy who looked like Nick—at least from the back. He was spreading a blanket about ten feet from where

Tim was sitting. His boyfriend was darker-complexioned, mixed race, part Hispanic maybe and he spoke with a French accent. Incredibly handsome. Then they started to make out and Tim couldn't take any more.

He ran on, down the hill to Dolores and left to 18th Street. He got in line for an ice cream cone at Bi-Rite Creamery. It was early enough that the wait wasn't long. He could at least satisfy part of his oral craving before he headed north again. As he neared Mission Dolores, Tim saw a television camera crew on the front steps. Something about the scene was familiar. Sure enough, there was Rosa Rivera, shooting another promo for her wedding series. Tim's first instinct was to hide, but she didn't notice him and what difference would it make? Even if she saw him, she wouldn't have placed Tim as the waiter who served her on her first visit to Arts on Castro Street.

And Rosa was busy making sure the camera angle had the entrance to the Mission in the background and the light was perfect to flatter her cheekbones without causing any shadows. Her assistant Bruno didn't *recognize* Tim either, but he *noticed* him. Bruno wouldn't let any good-looking bare-chested guy jog by without getting a good look, although Bruno didn't look at Tim's face. Tim headed home with plenty of time for a long hot shower, when what he really needed was a cold one.

When Tim got to work later, the same camera crew from Mission Dolores was in front of Arts. They took up three parking spaces and onlookers blocked the first lane of traffic. "Tim... Ti-im!" Someone yelled at him. It was Artie, standing next to the van where he could watch the monitors inside. "Come over here. You can see better."

"Hey Artie... what's going on?"

"Publicity, that's what! Rosa's recording a spot to promote the wedding series and the show she's doing from here. The entry forms are already coming in like crazy."

"Really...?" Tim couldn't imagine anyone wanting to be part of such a tacky event. Rosa had paused between takes while an ambulance screamed by. "I think I'll go around the back way through Hartford. It looks like this might take a while."

"Wait, I'll come with you."

"Are you working with Aunt Ruth tonight?"

"No, it's gonna be Scott and me behind the bar. Your Aunt Ruth asked for some time off. Didn't she tell you?"

"No, I guess we haven't talked in a while." As close as Tim was to his aunt, they could go without talking very much for long periods of time. Even at work they didn't have much time to visit, but Tim never worried about her. She was always the one to worry about him. "I guess Sam must be back in town."

Jake and Scott were already inside setting up, so Artie proceeded to the office and Tim helped set the tables for dinner. The employees bantered as they did their prep work, mostly about neighborhood gossip and subjects they'd covered a thousand times before. When they heard Rosa's laugh from the front of the restaurant it reminded them all of Artie's obsession with her.

"What's your impression of her, Jake?" Scott asked. "Do you think she's really 'going places' like Artie says?"

"Who knows? She's got a pretty good gimmick, I suppose. Gay men are so easily amused. It's part of our heritage going way back to before Stonewall, even."

"Look out, Scott! Here comes this week's gay trivia lesson," Tim groaned. "I thought Artie was bad enough when he gets on a roll."

"Well, it's true!" Jake persisted. "Joan Crawford wasn't really much of an actress, but the gays loved her because she was a star. If Judy Garland were alive today, she'd probably be at the Betty Ford Clinic, not doing movies and concerts."

"She'd also be ancient, wouldn't she?" Tim said, but Jake ignored him and kept right on going.

"And consider Madonna. She's not the greatest singer in the world, but she still knows how to market herself. Look at some of these new girls on VH1 these days."

"I'd rather not," Tim said.

"My point exactly... where's the talent?"

Scott laughed. "The other night I stopped at the Edge after work and they were having a benefit. Drag queens were trying to lip sync and do choreography on that tiny stage. You'd swear none of them had even rehearsed their songs— like they didn't even know the words—but the crowd was cheering like wild."

Artie returned from the office at the same time Rosa Rivera came in the front door, followed by her assistant Bruno and someone with a small hand-held camera. Artie rushed across the room toward her. "Rosa, how wonderful to see you! Come in; come in... how about a cocktail? Scott will get you something. Campari soda? How about you, Bruno?"

"Maybe just a short one, please," Rosa said, "with a twist of lemon. *Facciamo presto, però.*"

"Scotch rocks," Bruno said. "Dewar's."

"Nothing for me, Scott," Artie said. "I'll jump back there to help out just as soon as you get busy. Tim, reserve a table in your section for Bumps for three. I took the call in the office and they asked for you."

Scott noticed that no one reached for their wallets, so he made the drinks for Rosa and Bruno and started a tab with Artie's name on it. He could turn it over to Arturo later.

"Gladys Bumps?" Tim asked. "She hasn't been in for a long time. I hope she comes dressed. The last time her wig was so tall she had to duck to get in the door! She looked like some fabulous cartoon character."

"That must be her. Arturo took the call," Artie said. "You know... she's been around this town as long as I have. I imagine she's bringing both of her husbands."

"Husbands?" Tim asked. "Plural?"

"Yeah, the three of them have been together for years."

"How interesting..." Tim tried to ponder what that would be like. Would he and Nick someday get to the point where they wanted to open up their relationship to a third person? How would they go about it? Advertise on Craig's list for a special someone to fill out a ménage a trois—no femmes, fats, speed freaks or insecure types.

"And that's just what the rightwing nuts are always warning about." Jake stepped up to the bar. "If a man can marry another man, then why not his dog, his horse, his car… it'll open the door to all sorts of perversions… 3-ways… polygamy… horrors!"

Scott said, "And all the while they're fantasizing about having a 3-way with Ann Coulter and Michelle Malkin."

Jake said, "Some of those old geezers in Congress are probably still fantasizing about Nancy Reagan and Barbara Bush. Now there's a visual."

"Too scary for me!" Tim said

"Don't you boys have work to do?" Artie scolded and turned back to Rosa. "Now, before I forget, I've drawn up a list of musical numbers I'm considering for the ceremony. I've never performed at a wedding before and since it's a gay wedding I probably can't do typical wedding songs. I mean, a Carpenters' medley might work, but I'd have to change all the pronouns to 'he' and 'him.' Here's a copy of my list. You can look it over and let me know what you think. Then I'll practice with Phil, our piano player, when he has some free time. He's very creative."

But Rosa paid no attention to Artie. She stood up and walked toward the other end of the restaurant. "You know… if we got rid of the piano entirely it would give us more room for the ceremony. The lights and cameras take up a lot of space. We can use canned music."

"But my song…" Artie protested.

"It's only a thirty minute show—including commercials— so everything will have to be timed perfectly. The vows will be live, of course, but almost everything else can be taped in advance, all the planning, the wedding cake, the neighborhood. And I want to include a segment on the whole gift registry business."

"No piano?" Artie knew it would be harder to sing to tape. He was used to having the accompaniment follow him, not the other way around.

"I should also talk about wedding invitations, how to do the wording for same-sex couples, especially when the parents are involved. What a great idea! Maybe I could do an entire show just on invitations."

Artie realized this wasn't a good time to talk about his performance plans, but he tried not to fret about it. It was his place, after all, and he was glad to see Bruno taking notes about everything that was said, including Artie's remarks. Artie would try flattery for the time being. When Rosa sat back down at her drink, he said, "Rosa, you never cease to amaze me! You know so much about so many things and when it comes to weddings, you're an absolute genius! Tell me, have you ever been married yourself, dear?"

"No, I haven't." Her rapid-fire patter suddenly slowed as if her battery had run down. When she started again she spoke slowly. "I've had my share of offers, as you can imagine, but it wasn't meant to be. He loved race cars and speedboats and a life of danger. He loved strong women too, but only until he could tame them and then move on. *Che peccato. Era così carino.* What a pity…"

Artie listened to her story and got a tear in his eye, but Rosa Rivera's face was a mask of glass.

"*Bella Bambina!* Look at this little angel." Rosa jumped up and ran toward the door. "What a perfect little flower girl!"

Tim's downstairs neighbor Sarah, the magic child, ran in front of her mother, ignored Rosa and threw her arms around Tim's legs. Jane Larson was struggling with the baby's stroller and the front door at the same time. "Uncle Tim! Uncle Tim!"

"Hey there, kiddo!" Tim picked her up. "Are you here for dinner?"

"I don't think so. Daddy's still working. We were shopping at Walgreens and Mommy had to—"

"And Mommy had to use the bathroom," Jane interrupted and ran past the bar. "If my daughter is going to tell everyone, I might as well confess."

"Who is this delightful child?" Rosa Rivera asked.

Sarah turned toward the lady with the funny accent and smiled politely. "My name is Sarah Larson and that's my little brother. His name is Samuel Timothy and he's named after my grandpa and my Uncle Tim here."

Rosa looked down into the stroller. "What a sleepy little boy! He'd be a darling ring-bearer in a year or two. Is this really your niece?" Rosa finally spoke to Tim for the first time.

"Not by blood, but she might as well be."

"The Larson's used to live in the apartment building that Arturo and I have on Collingwood Street," Artie explained, although Rosa was barely listening to him. "Jeff and Tony live there now and the Larson's moved into the lower flat of Tim's duplex on Hancock Street. They have more room over there, with the growing family and all, plus they have Tim as a built-in babysitter."

"Aw, they hardly ever ask me to babysit, Artie, but I'd be glad to, you know…"

"You own a duplex?" Bruno asked Tim. It was his turn to sit up and take notice.

"Yes, well…" Tim started to answer, but he was still a little hurt that Bruno didn't acknowledge their episode in Buena Vista Park a while back. The encounter had been so real that Tim kept forgetting it was only a dream. "I, um… inherited it a while ago. It's not like I make the kind of money as a waiter that I could buy real estate in the Castro or anything…"

"Whew! I'm lucky I thought to stop here or I would have had to run all the way home," Jane said as she came out of the women's room. "There aren't too many places on this street for a girl to take care of business. Where's Ruth?"

"Where's *Sam*, your father?" Artie asked. "Ruth told me she needed some time off."

"I thought she was with your dad," Tim said. "Isn't he back in town?"

"No, he's in Rome," Jane said. "I just talked to him about an hour ago and he said he'd been trying to get a hold of Ruth. That's another reason we stopped by here was to ask about her. He said he tried calling her cell phone and it was turned off."

"Sometimes when she's at home she turns her cell phone off," Tim said. "Gee, I thought Sam was in Hillsborough and she was with him. Did he try her landline on Collingwood and leave a message for her?"

"He said he tried, but he had some trouble with the connection. Either the answering machine was turned off or else he was having trouble with an overseas operator, maybe. He said a couple of times it sounded like a drunken woman answering Ruth's phone. Well, we'd better get home so I can start dinner. If you talk to Ruth, please ask her to call Dad, okay?"

"You bet I will," Tim said.

"We'd better go, too," Rosa said. "Are you ready, Bruno?"

"Sure I'm ready," he said, chugging his scotch. "Bye, Artie. Seeya later, Tim."

"*Arrivederci…* I'll be in touch, Artie," Rosa said. "If the video bits we filmed out front today aren't good enough, we'll try again tomorrow. We might need to come a little earlier when the sun is higher in the sky. I'll call and let you know. And I'll have Bruno link your website to the section on mine about the wedding plans here at Arts, too. They can email the applications to be in the drawing or drop them off here in person."

"I know… I know," Artie said.

As soon as Bruno and Rosa were gone Tim asked, "When did you last talk to my Aunt Ruth, Artie?"

"It was a day or two ago, I guess," Artie said. "What's today, Friday…? It was Tuesday, I'm sure of it. Or maybe it was Monday. It was a day when she would have been off anyway, so it wasn't any big deal to cover her shifts right away."

"What did she say exactly?" Tim asked.

"She said she needed some time off, that's all. That's what I already told you. You know Ruth. She never takes any extra time off, so when she asked I could hardly say no. I figured Sam was back in town, that's all. He's been gone so much lately and I figured they were finally planning their wedding."

"How much time off did she ask for, Artie?" Tim persisted.

"She said she needed at least a couple of weeks or so," Artie said. "I didn't think it was really any of my business, but she did sound a little peculiar, come to think of it."

Chapter 14

The next afternoon Tim saw Rosa Rivera and crew on Castro Street in front of Arts again. She was dressed exactly the same—for continuity's sake, Tim could only assume—but she looked tired.

"*Ciao*, everyone! Let's make it happen! *Facciamolo accadere!* This is Rosa Rivera, standing in front of my latest dining discovery—Arts, the most delightful little bar and restaurant on Castro Street. As part of my *eccezionale* series on San Francisco weddings…

… Cut! God dammit! What the hell is that noise? Stop the goddamn tape, will you? … *Maledizione!*"

The siren of a hook and ladder rig almost drown out Rosa's cursing in English *and* Italian and grew louder as the fire truck crossed the red light at 18th and Castro. It passed by the restaurant and ascended the hill in the direction of Noe Valley.

Tim laughed as he watched Rosa lose her composure and he hoped the cameraman caught some of her true personality on tape. It might make good blackmail material, if it were ever needed. Tim kept getting jostled out of position, making it hard to see. The shoulder that blocked his view at the moment turned out to be that of his co-worker, James.

"Psssst! Hey, James! I didn't see you at first. Are you working tonight?"

"I don't know. I just got back from L.A. this morning. I came by to check the schedule and find out, but then I discovered all this excitement."

Rosa looked at her reflection in the plate glass window, scratched her scalp with one perfectly manicured fingernail, pursed her lips and forced the friendly 'On-Air' smile back to her face. "Okay, ready? Let's try it again…

As part of my series on San Francisco weddings we will include a beautiful gay wedding, *un bellissimo matrimonio gay… Delle belle nozze tra individui dello stesso sesso…* from right here at Arts restaurant on Castro Street!"

Tim whispered, "I'm sure Artie will want you to work if Rosa stays for dinner. He always likes to show off to *important* people how racially integrated we are."

"I'm hep! I'm the token black like Rosa Rivera's the token Italian around here. I think the whole thing is a put-on. Have you ever really listened to her?"

"Not really."

"I think her accent evaporates when the cameras are off. I'll bet she dreams in trailer-trash hillbilly talk. She's probably from Arkansas… or New Jersey!"

Tim laughed. "Maybe Minnesota, but I doubt it. I'll try to pay closer attention next time she starts swearing."

"Are *you* working tonight? You're here awfully early… or did you just come by to watch this?

"Yeah, I'm working later. I just came out of Walgreens and noticed the crowds up here. Rosa was here yesterday too. She said they might have to come back if everything didn't turn out right. Somebody must have gotten the word out to her fans. It looks like she's not having much better luck today. I'm on my way over to Collingwood to try to track down my Aunt Ruth. I've been calling around all over, but she seems to have disappeared."

"Really? Gee, I'm sorry to hear that. You must be worried. I didn't know. I like working with her…"

"I'm sure she's fine," Tim thought that the more times he said it out loud, the more likely it might be true, but James didn't hear him. He'd already turned his attention back to Rosa.

"So I am searching right now for a very special same-sex couple. If you and your partner would like to declare your love on live television in front your friends and family—and of course my beautiful audience at home—you and '*il vostro handsome marito*' … that's 'your handsome husband' for my non-Italian-speaking fans… can enter by going to my website or picking up an application and questionnaire right here at Arts. Just ask your favorite waiter or bartender. The lucky winners will…

Cut! Dammit! CUT!"

A couple of men with large dogs were cruising each other, but their dogs weren't happy about it. The guys might have hit it off if it weren't for the snapping and growling that the microphone was picking up. The dogs not only drowned out what Rosa was trying to say but they were dangerously close to her $300 Ferragamo sling-back shoes.

"*Maledizione!* Get those fucking dogs away from me! *Portate quei cagnacci fuori da qui!* I can't work like this! Are you people crazy? *Gesù!*"

Tim stepped away from the throng of bystanders and noticed Birdie Fuller directing traffic around the congested area in front of the restaurant. She looked like such a tiny thing in a crowd of people and she was trying hard to be as butch as her SFPD uniform. Having only one lane of traffic blocked wouldn't have been so bad, but a panel truck was double-parked to make a delivery at the plant store across the street. Tim saw Teresa at the edge of the crowd and headed in her direction. She too was watching the spectacle of Rosa's meltdown.

Once the dogs and their equally horny owners were separated, Rosa managed to continue. "The lucky winners will not only be television stars on their special day, they will also receive a bounty of gifts and prizes from our sponsors, including an all-expense-paid romantic cruise to sunny…."

Tim tapped Teresa on the shoulder and she turned around. "Hey, Tim, I didn't see you sneak up on me. Rosa's really something, huh? What are you doing out here... coming in to work early?"

"No, I'm headed over to Collingwood. Have you seen my Aunt Ruth lately? She doesn't answer her cell phone and I've tried calling around. I called you last night, but I didn't leave a message."

"She's out of town," Teresa answered without a moment's hesitation. Tim was relieved to hear that someone knew his mysterious aunt's whereabouts.

"That's what I thought. Artie said she asked for some time off, so I assumed she was with Sam, but it turns out he's been trying to call her too and he can't get through. It's funny she didn't tell anyone..."

"Well, she told *me*," Teresa said, but she was listening more intently to Rosa than to Tim.

"... so go to my website, listed at the bottom of your screen, or come to Arts Restaurant on Castro Street... stop by in person and pick up your copy of the rules and regulations. This is Rosa Rivera... Let's make it happen!"

"Well, what did she tell you?" Tim asked Teresa. "Where did she go?"

"Oh... that part I couldn't say. She just said she had to go out of town for a while. She did act kind of secretive, now that you mention it, but I was busy when she called to tell me. I've been kinda... seeing someone new, you know?"

"Since when? Teresa, you slut! So my Aunt Ruth caught you in the middle of it, huh? Who is he? Anyone we know? Where'd you meet him?"

"Hush, now! I shouldn't have brought it up, especially to you! And I'm not going to talk about it. I don't want to jinx it this time."

"Tell me about Aunt Ruth, then. What did she say besides 'going out of town for a while'? Didn't she give you anything more specific? Should I be worried about her?"

"I don't think so. She just asked me to feed the cat for her and I'm used to that. This time she brought Bart up to my place, though, with his toys and food and water dish and everything. When she's at Sam's just for a day or two, I run downstairs and feed him there. I've got my own set of keys."

"So do I… that's why I was thinking about going over there and snooping around a little, but I guess you've saved me a trip."

"Well, I'd say she's going to be gone for a while. She left enough cat food for at least a couple of weeks. I put the litter box out on my deck. That's the only part I don't much care to deal with, but please don't mention it to her. She's such a dear and I know she'd do anything for me… or for anyone!"

"I won't." Tim felt better knowing that his Aunt Ruth had made plans for the cat. At least she'd told *somebody* she was going away. She was a sensible woman. Tim wasn't going to let it worry him if he could help it. "So… you're seeing someone new, huh? I'll bet he's hot and hung like a stallion. I thought you had a glow about you. You're looking really good, lately. Has Artie got you on his weight-loss diet, too?"

"Thanks, Tim, but you're not gonna worm another word out of me, not even with flattery, so give it up. I'll let you know just as soon as it's any of your business, and not a minute sooner."

"Alright, but if you hear from Aunt Ruth, ask her to call me, okay?"

"That I will do. And right now I've got to be on my way home."

"Me, too. I've gotta work tonight. See you later, Teresa."

Tim thought he had plenty of time, but by the time he stopped at Cliff's for an appliance bulb for the refrigerator and waited in line at Walgreens for a refill on his HIV meds, the day was slipping away. He still had to run home and change for work. By the time he walked in the door at Arts, there were already two tables filled, both in James' section, and Artie was worried about him. "There you are, Tim! I was getting ready to call out the cops."

Tim was surprised to see Sam at the bar. "I'm sorry I'm late, Artie. I lost track of the time. Sam, when did you get back in town?"

"I just got in from Rome this afternoon. Do you know where your Aunt Ruth is? I was hoping someone here could tell me. I've left messages on her home phone and her cell phone is out of range all the time. Artie said she asked for some time off, but I can't imagine where she is."

"I haven't heard from her either, but Teresa's taking care of her cat. She said Aunt Ruth told her she needed to go away for a while and I guess she figured since you were out of town anyway, this was a good time. Teresa doesn't know where she went either, but she left plenty of food for Bartholomew."

A group of potential customers on the sidewalk were reading the menu and nodding their heads. Now they opened the door and started filing in, so Tim excused himself to get rid of his jacket and start work. He was just in time. Within another twenty minutes all the tables were filled with a line out the door. The next time he looked toward where Sam was sitting, he noticed Rosa Rivera was there too and she was making herself very familiar. She had one leg bent at the knee and it was pressed against Sam's calf while her fingertip was sliding down Sam's jaw. Tim had seen his Aunt Ruth use the same motion on Sam. Where did women learn this stuff? The next time Tim had a chance to look, Sam and Rosa were both gone.

Hours later, Nick arrived at the bar as Tim cleared the dessert plates from his last table. He found a place at the bar, ordered a drink and talked with Scott until Tim came up behind him and pinched his seat. "Hey, stud! New in town? I missed you last night."

"Snowman!" Nick nuzzled Tim's neck with his lips and gave him a pat on the ass. "I hate working on Saturdays, but I told you I couldn't come down. I'll make it up to you. Do you wanna join me for a drink here or do we have other plans?"

"Let's stay for one. I have to count out my tips. Order me a beer when Scott gets caught up… or better yet, let's move down to Artie's end. I want to ask him about something."

When Artie finally got around to it, he told Tim that Rosa just came in to drop off more entry forms. She'd insisted that Artie introduce her to Sam, but he wasn't interested in her come-ons and left right afterward. Even though Artie was one of Rosa Rivera's biggest fans, he thought her behavior was inappropriate. "I told her Sam was Ruth's fiancé, but that didn't slow her down one bit. She was like a desperate woman! It was downright tacky!"

"I wish Aunt Ruth had seen her flirting with him. She'd think twice about sneaking out of town."

"Especially now, since Rosa knows she's missing!" Artie said.

"Who's missing?" Nick asked, looking up from the current issue of the *Bay Area Reporter* someone had left on the bar in front of him.

"My mysterious Aunt Ruth has vanished. Sam hasn't been able to reach her either. He just got back in town today, so she probably didn't think he would worry. Artie said she asked for some time off and Teresa's taking care of Bartholomew."

"I didn't know there was anything mysterious about it," Nick said. "I just saw her yesterday."

"You did? Where? When? Why didn't you tell me? What did she say?"

"Nothing. I didn't talk to her, Snowman. She didn't even see me. I stopped for gas in Santa Rosa. When I was pulling into the station I saw her pulling out. There was someone else in the car with her, too."

"But I thought Sam just got back today," Tim said.

"Was it a man?" Arturo had just come out of the kitchen and was trying to catch up with the conversation.

"No, Arturo," Artie said. "We already know Sam was in Rome until today. Besides, if she and Sam were out for a drive, they wouldn't take her old car. They would take his car or a car with a driver. Unless they were going someplace secret."

"Artie," Tim interrupted, "we already know for sure it wasn't Sam. He was just here looking for her."

"Who else would Ruth have in her car?" Arturo asked.

"It was a woman… an older woman," Nick said. "Is Ruth's mother still around?"

"My grandmother died when I was just a kid. I showed you that picture of her and me, remember?"

"Oh yeah. Sorry."

"Did you follow them? Did it look like they were headed back toward the city?"

"No, Snowman, I was working. I was on my way to give an estimate on a big project, miles from there. I didn't have time to waste and I didn't know Ruth was missing. She was pulling out from one end of the station when I was pulling into the other. She had to wait for a logging truck to go by and then she turned left and went right past me. I waved, but she didn't even see me."

"Maybe she went up north to visit an old girlfriend," Nick said.

"Right," Artie agreed. "From when she was at Stanford."

"She must know lots of old classmates from her college days." Nick tried to be optimistic and dispel the aura of mystery.

"You went to college, didn't you?" Tim asked.

"Yeah, a long time ago."

"Not as long ago as my Aunt Ruth."

"What do you mean?"

"I hardly keep in touch with anybody I knew from before I lived in San Francisco. Maybe it's different for women than for gay guys, but how many of your old college friends are you still in touch with these days, Nick?"

Nick thought about it. "No classmates, but there are people I still know now that I knew then."

"Besides your parents and grandparents?"

"One or two… are you ready to head home?"

"Sure. G'night, Artie. G'night, Arturo… Scott. Seeya later, guys…" Tim waved to his coworkers.

Tim wanted to stop for a drink at the Mix to unwind after work, but there was no place to sit indoors and the patio was jammed. "Do you want to try Moby's?" Nick asked.

"Nah… it'll be just as bad and I'm tired of being on my feet."

Nick had parked on the street in front of Tim's house. As they got nearer, they noticed lights on downstairs and a cobalt blue Jaguar in the driveway. "Sam must be visiting his family," Tim said.

"I almost forgot I've got the belt sander for your kitchen floor in the back of my truck. Help me get it out, will you? I nearly wrenched my back getting it in there by myself."

They struggled up the stairs with the sander and left it in the middle of the kitchen floor. Then they undressed each other without turning on the lights. Afterward, Tim said, "You were in a big hurry this time, huh?"

"I'd been saving it up all week." Nick stroked Tim's thigh.

"I was just thinking. I guess I don't need to worry about you messing around with other guys when I'm not looking." The words came out of Tim's mouth and he regretted them right away. He didn't even want to think about that, much less talk about it. Nick didn't pick up on what Tim had said, but rubbed up against him closer instead.

Tim grinned and pushed Nick's hair away from his face. Tim almost forgot to take his pills that night, but he could tell by his dreams that his drugs were hard at work in his system. He was riding in the back of Nick's truck, trying to keep the belt sander from bouncing around. Then the truck became a car and the sander disappeared. Tim was in the back seat and his Aunt Ruth was driving. A gray-haired woman was asleep in the passenger's seat.

Then the car became his father's car. Tim was a little boy in the back seat listening to his parents arguing. His mother was drunk and his father was angry… nothing out of the ordinary, but she jerked at the steering wheel and Tim jumped as he woke up from his dream.

"You okay, babe?" Nick asked.

"I'm fine… just a dream." Tim had a sudden urge to turn on the light and see if Nick's eyes were really as incredibly blue as the day they first met on the back stairs. He slid down in the bed a little and Nick pulled him closer.

"Ready for round two?"

"Don't get excited. Morning will be here soon enough and we can spend it in bed." Tim extricated his naked body from Nick's, went to the bathroom, got a drink of water and swallowed a couple of aspirin before his headache could take hold. He looked out the east window at the driveway and Sam's car was gone.

Chapter 15

Tim's dreams got worse as the night wore on and his mother was in all of them. He felt searing pain. He was at the doctor's office in bandages. He was a little boy and he was scared.

Tim's tossing and turning woke Nick. "Snowman... what's going on? What's wrong?"

"Hmm? Nothing. I don't know. Dreaming. What time is it?"

Nick sat up far enough to look at the digital clock on the dresser. "Six forty-five."

"Oh."

"You okay?"

"Yeah... I mean no. Come with me. We've got to get dressed."

"Where are *we* going?"

"Over to Collingwood. I have to check on something at Aunt Ruth's."

"Can't we have coffee first?" Nick moaned, but he was already pulling on his jeans.

"I'll take you to breakfast later, I promise."

Ruth leaned over in the deck chair and took another sip of her coffee. A young mother at the pool was letting her kids run in circles and scream what sounded like an Indian war cry. Ruth thought she must feed them a steady diet of sugar. They were in #5 at the opposite end of the motel from Ruth's room, thank goodness. She'd had her first good night's sleep in a long time, even though it was in a strange bed. Now it was time to make some phone calls.

"Sam? Yes it's me. Sweetheart, I didn't mean to worry you. I'm so sorry. You were out of town so long and I was sure I'd be back in the city before you got home and… He is? Well, I'm planning to call Tim just as soon as we're done talking. I didn't even know you were back from Europe already, so I wasn't sure… No, my cell phone probably wouldn't have been… I'm still getting used to this new one and yes, I forget to charge it sometimes, I suppose. Oh, darn it! Hold on a second, Sam. I won't be able to hear a word until I can get this poor little girl to stop crying."

One of the little demons was screaming at the top of her lungs. Ruth saw a big yellow ball under the chair next to hers. "Is this what you're looking for, honey? Is this your ball? Don't cry. Here, I'll bring it to you." Ruth set her phone down on top of the Good Housekeeping she'd been paging through. The magazine rack in the knotty pine office held a *Newsweek* from the Clinton administration, three very old *National Geographic*s, four faded *Good Housekeeping*s and a half-dozen tattered copies of *The Reader's Digest*. On the rickety coffee table there was one called *Christian Home* and a yellowed issue of *Wine Country*. Ruth leafed through them all before she picked up the *Good Housekeeping*. She might at least find an interesting recipe.

"Yes, Sam… I'm at the Wagon Wheel Inn. It was the first place I could find after I got Betty admitted. They must get a lot of business from people in my situation. The sign says *Free Cable—Swimming Pool—Horseback Riding—Adult Movies*—I haven't checked those out yet. I haven't seen any horses yet either, but I think I heard some. It's quite the place!"

Tim still had keys to Ruth's apartment on Collingwood Street. It was Tim's apartment for a long time and she insisted that he keep a set, *just in case.* When he put his key in the gate he remembered that Arturo had recently changed the lock because of that homeless woman who'd gotten into the building. Tim wanted to think she'd left the Castro by now and moved on to some other neighborhood, but in the back of his mind he knew better.

"Now what?" Nick asked. "It looks like Ruth's front window might be open a crack. Should I boost you up?"

"Nah... I'll buzz Teresa." Tim pressed the top right hand button. "Even if we wake her, she owes me one."

There was a long silence and then a tinny voice came through the speaker. "Hlllllo! Whbyzzzit?"

"Hey, Teresa! It's Tim. Nick and I need to get in. Can you buzz the gate please?"

"Sssstresa's nagrombsssss."

"What the hell? Arturo needs to replace that intercom. I couldn't understand a word she said." Tim leaned into the speaker again, "Will you please buzz us in, Teresa? I need to check out something in my Aunt Ruth's apartment, but I don't have a key to the new lock on the front gate."

Nothing. Two more minutes ticked by without another sound from the static-ridden squawk box. "I hate to ring Arturo and Artie's buzzer this early, but it would serve them right."

"Are you sure you don't want me to boost you up, Snowman? Maybe we could get in from around back... you know, by the garbage cans?"

They heard a creak as a window opened high above them and Birdie Fuller stuck her head out. "Hi guys! What can do for you?"

"Where's Teresa?"

"Seattle. It was short notice, so she asked me to housesit for her... and your Aunt Ruth's cat. What's up?"

"I need to check on my Aunt Ruth's apartment, but I forgot Arturo changed the lock. Sorry to wake you, but could you buzz us in, please?"

"I guess it's okay, but if someone calls the cops I could get into a lot of trouble, especially since I *am* one." Birdie laughed at her own little joke. "Where's the button I need to push, anyway?"

"It should be on the wall in the hallway, just to the right of the intercom."

Bzzzzzzzzzzzzzzzzzz...

When they got inside, Birdie was leaning over the railing looking down at them. "Hi guys!"

It was the first time Tim had ever seen her out of uniform. "Hi Birdie, have you met Nick?"

"Hey, Nick!"

"Good to meet you, Birdie." Nick waved.

"What's up with Teresa?" Tim asked.

"She went to Seattle for her class reunion. She wasn't gonna go, but her ex-husband Lenny is going and he's bringing his husband Teddy along. They talked her into it. She can visit her mother, too."

"I know them... ... Theodore and Leonardo. Don't call them Lenny and Teddy to their faces or you'll be on their shit list."

"Thanks for the tip," Birdie smiled again and gave Tim the thumbs-up. She seemed awfully jolly for this hour of the morning. "Teresa went by the restaurant yesterday to tell Artie she was going, but he was busy with the Italian superstar."

"I'll bet."

"Anyway, *Leonardo* asked Teresa to come along for moral support. He figured if his ex-wife was cool with him being a big old homo it would be easier to face his old classmates... oh, sorry... no offense."

"Hah, no problem, Birdie. Have you ever seen Teresa's ex?"

"No."

"Well, he sure doesn't have to worry about getting beat up. I'll bet those two will be the biggest guys at the whole reunion."

"Bears, huh?"

"Yup. Nobody's going to pick on them, at least not to their faces."

"Well, Teresa's mother is getting up there in years too, so she can kill two birds."

"Thanks for letting us in, Birdie."

A little boy came out of room #5 to see what his sister was screaming about. He wrestled the yellow ball away from her and kicked it back into the pool. Then the mother appeared, holding an infant. Ruth said to her, "Excuse me, but you really need to keep an eye on your children out here by the pool. There's no lifeguard, you know."

"You really need to mind your own damned business, lady!"

"Did you hear that, Sam? She swore at me. I feel sorry for those kids, growing up with a mother like that. I wonder where the father is… Where was I? Oh yes… Betty. This all has to do with my sister, you see. Tim's mother is my only sibling and she's here. Well, she's just up the road. You've heard of the Redwood Valley Ranch. They have those TV commercials: *Stop the downward spiral of addiction! Call today. We can make you feel like your old self again.* I think they should make you feel like your *young* self instead of your *old* self and they'd do a land-office business!

"I should start at the beginning, I suppose… remember when they saw that woman in my building? The first time Teresa found her in the garbage room. She was drunk… no not Teresa, the homeless woman. That gate never did lock properly, so nobody thought much of it. Yes, I think Artie still is…

"Well, it was conceivable that a homeless person crawled in there to sleep. But she'd been snooping around at Tim's house too. She scared your daughter Jane half to death, peeking in the windows. She didn't realize Tim lives upstairs on the second floor—"

"Hold on. I'm getting to that part, Sam. You see, I was the next one to spot her and I didn't even recognize her first.

She was on the bench outside Buffalo Whole Foods—you know the health food place on the corner of Castro and 19th. I thought she was begging for spare change and I rarely give money to people on the street unless it's a musician I like. You never know whether they're really who they appear to be—

"Yes, I remember that was in the papers, Sam. I also remember a boy panhandling in front of the restaurant every Friday afternoon. He'd smoke joints and collect quite a lot of money. He was cute, in a way, or so the gay boys at Arts all said. Then his mother would come and pick him up in a limousine. I wondered if she was his pimp! But Betty… in front of the health food store that day… she was sitting there clutching her Bible. Her hair was filthy. Her clothes were torn and ragged. When I realized she was my sister, I froze in my tracks! I don't know whether she recognized me right away. My very own sister, dressed like a vagabond."

Tim opened the apartment door and turned left into the kitchen. He'd lived here so long that the place still seemed like home, but it was strange to be here now without his Aunt Ruth. The refinished hardwood floors glowed a deep honey-brown color in the early morning light. Tim remembered that the big belt sander was still sitting in the middle of his kitchen floor on Hancock Street. The work ahead seemed daunting, but it would all be worthwhile if his floors came out looking as good as these.

"Does your Aunt Ruth have a housekeeper come in?" Nick asked. "This place is spotless."

"Nah, she does it all herself." Tim opened the back door onto the patio and picked up the watering can. "It's clean alright, but what this place needs is some fresh air. I'm surprised she didn't give the plants a good soaking before she left. She could have asked someone to do it… like me!" Tim was hurt that she hadn't confided in him where she was going.

"You could eat off this floor." Nick had a look around the kitchen. "And she didn't leave any dirty dishes in the sink or any science experiments in the refrigerator. I guess she didn't leave in any hurry."

"She's always been pretty anal about housework. She wasn't so fussy when I lived here and she was visiting me, but when I lived with her and Uncle Dan in high school she was meticulous. I'd almost forgotten about that." Tim filled the watering can again and again. Then he glanced at the refrigerator. When he lived here it was covered with pictures. Now there was just the South of Market Bare Chest Calendar his Aunt Ruth must have bought at Under One Roof to support the AIDS Emergency Fund.

"Do you want to look in here?" Nick was outside the closed door to Ruth's bedroom. "What are we looking for, anyway?"

"I'm not sure, but if anything was out of place, it might give me a clue. Maybe she just needed time to think before she marries Sam. Maybe she wanted to talk things over with an old friend. I think I know her so well and then sometimes I have to admit there are secrets in everyone's life, even secrets they keep from their closest friends."

"Now you're sounding mysterious, babe…"

"Don't worry, I'm not that complicated."

"Well Sam, you can imagine the ordeal it's been to hide her, especially from Tim. And she's so noisy when she's drunk—even in her sleep, she cries out like a monster is attacking her. The boys upstairs must have heard her moaning a couple of times. Oh Sam! They'll think it was you and me. Ha-ha-ha… the next time they see you I'll bet they give you a long hard look! Oh, God! I shouldn't be laughing! It's to keep from crying, I guess. You know what the Romans say, '*In Vino Veritas*.' Well, that was sure true in Betty's case. She told me some things I would rather not have known, horrible things she did to Tim when he was just a little boy… no, … I have no reason to doubt them now. She hadn't drawn a sober breath in years! And if Tim has blocked any memory of all that, it's a relief. I don't want to go into all the details on the phone,

Sam, but the worst part is that she doesn't regret a bit of it! Her mind is so twisted, between the alcohol and some sick interpretation of the Bible, that she thinks she was doing the right thing all along.

"No… no… I don't care what else happens. I mean, I hope this place will do her some good, but even when she gets out of there and she's sober, hopefully, I still don't want her coming after Tim. She has no right to his house or his money. After what she did to him, she doesn't even deserve to call herself his mother!"

Tim started thinking about the old pictures that used to be on this refrigerator. Now they were in a box on a shelf on Hancock Street. He remembered some of the beautiful men who'd been in this apartment, some of them several times, some for just a night or only an hour… or less. Where were they now? Some hadn't even made it as far as the bedroom. A couple of times someone followed him home from Collingwood Park in the wee small hours. When he didn't want to worry about his valuables, just inside the gate was far enough. The rest of the tenants would be asleep by that time. No one would ever know.

He remembered a sexy PG&E repairman who'd been working on the pole out in front when Tim came home from an early morning run. Teresa had almost caught them in the laundry room. Tim told her he was just showing the guy where the circuit breaker was, but both of them were still fastening up their pants. He'd told the guy he had a uniform fetish and to leave the tool belt on. Tim wondered how many loads had been finished off in that laundry room that had nothing to do with clothes.

Times sure had changed, now that Nick was part of his life. Maybe it was time to admit to the changes. Outside of Tim's dreams, he hadn't had sex with a stranger in ages. He didn't think of them as strangers at the time, of course. To whatever degree, some part of him fell deeply in love, if only for a moment. Sex was always easier than "dating" and

Tim would never believe there'd been anything wrong with learning to love as many other men as possible while he was on his way to loving Nick.

Tim headed toward his Aunt Ruth's bedroom – his old bedroom – and tried to remember the last time he'd made love with anyone else but Nick with as much trust and honesty, closeness and comfort and still so steaming hot! He couldn't remember anyone else. Nick had been pressuring him for a stronger commitment. Maybe it was time.

"Gosh, it's a relief to lie here in the sun and relax. I've been reading a Stephen King paperback the last couple of weeks, but I must have left it in my car. It's one of those books where he takes thirty pages to move the plot along by about five minutes. At the rate I'm going, it might last me all summer. Sometimes I just want to throw it across the room and scream, 'Get on with it, already!'

"No, I didn't buy it; someone left it on the bar, a lovely couple from Cleveland visiting their gay son. They were staying at Family Link. It's a place for people from out of town who are visiting loved ones who are sick. It started with AIDS families, but I think it's broader now. They did a benefit a while back at Arts; that's the only reason I know. It's just a couple of blocks from the restaurant. Anyway, they left the book on the bar. I would have returned it if I could, but they already told me they were on their way to the airport. Their son was doing much better and the father had to be back at work on Monday morning... back in Cleveland. Maybe they'd already finished the book...

"Oh, you're so funny. You're right, I'm digressing worse than Stephen King. I didn't mean to go on and on like this, monopolizing the conversation and I still haven't explained everything, but it's so good to hear your voice. I just wish it weren't over the telephone.

"I'm sure you've been to this part of California, haven't you? When I was in college we drove up here once or twice, but I'd forgotten how lovely it is, all the sunshine and the trees and the warm smells of nature. I went for a long drive yesterday after I got Betty settled in and I even toured a couple of wineries. I tasted a Petit Syrah and ended up buying a case. It's in the trunk of my car. I hope it doesn't boil in this heat. I'll cook us a nice dinner to go with it. Maybe lamb? It seems funny that people come to the Redwood Valley Ranch to *dry out* in the heart of the wine country.

"I ran into Terry and Chris, some customers I know from Arts. You met them both that day at my surprise party. They're the sweetest guys and both of them were born female, you know? Yes, the opposite of what Marcia went through. I got to know them over the bar a bit before they told me. I'd never known anyone before who was, either, but I felt flattered that they confided in me. I guess it's because the bar is just like an analyst's couch for a lot of people, but I like to think that I always listen with an open mind and a certain degree of empathy. I hope I project that.

"No, Sam… I think they're just the best of friends, going through something like this together. Yes, like Chastity Bono… 'Chaz', now. By the way, they told me they don't much care for her, I mean him, being a spokesperson for all of them. Each of them is an individual and has his own story to tell. Friends come in all forms, don't they? The whole idea of sex-change surgery planted the seed of an idea… Oh, goodness no, Sam, not me! I couldn't be happier being a woman, but I'll tell you one thing, if I woke up one morning in a man's body, I'd do everything I could to make things right again. And if I'd felt that way my whole life, that I was stuck in the wrong gender, I can hardly imagine it, but that's what these poor souls are going through. Wouldn't you do everything in your power, Sam, if it were you?

"Exactly. Anyway, this whole thing got me to thinking how some people will never understand anyone who's different—gays, even—or people from different religions, other than their own, and that we're all just human beings at heart. Well, they insisted on treating me to lunch and it was so nice to see them. They had fascinating stories, both of them, and all the while they were telling me about their families and their childhoods and their backgrounds, I was coming up with a little plan of my own. I can't go into it all on the telephone, no… They were staying at one of those resorts over in Guerneville for a long weekend and wanted to make a little side trip for some wine-tasting too…"

"Yes, well… Betty. She'd already tried the program at Hazelden in Minnesota. It's highly reputable. I guess Bud gave her an ultimatum, so she went through with it, but within a few weeks she was drinking again and when she went off the wagon she got even worse than before. She and I inherited plenty of family money, you know, but Betty's problems must have cost them most of her share. Bud was angrier that the money was wasted than he was about her drinking again. Whenever she passes out, he can go live the life he wants.

"I told her that day I found her outside the health food store that she could stay with me if she made an effort to get sober. I found a notice on the bulletin board across from the Badlands for one of those recovery groups and I gave her the number. She went to a couple of meetings, but then she'd walk right out and get another bottle. You should have seen her that first day. We must have laundered her clothes four times. I wanted to burn them, but she wouldn't hear of it. I told her that… what's that, Sam? Yes, she agreed to go to the Ranch this time, not that she had any choice in the matter… No, I'm paying for it. I promised I would.

"Oh, I just had the most wonderful idea! All this talk about Betty and religion and the sex-change operations. Oh, my! I think this could work, but I'll have to plan it very carefully and you can help me. No, not today. I need to roll it around in my brain for a while and then we'll discuss it in person when I see you.

Tim opened his Aunt Ruth's bedroom door and Nick stepped back to let him pass. "Wow, Snowman! This was the first place we ever got it on. There sure are a lot of good memories in this room, huh?"

"I thought our first time was in the Thunderbird out by the Legion of Honor."

"That doesn't count," Nick laughed. "We didn't finish."

"Maybe *you* didn't," Tim said with a grin. "Yeah, if these walls could only talk, huh? You getting horny again?"

"Always, but it's not the same with pastel ruffles around the bed. It doesn't turn me on like when you lived here. It's too clean, I guess, and these flowered curtains are *so* not sexy! I wonder how Sam can even perform in these surroundings—"

"Stop! Let's not go there. I don't want the vision of those two doing it stuck in my brain. They're family! Well… she is and he will be soon."

"Yes, my sister Betty was always religious, but it wasn't a case of having been raised that way. Our mother's spiritual beliefs were broader than any church could contain and Dad didn't care one way or another. Mother had her dreams, visions. That's where Tim gets it, but it's more subtle with him. He only sees things in his sleep, not when he's awake. Maybe when he gets older. Mother's grew stronger with age. I remember when people came from miles around to see her. They'd want her advice before they made any major life decisions.

"Nowadays I find it more interesting, especially as it affects Tim, but I didn't pay much attention at the time. When you grow up around something like that, you don't know that it's so unusual. Besides, I was always busy with schoolwork and parties and friends.

"Wait… What!? Oh my God! An ice pick! Hold on a minute, Sam."

"Let's go back to your place," Nick groped Tim and let him pass on his way to the living room. "I need coffee soon."

"Sorry. I know I got you up awfully early. As soon as we're done here we'll go have a romantic brunch… and then get to work on the hardwood floors."

"I wanna hear more about brunch." Nick grinned. "What's gonna be so romantic about it?"

"Oh, I don't know… we could be naked, for starters."

"An outdoor table at Café Flore?"

"In bed." Tim laughed.

"Sounds *real* good, Snowman. We haven't had breakfast in bed in a long time. You know… I'll bet your Aunt Ruth is just helping out a friend. I'll bet she got a call from an old classmate of hers from when she was at Stanford. Well, that woman looked to me to be older than Ruth, so maybe she was one of her professors that she admired. An important woman in her life might have been a big influence. Weren't they all feminists at Stanford in those days? Or else that woman she had in the car might have been someone she knew in Minneapolis and when she phoned up Ruth out of the blue like that and said she was in California and in some kind of trouble, Ruth said sure, she'd be glad to help…"

Nick wasn't usually one to talk so much, but now he was rambling on and on, a pure stream-of-consciousness pattern of one word right after another until he heard Tim yell, "Holy shit! Come in here!"

Ruth was gone several minutes this time. When she returned to the phone she was out of breath. "Sam? Are you still there? You won't believe what happened! That woman with the three little kids! The manager of this place, the Wagon Wheel Inn, just told me he caught her with an ice pick. She had her kids all piled into her car and then she ran back and grabbed the ice pick from on top of the ice machine. She was going after my tires! He caught her just in time! She threw the ice pick at him and took off. I'm not that worried about my tires; I have Triple A, but she could have put that poor man's eye out. Hold on, Sam. I may as well grab another cup of coffee as long as I'm up.

"Mmmm, good coffee. Now, where was I? Betty was always embarrassed by our mother. She over-reacted to the whole situation by becoming *ultra*-religious. Then she married Bud and within a few years after Tim was born she started to alternate between the Bible and the bottle. Tim's father's real name is Clarence—Clarence Snow—but everyone calls him Bud. He was the most boring person you'd ever want to meet, but he did his best. He was stable. He went to work every day as a mechanic. When he finally got up the gumption to put his foot down with Betty, she decided to come looking for me. She was actually looking for Tim, now that she thinks he's rich. I never should have let her know about Tim inheriting a house. I told her Tim doesn't have any liquid assets, but she didn't want to believe me. If it weren't for Jason leaving him the house, Tim wouldn't have anything. He will when I die, but even if he could forgive what his mother did to him, why would he want to see her, especially in the shape she was in?

"I told her if she stopped drinking and got her act together I'd buy her some new clothes and I could take her to see Rene, Tim's friend who does my hair and... oh... sorry, Sam... where was I? Oh yes, I was telling you about Bud, the mechanic. He was perfect for Betty. He was normal. Some people in the Midwest... I guess people are the same everywhere, but Bud has always been one of those people who just wanted to fit in. They go along to get along, never make waves, never say or do or even think anything that someone else might construe as the least bit controversial. An original way of thinking about things would be considered downright sinful.

"Tim always liked to run. He wasn't interested in any other sports, but he *lived* to run! It wasn't so much a discipline as a passion. When you consider all that he's been through, it's amazing Tim turned out as well adjusted as he is. It never occurred to me when he was a little boy that he might actually be running away from something."

Ruth's voice sounded muffled for a moment and Sam realized she was talking to someone else at the motel. "Good morning! Yes, it's a lovely day, isn't it? Yes, I'll be happy to watch it for you...sorry, Sam. More people are starting to come out of their rooms now. A girl put her bag down on the chair beside me. There, she's put on her headphones and crawled out onto a rubber raft on the pool—doesn't look like she could be much older than a teenager, but it's hard to tell these days. The music is so loud I can hear the bass beat blasting from here, so I'm sure she can't hear me. No wonder these kids have hearing problems when they get older.

"Now, where were we? Oh, it's so good to hear your voice too, Sam. I don't mean to be the one doing all the talking. I want to hear about your latest trip just as soon as I see you. Rome must be beautiful this time of year. I don't know why I should be acting so secretive, either. There's nobody here who knows anyone I'm talking about and the place isn't even full. There's one couple who checked in about the same time as I did the other night. She drove a car with Nevada plates and his were from Oregon. I suspect that they're married, but not to each other...

"I know... anyway... Betty had Tim at the doctor constantly. He didn't look frail to me, but he seemed to catch every typical childhood illness that came along and a few others I'd never heard of. Betty said he was accident-prone. He always had an upset stomach or a strange rash or she'd say he couldn't come out of his room because he was sleeping. Tim slept a lot when he was little. He had an awful lot of scrapes and bruises. I had my hands full raising Dianne at the same time, so I wasn't too concerned. Dianne was a couple of years older than Tim, so it only seemed natural when she sprouted up first, the way girls do. Dianne got into enough of her own troubles to keep me busy. If Tim had more sprains and bruises and broken bones than Dianne, I figured it was just because boys were rougher."

Sam spoke for a few minutes again and Ruth replied, "Yes, but in those days we had never heard of that... whatever they called...? Yes, you're right. I think it *is* called Munchausen's Syndrome... but we didn't know in those days. That's right... by proxy. Well, no, they never diagnosed it as such. I suspected something funny was going on between Betty and that doctor she was always dragging Tim to see though. He was *her* doctor in the first place and then he started treating Tim. I guess she wouldn't have any trouble with a guilty conscience getting undressed in front of a doctor.

"No, you never told me about that, Sam. How interesting. There's still so much you and I don't know about each other. I guess we'll have all our married years to find out all those things. Yes, of course, I still intend to marry you, Sam. Don't tell me you've changed your mind!

"Well, that's good… Anyway, the stigma of Betty's alcoholism was bad enough, especially for a woman, but people were so vicious, too, saying she should have paid more attention to her husband than the bottle. When Bud started fooling around, it didn't surprise anyone and she was so devout, she still looked down on the rest of us like we were heathens. I almost felt sorry for Bud until he turned out to be such a homophobe, but that was probably a blessing in disguise. It got Tim out of their house where I could look after him. Dan and I did, I should say. For all the negative things I could say about Dan since our divorce, he was a good father to Dianne and he was good to Tim. He wasn't a bigot. He's in advertising. He knew gay people. We both did. It was no big deal and the times were changing.

"I miss you too, Sam. I miss you terribly. Well, you *could* drive up and meet me here. I told Artie I needed at least a couple of weeks off, so I don't have to rush back. It might be fun to spend the night at the Wagon Wheel Inn but tomorrow morning I have an appointment with the director of the Redwood Valley Ranch before I was planning to drive back to the city. He wasn't there on the weekend and I have a few more questions for him.

Tim was on his hands and knees by the living room window. Nick knelt down next to him and saw the battered suitcase beside the desk that held Ruth's computer.

"What is it, Snowman? What's wrong? Who does that old suitcase belong to?"

Tim held the luggage tag up to the light so Nick could read it.

> Mrs. Clarence Snow
> 1834 32nd Avenue South
> Minneapolis, Minnesota 55406

"It's my mother's." Tim's mind raced back to a terrible place in his childhood, a nightmare he had long ago forgotten. "Nick, she's looking for me. I just know it. And I don't ever want to see her again."

"Come on, Snowman. Let's just go back to your place. I'll make us breakfast. And I promise I'll be with you through whatever happens, no matter what. There's nothing more for us to do here."

"She did? Delia and Frank both gave notice? After all these years? Oh, my… we do have a lot to talk about when I see you.

"Yes, I've had the *pleasure* of meeting Miss Rosa Rivera, Sam. Artie seems quite taken with her. He talks like she's the next big thing. I'm not sure if he means it or if he's trying to get his big break on television. He's dying to polish up his old act, you know…

"Yes, I caught some of her show last night. I told you they have cable here. She was covering a wedding at Holy Trinity out by Lake Merced. I can only imagine what she had to pay the Greek Orthodox to allow her film crew in there. She's always oblivious to being an intrusion, but some of the food looked awfully good.

"You did? She was? Sam!"

Ruth laughed so hard she had to sit up and in doing so her coffee spilled all over the old *Good Housekeeping Magazine*. The chocolate soufflé on the cover looked like it was melting.

"I would have knocked her right off her barstool! Oh, she was standing? Almost on your lap? Well, that's even worse!" Ruth laughed out loud again.

"Yes, you're right, Sam. I'm going to call Tim as soon as we finish. I can't put off talking to him any longer. He's going to find out sooner or later that his mother is looking for him and it ought to be from me. Oh, that's a wonderful idea, Sam. And we can try a bottle of this delicious wine I just bought. See you then, Sam... unless you want to call me again later this evening. My cell phone seems to be working fine. I must not have had it charged up before."

Chapter 16

Artie might have let the relentless gloom get him down without his big comeback to look forward to. Sometimes the summer days in San Francisco all look alike... cold, damp and gray. Each morning that week the fog was so thick that it blocked out the sun until noon... or one... or five. But each time Artie pulled one of his old gowns out of the trunk he could almost feel the heat of the spotlights again and the warmth of the loving crowds.

Tim kept busy too. He worked at Arts every night that week and worked on his kitchen floor during the daytime. The first sanding exposed the tiny nails in the hardwood floors. Now he gave each one a tap with the hammer and a little steel tool that looked like an awl—exactly the way Nick taught him.

On Saturday Nick drove down from Monte Rio and they spent the afternoon filling the tiny holes with wood putty. They tuned in a classical station and didn't talk much. Tim's back ached and he hadn't mentioned his mother once since Aunt Ruth called on Sunday from the Wagon Wheel Inn.

Nick was frustrated that Tim wouldn't confide in him and he couldn't remember the last time they spent a Saturday night without sex. Sunday morning over breakfast, Nick brought up the subject. "Are you sure you don't want to talk about your mother, Snowman?" Nick had managed to cook up coffee, pancakes and eggs in Tim's dusty torn-apart kitchen, which they ate in the living room.

"I've already told you all about my parents. I thought I'd never have to see them again after they threw me out. They're in the past and they can stay there."

"But she's here, now, Tim. Your mother is only a couple of hours north of here. Your Aunt Ruth said she'll—"

"I think I need to go for a run. You want more coffee?" Tim stood up and walked to the sink with his dirty dishes.

Nick ignored the question and walked over to put his arms around Tim's shoulders. "At least you ought to think about what your Aunt Ruth said on the phone. You need to make a plan, just in case what she told you really happens. When your mother gets out of there, she might just—"

"I appreciate you being here for me. I really do. Maybe we can talk about all of this later, okay? I just think I need to be alone for a little while. I feel kind of numb these days. Maybe some fresh air and exercise would…"

"Sure Babe," Nick tousled Tim's hair with his fingertips and kissed him again.

Sunday morning started earlier than usual at Arts restaurant on the 500 block of Castro Street, fog or no fog; Artie was rehearsing.

While he waited for his accompanist Phil to arrive, Artie lifted jeweled and sequined gowns out of their boxes and held each of them up to the light on the little stage. They looked awful, but it wasn't the dresses' fault; it was the lighting. He had to order new gels first thing Monday morning. He would call Holzmueller, down off Bayshore Boulevard—maybe even take a drive out there and see if they still carry "surprise pink." Artie picked up a pen and made a notation on his rapidly growing list on top of the piano.

Phil was the only employee without his own set of keys, since he never had to open or close the place. When he knocked, he was surprised to see Arturo let him in. "Where's Artie?"

"He's around here somewhere."

"What are you doing here so early?"

"You know how Artie is. If he had to get up early he wouldn't let me sleep in. He's so excited you'd think he was going back on stage at Finocchios."

"I can't believe he dragged either one of us out of bed at this hour."

"Phil! Stop complaining and get in here!" Artie shouted from the far end of the room.

"Speaking of drag…"

"You know this is the only time we can practice, when the place is closed. Besides, the gay parade is only a couple of weeks away. That's the last day to enter the contest and the entry forms are coming in like crazy! Rosa's live TV special from Arts is the weekend after the Fourth. There's no time to waste!"

"What's with all the sequins? Are you redecorating the place for Pride? Isn't it gay enough already?"

"I'm trying to decide which outfit to wear for my television appearance. Out of one whole steamer trunk full of beaded gowns, I've narrowed down my choices to three, but I might still change my mind. At least with two grooms at this wedding, I don't have to worry about upstaging the bride, but I don't think I've lost enough weight to squeeze into something white. Arturo likes that blue one. This is one Pat Montclaire made for me. It's an Edith Head knock-off."

"Who's that?"

"Pat Montclaire was a fabulous drag queen—what a transformation!—but she was an even better seamstress, used to do costumes for some of the big shows in Vegas. She was Empress once too, over twenty years ago."

"No, the other one."

"Edith Head? She did costumes for movies and, contrary to popular belief, her middle name was not 'Givesgood.' Edith gives good head, get it? Oh, Phil… you young kids don't know half the fun you missed out on back in the day. Which one is your favorite?"

"It's too early for me to think," Phil grumbled. "I had a new client at the Hyatt Regency last night. Whatever drugs he was on made it impossible for him to get off, so he hired me overtime. That's when I can really rake in the bucks, but I've hardly had any sleep. You're lucky I'm so damned responsible that I showed up on time."

"I don't want to hear about your tricks and I don't approve of drugs, you know."

"I wasn't doing drugs; he was."

"Whatever. Don't you make enough money here playing the piano? Do you really have to resort to prostitution?"

"I'm an *escort*, Artie. What I do is completely legal and above board. People pay me for my *time*. That's all!"

"Oh, sure," Artie snorted. "I suppose they want you to don a tuxedo and they take you on a date to the Symphony on a Saturday night, walk into Davies Hall on your arm and then to Farallon for a quiet dinner afterward."

"I do own a tuxedo, Artie, and it has been known to happen, but not on a Saturday night. I'm always right here playing this damned piano for you."

"And whoring after you get off work…"

"Escorting," Phil insisted, "We might meet at the bar in his hotel lobby and then if we happen to hit it off, we might connect, that's all."

"Do you wear a yellow hat or a rose boutonnière for him to recognize you?"

Phil ignored Artie's last remark. "Right this minute there are probably dozens—no—hundreds of couples who paired off last night, waking up in hotel rooms all over San Francisco. Or in apartments or in dungeon playrooms or at one of their grandma's house—what difference does it make? It's nobody's business and with me, no bodily fluids are ever exchanged. I'm not stupid!"

"Yeah, right!"

"Don't be such a prude, Artie. Besides, I intend to buy real estate before I'm forty. I don't see anyone leaving me a house, the way Tim got his."

"You never know." Artie realized when he was defeated and it was time to change the subject. "Look, Phil, I dragged out all my old sheet music. I was looking for a love song, something suitable for a wedding show. I've performed each and every one of these in my illustrious career. There's got to be one we can whip into shape."

Phil picked up one of the folders, spread it out above the keyboard and plunked out a few notes of *La Vie En Rose*, Artie stopped him. "No, my French is too rusty and I can't get into that little black dress."

"You did Edith Piaf?" Phil laughed out loud.

"Don't be a such a smart ass. I did a couple of Piaf *songs*. I never *looked* like her, but I had a beret and a little black dress—I was a lot thinner then, okay?—never mind! Rosa's Italian, not French and black wouldn't be right for a wedding show, anyway."

"How about this one?" Phil began to play *My Funny Valentine*.

"Too slow, I think, but it *is* in my range."

"What range is that? Baritone?"

"Find another one! We've only got a few weeks to resurrect my persona *and* my singing voice."

"*I've Got You Under my skin*? Or maybe *Stardust*? Phil played and sang:

"Beside a garden wall where stars are bright
You are in my arms
The nightingale tells its fairy tale... of paradise where roses grew..."

"You have a lovely voice, Phil."

"Thanks, Artie."

"Maybe someday we should work up a duet."

"Yeah, right." Phil tossed Artie's phrase back at him.

"But not this time. I'm the one who's making a comeback and I'm doing it alone and I'm doing it my way."

"Sinatra? I don't know. *My Way*? For a wedding?"

"Shut up. Here, try this one. *From this Moment on.*" Artie sang,

"From this moment on,
You for me, dear, Only two for tea, dear, From this moment on..."

While Tim got ready to go for his run, Nick pulled on his jeans and boots, then put a finer grade of sandpaper into the machine and began the next phase of the kitchen floor. Tim came out of the bedroom in sneakers and running shorts and stared at Nick a while. He was amazed sometimes at how hot Nick was, especially when he didn't know anyone was watching him. His muscles moved under his broad shoulders as he pulled the machine across the floor as easily as mowing a lawn. Nick's white paper facemask reminded Tim of a surgeon.

Tim still saw himself as the sickly, skinny Minnesota kid who was never very good at anything. Why would this big handsome Nick want him? "What could he see in me?" Tim asked himself the same question over and over again.

Nick looked so sexy that Tim almost changed his mind about going for a run. Instead, he opened a couple of windows to let the dust out, kissed Nick on the forehead and mouthed the words "see you later" over the noise from the sander. Tim intended to run around Dolores Park, but the sun was breaking through and the top was down on the Thunderbird. He climbed behind the wheel and headed south under the palm trees of Dolores Street and slid out onto 280.

A few minutes later a huge tanker truck slowed in front of him and Tim couldn't see to pass, so he pulled over to the right and turned off at the next exit. Rockaway Beach in Pacifica wasn't a place he usually stopped on his way to San Gregorio or Devil's Slide, but an old VW bug covered in daisy decals vacated a parking space and Tim grabbed it. Sunlight played across a layer of late morning haze above the waves and the fog had burned back to the horizon. The sun was nearly overhead by now and felt hot on Tim's shoulders.

He pulled off his T-shirt and took a sip of water, then climbed over the boulders and started to run, trying to focus on something outside of himself. He thought about the plans Nick had showed him for the new deck. He pictured Artie in drag at his Aunt Ruth's surprise birthday party. He tried to imagine Teresa's new boyfriend and hoped that this time she'd found someone who wasn't a jerk. He tried to think about Rosa Rivera's television show and her sexy assistant, Bruno. Tim tried to think about anything besides what he feared most, the imminent reunion with his mother.

This was not a gay beach. It was dotted with families, dogs and kites. Like any California beach, the roar of the surf and cries of seagulls drowned out most other sounds, even the screams and giggles of children. Tim didn't need a gay beach today. He had Nick waiting for him at home.

Things were going well these days. Tim's life had settled back down. It had been a couple of weeks since they'd found the suitcase and even longer since his mother had gone into rehab. Yes, life was just fine the way it was. He'd gotten used to having Nick drive down from the Russian River every weekend, always affectionate and horny. He could still flirt with his regular customers and the tourists who showed up at the restaurant on Castro Street. He even had the freedom to meet someone new from time to time, although he hadn't been tempted to take things any further than flirtation in a long time. And Nick hadn't mentioned *marriage* in a while either, thank heaven. Maybe he'd forgotten about it. Tim didn't want change. Things were *perfect* the way they were.

Tim ran south along the surf's edge. Ahead of him the cliffs rose out of the sea and he would have to turn back. There was a runner ahead, a little taller than him and a lot more muscular. He was about Nick's build, but darker complexioned. Tim checked out the long legs and the ripe buns sliding in perfect rhythm under his gray shorts. The other runner reached the end of the beach and turned back. Now Tim watched as each step created a rhythmic back and forth a few inches below the man's waist, a swaying pendulum barely under wraps. When they met there was no smile, no sly grin, no lasting eye contact… definitely not a gay beach.

Tim reached the end and turned back too. This run felt good, the fresh salt air and the sunshine. He'd spent years trying to forget about his parents. They didn't want him when they found out he was gay and threw him out of the house back in high school. That seemed like a lifetime ago and he barely remembered the mistreatments of his earlier childhood. He didn't want to think about those times and he didn't need his mother trying to finagle her way back into his life now.

Tim watched the other runner drop to the sand, pick up a water bottle and take a long swallow. A woman beside him was all cocoa-buttered legs and fleshy breasts held inside a few scraps of silver fabric.

"Be careful!" she yelled at the man. A drop of his sweat must have landed on her and Tim couldn't believe anyone would complain about a little thing like that. Some guys Tim knew would almost pay to taste the sweat from the pores of a hunk like him. Then she reached for him and smiled. She was a knockout too. Her fingers moved back and forth across his chest in the motion of a hand wiping steam off a window or a mirror. She licked her lips as her fingers slid below the waist of his shorts as he nestled in closer.

Tim picked up his pace again. A small blue jet, like a fighter plane, appeared out of nowhere, did a death spiral and shot out a stream of pink smoke. Why? Fleet Week was still months away. Tim half expected to see it skywrite SURRENDER DOROTHY and he wasn't even stoned.

Tim stepped up over the rocks again and looked back at the couple on the beach. The man was on top of her now and it didn't look like she was complaining. Tim climbed behind the wheel of the Thunderbird and took another swig of water. It had been a long time since he'd cruised a straight guy by mistake. That was one good reason to live in the Castro. Now he wondered how soon he could make it back to Hancock. He hoped Nick was still ready for him. Silly thought… Nick was always ready. This time Tim was ready too… ready and horny and longing for it.

Artie snapped his fingers and said, "Pick up the tempo a little… that's it. *From this moment on. For you've got the love I need so much, Got the skin I love to touch, Got the arms to hold me tight.*"

Artie sang the next few words staccato:

*"You've
got the
sweet lips
to-ooh
kiss me
go—od
night.*

"Okay, Phil, big finish, now…

*"From this moment on,
You and I, babe,
We'll be ridin' high, babe,
Ev'ry care is gone
From—this—mo—ment—on.*"

Arturo and Phil both applauded, but to Artie it sounded like the empty restaurant was SRO with his adoring fans.

Chapter 17

Tim was vomiting into a toilet bowl the size of a six-man hot tub. He'd call it a six-*person* hot tub outside of San Francisco, but Tim hadn't been in a co-ed hot tub since he left Minnesota. He'd been dreaming about Minnesota most of the night, but this was the dream that woke him. He ached everywhere and the hacking came from deep in his body, below his center of gravity, below the stomach, maybe below his knees. Yes, even his toes hurt from puking so hard.

His mother stood over him. She moved in slow motion and he couldn't hear her words, but she was clapping and shouting and he could read her lips: "Good boy, Timmy! Throw it all up. There's a good boy!"

He almost didn't recognize her with so much henna in her hair. She wore a pink gingham apron over a green print housedress with a strand of pop beads. Tim had tried not to think about his mother for years, but ever since he and Nick came across her old suitcase in Aunt Ruth's apartment he thought about her all the time and his dreams about her were even worse.

Then a doctor and a nurse appeared. They were smiling too. Everyone acted like they were proud of Tim for throwing up.

Tim lurched out of bed and ran to the bathroom. Why did Nick have to leave the lid down? He must have been raised better than Tim was. Everything about Nick was better than Tim was, but he tried not to let him know. He lived in fear that Nick would find out. No, he didn't. It was only when his dreams were so vivid. Dreams could bring on the paranoia. Everything was okay except the pain in that place below his stomach.

The normal-sized toilet seemed so small. Tim lifted his face from the cold rim and he wasn't sick at all, but he was wide awake now. He rose to his feet and figured that as long as he was naked at the toilet in the middle of the night he might as well empty his bladder. He hoped he hadn't woken Nick.

Dreams like tonight's reminded him that he meant to ask Aunt Ruth about his grandmother's dreams. Were they like these? Did she have visions that nobody wanted to talk about? Tim wasn't sure he believed in visions, but he knew dreams. If they could be traced back to his grandmother, his Aunt Ruth should know. Were they inherited or were they drug-induced? He'd been having the dreams as long as he could remember and he hadn't taken any drugs as a child—or had he?

Tim stepped into the kitchen. Sawdust was everywhere, spread so thick that the ridges on the wainscoting looked smooth. Tim stared out the window at where the redwood tree used to be. The view of downtown was covered in fog except for the light on top of the Transamerica Pyramid.

Tim heard a flute in the distance, but who'd be playing a flute at this hour of the night? The nearest bar was the Last Call, formerly the Men's Room on 18th Street at Noe. Sometimes he heard drunks singing their way home from Castro Street. Maybe the flute was only the sound of a strange summer wind that had come up in the night.

He meant to question his Aunt Ruth, but his desire to get to the bottom of things usually faded away with the dreams when morning came. Sometimes when Nick was around, when he heard Tim cry out in his sleep, Nick would encourage him to find out more, but tonight Nick was still fast asleep.

Tim looked at the footprints of sawdust he tracked from the kitchen to the bedroom carpet. The socks he'd pulled off earlier were on the floor beside his bed. He used them to wipe the soles of his feet and then tossed them toward the hamper. He pulled the covers back and there was Nick, half-hard, always ready for him. Tim was happy that Nick could spend the night, especially when he was having his dreams.

Tim slid into bed and felt the weight of Nick's sleeping arm wrap around him like a favorite blanket. Tim drifted back to sleep and it wasn't until nearly morning that he had any more dreams. This time he and Nick were on a rowboat on the Russian River. Nick's hair was thin and white and his eyes had a thousand tiny lines around them, but they were as blue and full of love as ever.

The kitchen floor spent the week under tarps and Tim spent the week dusting. Nick would come back down on the weekend to seal it, but in the meanwhile Tim gave the entire flat a thorough cleaning. He vacuumed the tops of every door frame and window. He dragged a soft cloth over every picture frame and tabletop. He dusted books and lamps and the leaves of plants. He washed clothes that weren't even dirty. On Saturday morning when the sun came in across the kitchen, he and Nick removed the tarps and put on the final sealant and it was perfect. Then they went out to eat and celebrate while the floor dried for 24 hours.

The Sunday brunch shift was busy and Tim was on automatic pilot. He kept forgetting the day's specials, but this time of year they were usually the same. Arturo mixed up an elaborate concoction of fresh fruit with three kinds of berries, seedless red and green grapes and melon balls of crenshaw and honeydew. Tim recommended this to people who wanted something light and healthy for brunch. Then he talked them into an order of French toast to go underneath the fruit (with lots of butter, of course) and warm maple syrup drizzled over it all.

Tim barely noticed when the canned music stopped and the piano started. He was taking an order for a young man and his partner and a set of parents. Tim tried to guess which of the gay couple the father resembled more. Tim's back was to the piano when the mother said, "Beethoven. How lovely. I'm glad you suggested this place, Ian."

Tim had never heard classical music at Arts before. When he got to the bar he asked Artie, "What's going on? Where's Phil?"

"I have him rehearsing with me so much lately for Rosa's TV show that I gave him the day off. Her name is Mimi. She's from the Music Conservatory. She doesn't speak much English, but she plays beautifully. When I called I told them I wanted someone to play instrumental music only. No sing-alongs."

Jake arrived at the waiter's station. "Two Mimosas, please. Artie, where's Phil?'

"He's off today. I think this will be a nice change."

"No show tunes, huh?" Tim asked.

"Well, that was another thought I had," Artie said. "You know that guy who's been coming in every weekend? The loud one?

"Oh yeah," Tim said. "He's built like Pavarotti and he thinks he sounds like him. What a jerk when he gets a few drinks in him. I think his name is Joe."

"He prefers Joseph," Artie corrected. "And his weasely little lover's name is Lionel, but at least you never hear a peep out of him."

"Josephina!" Jake said. "And look out! Here he comes now."

The enormous man stepped up to the bar and was about to order drinks from Scott when he noticed the change in atmosphere. "Where's Phil?"

"I guess he's not working," Scott said. "He has another night job when he leaves here, you know. Do you want your usual, Joseph?"

"I'm not sure if we'll stay or not. Does this new girl know her stuff? She looks like a child in an evening gown! What the hell is she doing here, anyway?"

"Artie says she's from the Conservatory."

"Where *is* Artie?" Joseph demanded.

Scott turned around and realized that Artie had *conveniently* disappeared. "He must be on a break."

"Here's my card. See that Artie gets it! If he wants *our* business, he'd better stop making changes willy-nilly around here and put things back the way they were. I'm sure my performances are a big draw, but if he doesn't appreciate talent, he can do without. Come on, Lionel. Let's get out of here!"

Joseph and Lionel had barely set foot outside the door and onto the sidewalk when half the room burst into applause. The brunch crowd at Arts was apparently no more fond of Joseph's singing than the staff was. Artie stuck his head out of the kitchen and smiled. "That went well, I thought."

Chapter 18

"**S**ure, Ruth... okay, I'll tell him. It's no trouble. I'm on my way over to Arts right now. See you in a bit." Nick hung up the phone and grabbed his jacket. He walked down to 18th Street so that he could stop at the Bank of America ATM on the corner and get some more cash. He wanted to arrive at the restaurant before Ruth and Sam did, but there was no hurry, even when he took into account the need to negotiate the usual Sunday afternoon obstacle course of worthy causes on Castro Street. Two little boys in matching school uniforms with clip-on ties were selling raffle tickets for a trip to Hawaii. Tickets were a dollar apiece or six for five dollars and the proceeds were going to help their school's music program. Nick already had his wallet out to get his ATM card, so he handed them a five-dollar bill and scribbled his name and phone number six times.

Further along were another couple of guys about twenty years older than the little boys. They sported matching nipple rings on nearly identical perfect bodies. Nick wondered if they were twins in their matching haircuts and expensive orthodontia. Their raffle tickets were fifty dollars each for a new silver BMW convertible parked at the curb. Nick didn't see what the proceeds were for, but as he retrieved his cash from the ATM he noticed Birdie Fuller in her SFPD uniform heading toward them. Nick wondered if Teresa was back from Seattle yet, but didn't have time to ask.

"You can't leave the car in the bus stop, fellas," Birdie said to the BMW boys. "The next two spots are for taxicabs, but the one in front of the Sausage Factory is about to open up. How about backing it up a few feet? You don't want to make me write a ticket on that pretty new car, do you?"

The one with the raffle tickets handed them to the one holding the money so that he could reach into the pocket of his skin-tight shorts for the car key. Even though both of them towered over Birdie Fuller, they seemed accustomed to acquiescing to an officer in uniform. Her demeanor helped, too. She always tried friendliness first. If that didn't work, her natural butch intimidation tactics could come later.

Nick would have continued on his way to Arts if Birdie hadn't spotted him first. "Hey there! Aren't you Tim Snow's friend?"

"Yes." Nick smiled. It had been a while since anyone used the term *friend* to describe what he and Tim had together, but Nick wasn't one to argue with a cop, either.

"He used to live in Teresa's building, right? You were the guys without the gate key. I remember you now."

"That's right. I'm on my way over to Arts to see Tim now. My name is Nick."

"Nick! Right… I'm Birdie Fuller… at your service!" The policewoman grinned and gave Nick a firm handshake.

"I remember you too. How's Ruth's cat? Are you still stuck with the feeding chores?"

"Teresa gets back tonight sometime, so she can take over."

"She won't have to," Nick said. "I just talked to Ruth on the phone. She and Sam are meeting us at the restaurant, too. They're on their way into the city right now.

"Sounds like a party. Maybe I'll stop by and say hi to Artie if he's working, but first I've got to go over and pet me some dogs. Seeya, Nick!"

"Seeya, Birdie," Nick watched her head toward the animal lovers from Rocket Dog Rescue on the corner. He'd tried not to look when he walked by them or he'd have wanted to adopt them all. With his schedule lately, it wouldn't be fair to have an animal, but he hoped maybe someday he and Tim could adopt a dog together. And it wouldn't be some prissy little neurotic gay show-dog, either. They'd get a real dog, a butch dog, a country dog.

Mimi broke into *Rhapsody in Blue* just as Rosa Rivera came in the door, followed by Bruno with his hands full of applications for the big gay wedding at Arts.

"Rosa Rivera!" Artie shouted across the room. "*Bienvenuto!* Don't you look lovely today? *Non sembrate oggi belli?*"

"*Grazie tante,* Artie! *Che piacere vederti.*" She was talking fast and gesturing wildly. "*Oh mio dio!* We have nearly sixty applications already. How many have you got?"

"At least that many," Artie said, "And it's not even Pride until next Sunday. They're coming in every day. What are we going to do?"

"I don't know. I'll be in the parade, you know. More couples will want to enter after they've seen me in person. Some of them sent along their photographs. You wouldn't believe how graphic the pictures are. Some are even nudes!"

"Really?" Artie had to see *those* pictures. "You'd better leave them all here with me. What do we need to confirm, exactly?"

"Make sure they're legitimate. Both entrants must be over twenty-one, they have to live within a San Francisco zip code. I should hope that they're photogenic for the cameras, but we didn't *ask* for pictures, so we can't rule out the ones who didn't send them. If I ever do something like this again, I will…"

"How many finalists do you want?" Artie asked.

"How many people will this place hold? Don't forget the cameras and technicians need room. They'll run cables out to the van where they'll take care of the technical things. Bruno can help with that and it will save up *some* of our precious space…"

"We'll have to rent some chairs. We could fit a hundred in here, maybe more if we took out the larger tables and put the chairs in rows with an aisle down the center, but which one would walk down it?"

"Neither. They'll get in position on the commercial break, before the cameras start rolling. After you weed out the ones that don't qualify, we'll draw twenty-five couples for finalists and each winning couple will get four tickets, so they can bring two friends as witnesses. Everyone will dress up, just in case they're going to be on TV and it will be a good-looking crowd. That's a total of one hundred for the studio audience—I mean, the ceremony—with room for a few extras."

"That's good," Artie said. "I want to invite some people to hear me sing. I'll call up some of the old gang from Finocchios, if any of them are still alive. Arturo will want to invite our tenants from Collingwood Street and the gay papers should send reporters. Donna Sachet might write about it in her column, if she's not busy at Harry Denton's... no, come to think of it, that's only on Sundays... and maybe the *Chronicle*. I'll bet Leah Garchik will come if she can. And I'm sure Ruth will want to invite Sam. Each of our staff should be able to invite a friend. Let me see... who else?"

"Whatever!" Rosa wasn't here to listen to Artie's blathering. Some days it took all her patience just to remain civil to him. "We're filming some local florists today. I can't stay here all afternoon chit-chatting. Let's see... I'll be on camera in the center of the room, and we'll have another camera close up on the couple's faces with the audience in the background and one camera from the opposite direction to get the person who is officiating at the ceremony... Oh, did I tell you... we might have Gavin Newsom?"

"No kidding!" Artie said. "What a coup!"

"He's big on gay marriage, you know."

"He likes gays and the homeless, as long as he doesn't have to sleep with either," Jake cracked and Artie gave him a dirty look.

"Don't say anything yet, Artie," Rosa warned. "I'll firm things up when I see him this week. We're taping one of my wedding episodes of *Let's Make it Happen* at St. Mary's Cathedral. He'll be there as well as two other former mayors, the governor, and a lot of people flying in…"

"Who's getting married?" Artie asked.

"Natalie Rhodes."

"Doesn't her father own that new hotel they're building down on the waterfront?"

"He already *sold* that one. He's building an even bigger one a block away! They won't let me bring cameras into St. Mary's, but I'll get the guests coming and going. It'll be the red carpet treatment and we'll have full access to the reception. I shot an interview yesterday with Natalie in her childhood bedroom at their home in Seacliff. It's *così dolce*… such a precious setting with her trying on her veil and in the background are her little teddy bears and the view of the Golden Gate Bridge."

"Who's the lucky groom?"

"Terry Winthrop, the sole heir to his grandfather's pharmaceutical company. It will be a good *first* marriage for both of them."

"He should be the one wearing white," Jake interrupted. "… just in case anything falls out of his nose."

"Don't you have work to do?!" Artie scolded.

"Come to think of it, maybe I ought to do an episode on prenuptial agreements, but that wouldn't be very romantic."

"Which camera will be on me when I do my number?"

"Oh, Artie… there'll be plenty of time to work that out later," Rosa cut him off.

Mimi started playing again and Artie sang along, "*Take my hand*… Hey! Wait a minute! That's *Stranger in Paradise*. She's supposed to be playing classical music that nobody could sing along to. I just did!"

A stranger at the bar heard Artie and explained, "It *is* classical music. That's from Borodin's opera *Prince Igor*. The melody was the inspiration for *Stranger in Paradise* in the Broadway show *Kismet.*"

"Well, excuse me…" Artie turned to the stranger. "How do you know that?"

"I'm from New York… big Broadway fan… it's a hobby of mine."

"Smart-ass queen" Artie said under his breath. "Where did Jake disappear to? He's supposed to be the trivia buff around here. Oh well… as long as that loud-mouthed Joseph is gone, it's a lovely tune and she's playing it in my key."

When he arrived at the restaurant, Nick didn't see Tim right away, but he spotted Rosa Rivera at the bar. Her assistant Bruno turned all the way around on his barstool to flirt with Nick before the front door had even closed. "Hello there, handsome."

Nick looked behind him to see if Bruno was talking to someone else and Rosa spun Bruno back with a tug on his shoulder. "Can't you stop cruising for one minute? Pay attention here! *Buoni a nulla!* What do I keep you for?"

"Hello Nick!" Artie said over the chaos. "Tim must be in the kitchen. You know Rosa Rivera, don't you? And her assistant Bruno?"

"How do you do," Nick shook Rosa's hand as she turned to face him. "I'm very pleased to meet you, Miss Rivera."

"*Ché uomo* handsome! How do *you* do?" Rosa batted her eyelashes. "*Sono estasiata di conoscerla*. The pleasure is all mine."

Tim appeared from the men's room wiping his hands on a paper towel and made a fast approach. "Hey stud… what's up?" Tim put his arms around Nick, which prompted Nick to return his affection with a kiss.

"*Merda*! The best ones are always taken. *Quelli belli sono tutti* gay." Rosa was disappointed that Nick wouldn't return her flirtations, but her smile reappeared as she handed him an entry form. "You two ought to enter. Maybe you'll be the lucky winners."

They both ignored her and Tim asked Nick, "What's going on? I thought you were gonna wait for me at home."

"I just got off the phone with your Aunt Ruth. She thought you'd be done with work by now."

"I normally would, but…" Tim cocked his head in the direction of the only occupied table—a pair of young blond love-birds at a corner table.

"Did you say you talked to Ruth?" Artie asked Nick. "It's about time someone heard from her. Where is she?"

"She and Sam took a little trip together."

"Thank goodness. I was worried that she'd gone the way of Madalyn Murray O'Hair!"

"Who's that?" Tim asked.

"She was that infamous atheist women who disappeared. Don't you ever watch the History Channel?"

"Sometimes, I guess, but I must have missed that one."

"Your Aunt Ruth's not an atheist, is she?" Jake was back.

"Only if you compare her to my mother, but… never mind! Where is she? Where have they been?"

"They went to Wyoming—the Tetons—but they're back in Hillsborough now. She asked me how you were doing after that phone call a couple of weeks ago. She said she thought you might have needed some time to process the news about your mother, but she hoped you would have called her by now."

"I've been trying not to think about that phone call."

"Why? You still haven't told me everything, have you?"

"If what Aunt Ruth thinks is true, the main reason my mother came out here was because she thought I was dying of AIDS."

"Why would she think that?"

"Because *all* gay people are dying of AIDS, that's just how those people think."

"Well, then her intentions were good, anyway. She must have gotten over your being gay, at least enough to want to see you *one last time*. She wanted to smooth everything over with you. That's not so bad, is it?"

"She didn't care about me dying, Nick. Aunt Ruth told her way back when I inherited Jason's house and that's what she wants. My dad's just about through with her and her drinking and who could blame him? He's got his own life now. She figured she could get her hands on my house, sell it, and the money would support her in grand style in Minnesota."

"Oh, I'm sorry, babe. That's a whole different story."

"No kidding."

"What an evil bitch!"

"Yep…"

Tim started to walk away, so Nick changed the subject. "I thought you carried your cell phone with you. Don't you know how to change the ring from *The 1812 Overture* yet?"

"I thought I already did. That must be its default. I know how to put it on vibrate."

"I'll bet you do," Artie said with a wink.

"Am I a sitting duck here? Is my mother about to walk in that door any minute… after all these years?"

"No, babe, I can tell you that much, but your Aunt Ruth will have to tell you the rest. She should be here any minute."

"My mother is part of the past and I want her to stay there. I like my life the way it is. I don't need some phony tearful reunion and I sure as hell don't need to hear how much I upset her by being gay. If I could deal with it, she can too—or not! I don't care! I don't need any changes in my life right now at all… like getting married and moving to the country." Tim stopped, took a deep breath and turned to Nick with a sorry smile. "Oh, man, you didn't deserve that. I apologize. One thing doesn't have anything to do with the other, I know…"

"That's okay, Snowman, I hear you," Nick had winced at how Tim said the word *married*, but he understood the need to vent. "But this thing with your mother… don't you think you need to make a plan?"

"I don't know!"

"Okay, okay, I'll leave it alone, then. Your Aunt Ruth can help you figure it out. I'm going to the john."

As soon as Nick was gone, Artie asked, "What's pissed you off so much?"

"I'm not pissed off," Tim practically screamed.

"You could have fooled me. You and Nick aren't having marital troubles, are you?"

"No, we're not. Because we're not married! And we're gonna stay that way. Rosa Rivera can find some other suckers for her stupid TV show!

"Whoa," Artie tried to calm Tim down. "I didn't even see an application in there for you two and I've checked out dozens of them already. I need to hire a secretary. Maybe there's a business school where I could find a student cheap."

Tim took a deep breath and totaled up the check for his last table. They were standing up now, but still in a lip-lock. Tim thought about asking Artie for one of the entry forms behind the bar and handing it to the love-birds, but the phone rang and Artie was distracted. Rosa didn't miss the opportunity, though. She raced across the room with the entry form in a whirl of skirts and Italian flattery.

Then Birdie Fuller walked in, followed by Marcia and Jeff and Tony, the boys who lived in the apartment upstairs from Ruth's. They all gathered at the bar and ordered drinks from Artie. There was so much commotion that nobody besides Tim even noticed when Ruth entered. She put her arms around her nephew as he said, "Well, where's my mother? What the hell is going on? I keep expecting her to walk in that door any minute."

"That won't happen, honey. Don't worry. Right now she's a couple of hours from here, but she still wants very much to see you and I just don't know..."

"Where's Sam?"

"Parking the car. Where's Nick?"

"Taking a leak. Aunt Ruth, you remember that day I found out that Cousin Dianne wasn't really my cousin after all?"

"Everything happened so fast and it was all so confusing. I never intended to tell anyone, but the truth had to come out."

"Well, I remember it very well. We were at Davies Hospital and Dianne was barking orders and snapping at all the people who were trying to help her. When you finally told her she wasn't your real daughter, I was never so jealous of anyone in my entire life."

"I don't understand. Why were you jealous? Were you jealous of me?"

"I was jealous because I wished it was *my* mother telling me that *we* weren't related to each other, that there'd been a big secret she'd been keeping from me all these years. What a relief that would have been! My mother turned her back on me every time my father beat me up and then she'd recite some Bible verses like that would make it all okay. Anything that ever went wrong was my fault in her eyes. When they found out about me and the track coach all the shit in the world hit the fan. I've never laid eyes on my mother since that day you came to pick me up and I went to live with you and Uncle Dan. I was barely sixteen years old! Don't you see? I have no use for her now."

"Tim, do you remember all the times she took you to the doctor when you were little?"

"It's a little too late for a laundry list of her good qualities now, don't you think? All the little kindnesses she did that I might have forgotten?"

"No." Ruth placed her hands on his shoulders. "That's not what I'm talking about. It wasn't the good things. I'm wondering if you remember all the bad things she did to you."

"What do you mean?"

"Do you remember how often you were sick when you were a little boy?"

"No," Tim said. Nick had come to stand behind him now and had his arms around Tim's shoulders. "I hardly remember anything before those weeks when I was seeing Dave Anderson. It was as if I discovered a whole new part of myself and there were so many emotions welling up inside me that I couldn't understand."

"I didn't know about all this either until the last few weeks. When she showed up on Collingwood Street… when she was still drinking she let slip a lot of things. Then I did a little research and Sam and I talked to some doctors. Psychiatrists, really. There was more to it than just her alcoholism. She physically hurt you. She's a very sick woman, Tim. I'm so sorry I didn't understand all that back then. Maybe if I'd been paying closer attention I could have taken you away from her sooner."

Boisterous laughter was coming from the bar. Rosa Rivera was in no hurry to shoot footage at the florist's shop, now that she had an appreciative audience here at Arts. She also thought that Jeff and Tony, the young couple who lived across the hall from Marcia on Collingwood Street, might be perfect for her gay wedding plans.

Ruth said, "Come on. You too, Nick. Good, here's Sam. Let's all go someplace else where we can talk.

Chapter 19

Sam had looked for parking so long that he'd finally left his car in Tim's driveway on Hancock, so the four of them headed back there on foot. The temperature was already dropping when they left the restaurant. The wind tunnel down 18th Street was wide open now and the summer fog had enveloped the hills that separated Eureka Valley from the Inner Sunset and the Avenues. Patches of fluffy white cotton broke off from the bulk of it and darted across Castro Street from west to east like jaywalkers among the car traffic. The Sunday afternoon street corner vendors had already packed up and headed home.

Sam talked about his recent business trip and asked Nick how the nursery business was doing. Ruth and Tim listened to them and both had the same thought—that this was typical "man talk" meant to fill in the silence more than to say anything. Ruth didn't know whether it was a case of bad nerves or a change of heart, but when they reached Tim's, she became the one to need to talk about everything except the matter at hand.

Nick went to work building a fire and Tim plopped down in the overstuffed chair beside the fireplace. They all sensed a false note of cheeriness in Ruth's voice. "How about a nice glass of wine, everyone? I brought a bottle of Syrah from Sonoma in my big bag here. There's still a whole case in my car. Remind me, Sam, and you can carry it inside for me. I'll go find us some glasses and a corkscrew, shall I?"

Tim stroked Nick's hair as they stared into the flickering fire. Nick had pulled it back into a pony tail, but Tim slipped the elastic band off and let it fall around Nick's face. Sam was about to lower himself onto the couch when Ruth yelled from the kitchen, "What on earth happened in here?" and he rushed to join her. "What a big project you boys took on. I'll bet this was your doing, Nick. Am I right?"

"There's nothing like a good oak floor," Sam said, still trying to do his part to fill in any holes in the conversation. This house is pre-earthquake, isn't it, Tim?" The end of his question might have been cut off by the splashing of the faucet in the kitchen sink, but for whatever reason, Tim didn't answer. "Maybe I should go down and check on Jane and Ben and the kids," he said to Ruth while the water was still running.

"You're not going anywhere," Ruth said. "I need you now. Open this bottle and take it in the other room, will you?"

Sam smiled and did as she asked.

"These glasses were so dusty," Ruth shouted toward the living room. "Is it okay if I use a cloth from this drawer next to the sink to dry them?"

There was still no answer. Tim was only half listening as he stared at Nick. He was infinitely grateful to have him there. Ruth returned to the living room, placed the four glasses on the coffee table and Sam poured the wine. "What a lovely idea to build a fire." Ruth handed one glass to Nick and another to Tim. "Here's to the four of us all back in San Francisco with a cozy fire on such a chilly summer evening."

Nick attempted a feeble smile, but Tim set his glass down without tasting it. "Okay, Aunt Ruth, what the hell's going on?"

Ruth took a deep breath and let it out with a sigh. "Well, as you know, your mother is at the Redwood Valley Ranch, Tim. She's always had a hard time getting control of her alcohol consumption and it's only become worse in recent years, from what I can gather."

"I know that place," Nick said. "You see it advertised on TV all the time. I sold them a bunch of plants and some big trees a couple of years ago."

"I'm sure I admired some of them and they're really thriving, Nick. You should see the place, Sam. It's really beautiful... such a peaceful setting and the landscaping is extraordinary. You'd think it was a luxury resort with all the pools and fountains. It was a whole lot nicer than the Wagon Wheel Inn up the road, I can sure say that for—"

"Can we cut the crap now?" Tim interrupted. "What about my mother?"

"Well, your mother seems to be doing as well as could be expected. I stopped back to see her on visitor's day and she didn't remember having been in San Francisco at all. Once again she asked me about you, Tim, and I told her that she'd have to finish her treatment first before there was any possibility of seeing you and then the decision would be entirely up to you, of course... not her."

"Good, I'm glad you didn't promise her anything."

"I wouldn't do that."

"You wouldn't because you *couldn't.* Nobody can make me see that woman again!"

"Tim, I'm not asking you to forgive her, but I think it might do you good to understand where some of your anger is coming from."

"She threw me out! Wasn't that enough? Wouldn't that make *you* angry?"

"Of course it would. That would make anyone angry, Tim, but I'm talking about an earlier time in your life. I didn't understand when you were little, but your mother did some terrible things to you... long before they threw you out. And throwing you out of the house wasn't just your mother. That was your father's decision more than hers."

"And she did nothing to stop him! She didn't even try!"
Tim glared at her. "What else are you talking about? What
else did she do?"

Nick laid the fireplace poker down and sat on one arm
of Tim's chair. He stroked Tim's back and shoulders now. He
didn't say a word, but he was listening as intently as Tim was.

"Your mother had more than just a drinking problem.
Whenever she was frustrated, she looked for someplace to
lash out and there you were." Ruth paused and looked at Tim,
trying to grasp how much he understood. "You were such
a good little boy, always cheerful, trying to please people,
but she found ways to punish you, even when you'd done
nothing wrong."

"What do you mean?"

"When I was hiding her out at the apartment on
Collingwood a few weeks ago, I thought I could convince her
to get some help right here in the city. It was no use. She kept
right on drinking. Some nights she'd pass out for a couple
of hours and then I'd hear her crying and sometimes even
screaming. I thought she'd wake up the whole building. It
was a terrible sound!"

Ruth turned to Sam and said, "I tried to make light of it
when I called you, Sam. I didn't want you to worry and I was
so relieved to have her out of my hair and into someplace
that professionals could watch out for her. I was still trying to
make sense of the things she'd said."

Ruth took a sip of wine and a deep breath and turned
back to Tim. "Sometimes it was if she was talking to you, like
you were still a little boy and she was lashing out at you. She
said terrible things about what she was planning to do to you,
things she'd already *done* to you. Your mother is a very sick…
very unhappy woman."

"So that's why I've been having these dreams lately.
They've been worse since Nick and I found her suitcase,
you know. There was one where I was throwing up, sick to
my stomach, like I'd been poisoned. Do you really think she
wanted to hurt me?"

"I'm not sure of anything, but I think some part of her was trying to make you sick. There are rare cases in the medical books. Maybe she wanted to punish you for the pain she felt or maybe she was trying to get attention and sympathy for herself."

"Munchausen syndrome?" Nick asked.

"By proxy," Ruth didn't expect anyone to come up with the technical term. "She was never diagnosed as such, but tell me more about these dreams you've had lately, Tim."

"I told you the one about your wedding already."

"No, I mean about your childhood."

"Just that I'm sick... throwing up... or that I've been burned or scalded. I always hurt someplace on my body and then when I wake up I don't hurt anymore, or only for a minute and then the pain fades away with the dreams. I don't remember them very well and I don't remember anything that really happened back then... just in my sleep."

"Maybe that's a blessing, dear."

That night when Nick and Tim were getting ready for bed, Tim reached across to the bedside table. Most of the old photographs that were on his refrigerator on Collingwood were now in storage, but he'd put a couple of them in small frames beside his bed. And there was always the one of his grandmother, from whom he'd inherited this power of dreams. That was the picture he stared at now. He was a little boy with his grandmother's arm around him on a rough plaid blanket on the shore of the lake in Powderhorn Park in Minneapolis. It was the Fourth of July and he was holding a tiny American flag. He was wearing red swim trunks and he had a bandage on the big toe of his left foot.

That night Tim dreamed about Jesus. He knew it was Jesus because his mother had pictures of Jesus all over the house. Tim was in the kitchen of his parents' house in south Minneapolis. He sat on the counter and his feet dangled in the sink. He had on green shorts and he was kicking the side of the sink in time with the rhythm in his head. A man with long

hair stood over him and washed his feet. Tim thought it was
Nick at first and he laughed because he was ticklish. Then
the man's hair fell back and Tim looked into the face of Jesus,
who spoke in a soothing voice, "A person who has had a bath
needs only to wash his feet; his whole body is clean."

Tim was frightened, but Jesus had a kind face and loving
eyes like Nick's eyes when Nick was smiling at him. The
water from the tap ran hotter and Tim tried to pull his feet
away, but he was overpowered by hands that were stronger
than he was. One of the hands wore a small diamond ring
and when he looked up again, he didn't see Jesus or Nick. His
mother was holding his feet under the hot water. She sneered,
"In the book of John it says that you are not clean. Jesus knew
which of his disciples would betray him."

The grown-up Tim watched from the ceiling now, looking
down at the back of the woman's head. The little boy Tim
cried out in a sing-song voice, "Wash not just my feet, but my
hands and my head as well."

The woman who said she was his mother slapped the
little boy's face with the back of her hand and picked up the
stiff brush she used to scrub the floor. "You are not clean! I
will teach you to betray me!"

A bottle of bleach appeared in her other hand and the
little boy Tim saw his blood in the eddy of water from the toe
of his left foot running down the drain. He pushed his mother
as hard as he could. She fell to the kitchen floor screaming
and Tim climbed out of the kitchen sink and ran barefoot out
the door.

Tim ran for miles in his dreams that night. He ran around
Lake Nokomis and Lake Harriet and Lake of the Isles. He ran
past the Calhoun Beach Club and south along the shore of
Lake Calhoun. When he looked down at his bare feet in the
sand, there was no more blood. He ran west out of Minneapolis
past the cornfields and farmyards of Minnesota. By the time
he crossed the South Dakota Badlands his little boy's feet had
grown to the size of a teenager's. He ran across the Rocky
Mountains and soon he could smell the salt spray of the sea

and hear seagulls scolding him. They might be screaming about Jesus too, but Tim didn't listen. He was standing in the sand and the bandage was gone. He looked up toward the sun and the water and now he was a man with a man's feet standing beside the Pacific.

Tim had said that he didn't remember those awful things his mother did, but they remained in a dark dusty room in the back of his mind. A crack of light threatened to expose them now and he didn't want to see. Tim wasn't sure if he'd been running all night. He took a long time to come around on Monday morning and when he reached for Nick the bed was empty. Then he heard an engine that was way too loud for Hancock Street. A voice yelled, "Crank it to the left, now… about a foot more… that's it."

Tim remembered riding through the countryside, craning his neck to look out the back window at a shirtless Minnesota farm boy in bib overalls, maybe sixteen… seventeen, a few years older than Tim. He had clumps of manure on his work boots and bits of straw in his hair caught the sunlight. He was waving directions to his father to back up the truck to the barn. They were loading up cattle to take them to the stockyards in South St. Paul.

Tim was jealous of that boy. He wished he lived on a farm. He wished his father had a job where they could breathe air that smelled of hay and clover. He wished he wasn't sick so much. He wished the doctor was nicer. He wished his mother still baked cookies and didn't quote from her Bible all the time.

Still naked, Tim walked down the hall to investigate. Nick was yelling to the truck driver, "Crank it a little harder… that's it… right there… stop." Nick was still barefoot and shirtless, showing them where to stack the lumber for the new deck. Tim was so grateful to have Nick around. He could even smell coffee.

Chapter 20

"The gay parade in San Francisco is always the last Sunday in June, Aunt Ruth. I can't believe this is your first one. They celebrate PRIDE in Minneapolis too, you know, but they don't have half a million people turn out."

Arts was always closed until the evening shift on Pride Sunday, so the two of them had scored a window table at the Cove Café for an early breakfast. A steady stream of revelers passed by their window headed to the MUNI station. Even though Ruth had lived and worked in the Castro for some time, she'd never seen it quite this festive. Muscular men were bare-chested, sparkling drag queens teetered up the sidewalk in spindly high heels, young gay couples pushed baby strollers or pulled dogs on leashes and everyone displayed at least a splash of color, even the leather boys.

"I'm amazed so many people are out this early, after the Pink Saturday festivities last night." Ruth blew on her coffee and took a sip. "Lucky neither of us had to work. You know, Tim, the Twin Cities Pride celebration is one of the biggest in the country nowadays."

"Really? How would you know?"

"I've lived in Edina all these years; that's suburbia, not Siberia. I keep up on things."

Tim could almost imagine his Aunt Ruth marching down Hennepin Avenue carrying a PFLAG banner. Or organizing their whole contingent. But wouldn't she have told him? That might have been reason enough to go back for a visit, as long as he didn't have to see his parents.

"The parade is to commemorate the Stonewall Riots in New York way back in the 60s," Tim explained. "The cops were busting gay bars for no reason and the drag queens got fed up with it and then some movie star they all loved had just died and everyone was upset about that, so they decided to fight back."

"Which movie star?" Ruth asked while she spread jam on her toast.

"I'm not sure. I think it was maybe Joan Crawford."

"Joan Crawford?" The voice belonged to a tall man in an apron who refilled their coffee cups. "It was Judy Garland, you silly twinkie!"

"I'm not a twinkie," Tim protested. "I'm almost 31!"

"Ooh, ancient! You're Tim, right?"

"Yeah, how did you know?"

"We were at Arts for dinner the other night and my roommate was drooling over you. It's a good thing we were in Jake's section or he would have made a fool of himself. Jake told us your name."

"Oh." Tim was never sure what to say to such a blatant compliment. "Thanks... this is my Aunt Ruth."

"I know. She makes excellent Cosmos. I'm Steven." He had a contagious grin, Tim and Ruth both thought at the same time.

"Thank you, Steven." Ruth smiled up at him and shook his hand. "I remember you two boys at the bar. What's happened to our other waiter?"

"He just got slammed, so I'm pouring some coffee, helping him get caught up."

"Do you have to work all day and miss the parade?"

"Nah, I'll get off by noon. Castro Street will be a ghost town in a couple of hours before it fills back up again. But YOU, young man... you need to get your gay history straight. Haven't you ever seen *The Wizard of Oz*? Haven't you heard

Judy Garland sing 'Over the Rainbow' like a thousand times?
Look around you! There are rainbows everywhere! You're in
Oz, honey! Joan Crawford, my ass! She would have played
Dorothy Gale like a slut. Joan Crawford would have been
shagging the tin man!"

"Judy Garland... right," Tim said sheepishly. "Of course
I've seen *The Wizard of Oz,* lots of times. Gosh, I must have
heard that too. I just forgot."

"Joan Crawford... humph... instead of rainbow flags
hanging from every lamp pole down Market Street we'd
have... what?... wire hangers? Hah! Joan Crawford!"

Tim was too embarrassed to go on with his incomplete
history lesson. "Jeez... sorry..." He turned back toward his
Aunt Ruth. "What's new with you and Sam?"

"Oh... I haven't told you, have I? Delia and Frank gave
notice, after all these years. They're moving to Chicago.
Alexandra is expecting, so they've moved their wedding
plans up, but she also wants to get back to her modeling
career as soon as possible. Now she'll have Adam's mother
nearby to help with the new baby."

"So that means one less conflict for you," Tim said.

"Well, I don't know," Ruth popped the seedless grape
from the breakfast garnish into her mouth. "I'm still not
comfortable going to a wedding like part of the family when
I'll hardly know anyone."

"I meant one less conflict about marrying Sam. With Delia
gone, he'll need a new 'Lady of the House,' won't he?"

"You make it sound like a bordello! There's no conflict.
Sam and I just haven't gotten around to setting a date and
I'm not going to think about it today. Tell me more about the
parade."

"You'll see for yourself. It'll be fun. It's pretty much the
same every year, I guess. The biggest variable is probably the
weather. Sometimes the Sisters of Perpetual Indulgence do
an outrageous contingent and it's always fun to see which
celebrities show up. One year Nancy Sinatra rode all the way

down Market Street on the back of a convertible kicking her boots in the air."

"I remember that song," Ruth said. "These boots were made for walkin'?"

"Yeah, but her sign must have fallen off the car, so nobody recognized her. Anyway, the parade always starts with the Dykes on Bikes. They take about half an hour to go by— literally. There are thousands of them and more every year. And it usually ends with the biggest floats with the best sound systems. They blast their music and get the crowds revved up to follow them into the Civic Center for the celebration afterward. All the hours in between are filled with the usual suspects... the gay marching band, the gay men's chorus, the SPCA, the Fire Department, local TV and radio stations, groups who've come from out of town, politicians on fancy cars and contingents representing corporations, religious groups..."

"They allow religious protesters in the parade?"

"Not protesters, *gay* religious groups, churches like MCC and Dignity for gay Catholics. There must be a Jewish bunch, too. In spite of what the far right says, we're not all a bunch of Godless hedonists, you know."

"I never said…"

''I never said you did, Aunt Ruth."

"Well, I just hope it's not as crowded as the parade down Market Street when the Giants won the World Series. It was worth it to see Tim Lincecum in person, but I thought we'd never get back to the Castro afterward with all those crowds packed into the MUNI station."

"There were a million people downtown that day. This will only be half a million and it'll be much more colorful than just orange and black." Tim snatched up the check and pulled out his wallet. "My treat, I insist."

"You don't have to…"

"I know I don't. Happy first Gay Pride, Aunt Ruth! I remember Jason telling me how the parade started in the Castro one year. All the floats lined up right here in the neighborhood. And it used to go down Polk Street in the beginning. That's where most of the gay bars were before the Castro. Can you imagine? Compared to Market, Polk Street is so narrow!"

"When was that?"

"Way before my time. You know, you've been trying lately to get me to remember things that happened when I was a little boy, but I can only remember them in my dreams."

"It isn't necessary, Tim. I'm only concerned about your well-being."

"I know and I love you for it, but I don't think I want to remember. And I'd rather dream about San Francisco. Jason told me so many stories and Artie still talks about the things I missed, the way it was before I got here... before AIDS, even. You could have come to the San Francisco parade before. I mean... they must have been having Pride back when you were at Stanford."

"Well, I guess I didn't know about it then. I lived such a sheltered life in those days. I only wish I could have sheltered you more. If I had known about what your mother—"

"You did just fine, Aunt Ruth."

Steven interrupted to offer more coffee, but they both declined.

"I'm coffee-ed out," Ruth placed her fingertips over the rim of her cup as she looked up and smiled.

"Jason he taught me so much. Artie and Arturo go back even farther. The guys here are more like my family than my parents ever were—even the ones who are gone... like Jason." Tim became quiet for a moment. "We don't have any choice about the families we're born into. Other than you, my family has always been right here in San Francisco. It was like they were waiting for me to arrive. My chosen family will always be here and now you are, too. I get the best of both worlds."

Ruth gave Tim's hand a squeeze. "You sure do, honey. Even Jason and all the others are still here in spirit. Whenever you walk down Castro Street you walk in their footsteps."

"Here's your change," their original waiter said as he wiped the table.

"Have fun at the parade!" Steven waved from across the room as they stood up and stretched.

"Thanks. We will." Tim fingered the change and added to it for a very healthy tip. "Come on, Aunt Ruth. We don't want to miss the Dykes on Bikes!"

"*Only* half a million people?"

Nick found his way through a snarl of traffic and street closures to the Embarcadero, where participants were lining up for the parade. The Bay Bridge loomed above the fishy smells of the waterfront. Nick found the Russian River float on Front Street. He'd loaned them potted ferns and trees, so he wanted to see how it looked and to wish them well.

"It's great! I love the hot tub." Nick walked around the float and checked it out. "But I think you should secure those trees a little better. I've got some wire in my truck."

"There's room for one more in the hot tub, Nick," one of the burly bears said with a grin. He was armed with a staple gun trying to straighten the "R" on the *Russian River* sign. "You can sit on my lap, darlin'."

"No thanks, Ralph," Nick laughed, "I've got to get back to the nursery today—got a big job this week and I want to get a head start. Drop off the plants at the north greenhouse when you're done, okay? No hurry."

"You ought to join us one of these years."

"Thanks, but no thanks. Too many people… I get claustrophobic enough just going to the Guerneville Safeway during tourist season. You guys have fun without me."

By the time Tim and his Aunt Ruth left the Cove Café, Nick was passing Petaluma. He'd already changed his mind about going to work and sailed past the exit to the nursery. When he got to Santa Rosa he headed east instead of toward home. He arrived at the Redwood Valley Ranch as Visitors' Day was just beginning.

The grounds were beautiful. The plants he'd sold them a couple of years ago were perfect for this lush environment. The lady at the reception desk took Nick's card and lifted the glasses she wore on a chain around her neck. "You look familiar... ah... Nick Musgrove, the tree man. How is the nursery business? If you're here to sell us something, you'll have to come back during office hours and talk to the director, I'm afraid." She wasn't being rude, just business-like.

"Miss Austin, is it?" Nick squinted to read the name tag she wore on her blouse collar. "I happened to be in the area and wanted to have a look around, if that's alright. I like to follow up on my projects when I get a chance, make sure the plants I sold you are thriving."

"Of course—" she started to reply when the phone interrupted her. "Excuse me... Redwood Valley Ranch... yes, that's right. There's plenty of free visitor parking in the lot. You'll see the sign when you turn off the main road."

When Miss Austin finished her call, Nick decided to be more straightforward. "Also... there's another reason I came today. You have a client... Mrs. Snow?"

"Are you a relative?"

"No, she's the mother of a good friend of mine and I offered to check on her... since I was in the neighborhood." Nick felt nervous, as if this woman would catch him in a lie. It *was* a lie, after all. He hadn't told anyone he was coming here. He wasn't sure of it himself until this morning. He'd thought about it ever since Ruth told them about the terrible things Tim's mother had done to the little boy who grew up to be the man Nick loved.

This morning had clinched it. This morning in San Francisco, while the fog was burning off the bay and thousands of people got ready for the big parade; Nick made up his mind. The PFLAG contingent was gathering in front of the Russian River float. When Nick saw all those friends and family members of gay people—especially mothers—

carrying signs spelling out their love and support, he decided he had to see this monstrous woman in person.

"Mrs. Snow has been rather withdrawn lately. I believe her sister has been here, but a visit from a handsome young man like you might be just what she needs." Miss Austin had warmed up in a short time. Nick didn't think he was much younger than she was. She answered the phone again, but it must have been a wrong number. "Do you need someone to show you around, Mr. Musgrove? I can't leave the desk right now, but I could page someone to take you to Mrs. Snow. She's in number eighteen."

"No, that's alright. You're busy. I'll find her and as I said, I do want to check on the trees."

"Ah… there's the phone again… excuse me…" Nick walked away as she told the caller, "No, you must have taken a wrong turn. Backtrack to the winery and take a left, not a right…"

Nick wasn't sure what to expect from Betty Snow, a modern-day Medusa or one of her Gorgon sisters—snakes coming out of her head and fiery flames licking the backs of empty eye sockets, fangs instead of teeth. He'd never even seen a photograph of Tim's mother, but he recognized her right away. She was sitting on a bench beside a willow tree with a floppy hat pulled down over stringy gray hair. The hem of her dress fell past her knees and the sleeves were snug around her wrists. Ruth had mentioned that her sister was younger than she was, but Tim's mother looked much older. She looked exactly like Ruth might look if she let herself go.

Nick snapped a twig off a tree and pretended he was inspecting the flora. He got closer, but she didn't look up from her open Bible. A bird screeched as if to scold him and she glanced up at the noise. The sun's glare blocked her from seeing Nick, but it exposed to him the tendrils of age around her eyes and deep vertical lines above her upper lip. He saw purple veins across her nose, a sign of the ravages of alcoholism. He imagined a flicker of flame in the backs of her eyes. Nick looked down at his hands and realized how easily they could reach around her wrinkled neck and choke the life out of her. He'd seen enough… at least for now.

Miss Austin glanced up from her desk in time to see a cloud of dust as Nick's truck peeled out of the parking lot of the Redwood Valley Ranch.

Chapter 21

"Well, he was awfully nice," Ruth said to Tim as they left the Cove Café.

"Who was?"

"That waiter… Steven, silly!

"Yeah, I guess so," Tim laughed. "He called me a 'twinkie.' I haven't been called a twinkie in years!"

The platform at Castro Station was so crowded that only half of the people could get onto the first train that came along, a double M-Oceanview. They managed to squeeze into the next one, though, a two-car L-Taraval. Once inside, Tim apologized for getting pressed up against a handsome man with a little boy, but everyone rolled with the punches on a day like this. The little boy was perched on one of the side seats and gesturing toward something above them. "Daddy, what's that say?"

The man stroked the bangs away from the little boy's forehead and looked in the direction his tiny index finger was pointing. "That sign says *L-Taraval*. That's the name of this subway car we're on."

"No, not that… that!" The boy pointed again. Other passengers watched and listened and Ruth wondered what the grown-ups were failing to see. The train pulled into Church Street Station where a man in a business suit tried to exit by yelling, "Coming out!"

"It's about time! I came out years ago," someone yelled and everyone laughed. It reminded Ruth of the nervous laughter of strangers on a crowded elevator or the collective joy of people who'd been stranded at an airport together when their flight is finally called. It reminded her that people—gay and straight—were alike in so many ways.

The father said to the little boy, "That sign says *Church Street Station*. That's where we are now, but we're going to take this all the way downtown to the parade, okay?"

"No, Daddy. Not that. That!"

The man patiently looked around again. "That one says *Emergency Exit*. Is that the one you mean?"

"What's e-mer-gen-cy?" The little boy was proud of repeating such a big word.

"An emergency would be if you lost your stuffed doggie out the window. You would push that button to stop the train and everyone would get out and look for him."

"Oh…"

"Your little boy is just *adorable*," Ruth said.

"Thanks. He's at that inquisitive stage. I'm the one he likes to have feed him and tuck him in, but his other dad is better at answering questions when he gets like this." The man glanced at his watch. "We're supposed to meet him in ten minutes in front of the Sheraton Palace and he'd better be on time."

"I'm sure you'll do just fine until then," Ruth smiled. She could almost remember Dianne at that age, though Dianne was never this sweet. Tim was. The train lumbered into Van Ness Station and Tim and Ruth were pressed deeper inside as more rainbow stripes pressed onto the car.

They finally piled out at Powell Street Station and had no sooner stepped off the escalator when someone shouted, "Tim!"

Tim recognized the man as someone he'd gone home with a couple of times, but he couldn't remember when, exactly. His best guess would be post-Jason and pre-Cory and he thought the guy's name was Denny.

"Hi! How are you? Happy Pride!"

"Thanks, same to you. Tim, do you know my husband Elliot? And this is Clarisse." Tim shook hands with Elliot, who had knelt down beside the stroller to adjust the baby's bottle. "The adoption papers were finalized just this week."

"Congratulations. This is my Aunt Ruth."

Ruth crouched to get a better look at the baby. "She's just beautiful! Look at those cheekbones. She could be descended from a princess."

"She's part Native American," Elliot said. "One of her grandmothers thinks she *is* a princess, but *my* mother has completely disowned me."

"She'll come around," Ruth said. "How old is she?"

"Nearly seventy… oh, you meant Clarisse. She'll be nine weeks tomorrow."

"Aw, Denny," Tim said. "You must be so proud of her."

"It's Danny."

"Right. Sorry."

"Come on, Elliot, we're going to be late. It was nice to meet you, Ruth. We're marching with the adoption rights group."

"It's not like we could miss them, Danny. What's the big hurry?" Elliot said, but he was speaking to Danny's disappearing backside. "Seeya, Tim. Ruth, I'd better go before I lose him. He's so anal and he's such a stickler for being places on time. Happy Pride!"

Tim tried to remember why he'd never had a third date with Denny. Danny? He couldn't even remember the guy's name, much less the time they'd spent together. There must have been something halfway decent about him or there wouldn't have been a *second* date. Maybe Tim wasn't his type, although *anal* was all relative.

Tim saw a bare spot at the barrier and pushed Ruth toward it. "Quick! Stand right there. You'll be able to see everything."

Tim fell in behind his aunt so he could look over her shoulder and Ruth started chatting with a couple of butch lesbians from Fresno. They were wearing matching blue denim men's work shirts and suede visors. "It's pretty different where we come from. Everyone thinks we're just roommates."

"I'll bet they do," Tim was trying to be nonchalant, but Ruth stepped on his toe before he could make any worse smart remarks. She knew he had it in him.

"Welcome to San Francisco," Ruth said. "I'm so excited to be at my very first parade. My name is Ruth Taylor and this is my—"

"Good to meet you, Ruth," said the larger one—Deb— who wasn't particularly interested in meeting Tim. "This is our first parade, too."

The Women's Motorcycle Contingent, better known as Dykes on Bikes, started roaring past and the sound of horns and revving engines made it impossible to talk. Deb turned to her partner and shouted, "Just look at all those hogs, Maryellen. Next year... you and me, babe... right out there!"

Some of the riders were dwarfed by their enormous shiny machines. Ruth was startled more than once to see people she knew as customers at Arts. First was a pair of women who came in for brunch nearly every Sunday. They honked and waved and called her name, but it took a moment for Ruth to recognize them, wearing little more than G-strings below the waist and Band-Aids over their nipples. Ruth waved back anyway and smiled. Maryellen and Deb were impressed that Ruth knew so many people. They moved their beer cooler over to make more room for her to stand.

"Why, thank you," Ruth said and waited for some of the noise to die down. "Did you *gals* meet my nephew Tim?"

"Hiya, Tim," Deb acknowledged him with a crippling handshake. Maryellen was too far away to do more than nod and wave. "This your first time too?"

"Nah, I live here. I've been lots of times," Tim said, shaking his hand out behind his back to try to return the sensation to his fingers.

There appeared to be some kind of hold-up that caused a block-long gap between parade contingents. "This is going to be a long day at this rate." Tim looked at his watch and picked up a sheet of lavender paper off the sidewalk.

"What's that?" Ruth asked.

"It's a list of the parade entrants in order of appearance. There are over a hundred and fifty contingents this year. The Dykes on Bikes are always first and then *Mikes on Bikes*. They're number two, see?"

Ruth took the sheet of paper, but she didn't look at it. "There's a big gap now, Tim. The next thing coming looks like someone on the back of a convertible. See him way down there? It must be one of the Grand Marshals or the mayor or someone important."

"If it's a politician, it must be a Republican. They always hold up anything gay. I guess that'll give these Mikes plenty of time to ride around in circles."

"Look at this one on the bike with the baby strapped to his back." Ruth's enthusiasm would not be deterred by any long delays. "How adorable!"

"Yeah, everyone's raising babies these days. You know, between that hot daddy with the cute little boy on MUNI and those guys we just met—Danny and Elliot, with their girl, it almost makes me want to have a kid.

Ruth shook her head. "Have you ever in your entire life been responsible for so much as a pet?"

"No… when I was little, my mother said I was allergic to cats and dogs, but you know what? I'm not. I've spent lots of time with other people's pets and they don't bother me. Why don't you ever ask me to take care of Bartholomew when you're out of town?"

"I never knew you wanted to and Teresa's so convenient… maybe next time."

"Nick was talking about getting a dog, just the other night. We could share him, maybe keep him in the country part-time at Nick's and part-time in the city at my place."

"Maybe you should start with a goldfish, dear."

Tim rolled his eyes at his aunt.

During the next hour the Fresno lesbians twice offered Ruth a beer from their ice chest. She finally accepted one. "It's nice and cold," she took a sip, then handed the can to Tim and pointed, "My word! Look what's coming next!"

Tim was trying to find where they were on the lavender list, but he put it down and just looked. "It's Rosa Rivera. Great car!" The Italian TV personality was on the back of a shiny white Mercedes convertible. Her dress was white chiffon with billowing sleeves and a plunging neckline trimmed in gold sequins.

"Her makeup is awfully garish for daylight, don't you think?" Ruth asked.

"And look at that tacky dress!" Tim laughed. "She must have bought it on Mission Street."

"That's right... that's what she reminds me of... one of those beauty pageant winners in the *Cinco de Mayo* celebration!"

"She looks more like a drag queen!"

"A Mexican drag queen!" both Ruth and Tim shouted at the same time and then burst out laughing.

"She could be on stage at Esta Noche tonight!" Tim said. "Ooh, but look at those muscle numbers in Speedos escorting her car."

"How cute... they're all wearing bow ties and old fashioned men's garters."

"They must be some of Bruno's gym buddies. I wonder where Bruno is, anyway..."

"Look, he's the one driving."

There was a paper sign taped to the side of the car:

"Let's Make it Happen"
Watch Rosa Rivera's Wedding Season
~ LIVE from Arts on Castro Street ~
Saturday July 9 at 4PM

"At least the restaurant is getting some free publicity," Ruth said. "Artie told me he wants to ride in the parade next year… as Artie Glamóur, of course."

"He says that every year," Tim said, "but he always backs out."

"Oh look, those guys dressed as grooms are handing out something. Stand in my place, Tim. You're taller. See if you can reach out and get one."

"They're just applications for the wedding. According to Artie, they already have hundreds turned in. At this rate, she'll have to move the show to the Cow Palace!"

Rosa was gesturing wildly and yelling at Bruno, but a siren drowned out her words. Bruno slammed on the brakes and Rosa toppled over and slid down onto the seat. By the time she had assumed her regal position, the siren stopped and everyone could hear their voices. "Drive your own damn car, then!" Bruno threw the keys in her lap and climbed out. "I'm sick and tired of your bitching. You're never satisfied, dammit! I quit!'

"You can't quit. *Vaffanculo*! You're fired!"

"You can't fire me. I already quit! *Stronzo*!"

"You can't quit. *Vai a farti fottere*. I already fired you!"

"Mother… just shut the fuck up!" Bruno stomped off toward the other side of Market Street and leapt over the barricade.

"Wow, did you see that jump he took? Bruno must have been a gymnast," Tim said. "That would explain the great body. I'll bet he's off to find a Tenderloin bar that's open."

Ruth could hardly believe what she'd heard. "Bruno just called Rosa Rivera 'Mother,' didn't he?"

"I think you're right."

The Fresno lesbians nodded and Maryellen said, "Yes he did, Ma'am. We both heard him say it. If I'm not mistaken he called her a bitch, too!"

"Did you know Rosa was Bruno's mother?"

"No way," muttered Tim.

"I don't think anyone would have suspected," Ruth said. "She must have been very young—"

"And I thought life was hard with *my* mother. I almost feel sorry for Bruno now."

Ruth reached for Tim's arm and patted his hand. "Nobody ever said life was going to be easy for any of us, dear. Oh, look at all the balloons coming up. Look at the drag queen on the Moped! Look on your list there and find that float that Nick worked on. We'll have to tell him how nice it was. Oh, Tim, this is so much fun!"

Chapter 22

The Fourth of July weekend was relatively quiet in the Castro, downright dead if you compared it to Pride, the weekend before. Arts got by on a skeleton crew, which meant that Tim got to spend a rare weekend at the Russian River and Ruth stayed in Hillsborough. A few foreign gay tourists stuck around California for another week after the parade, but most of them moved on to visit Los Angeles or Portland or Seattle. Lots of the locals got out of town for the long weekend, too.

Ruth wanted nothing more than to relax at Sam's house before next Saturday's big event at Arts. But during the second week, Artie called her every day, begging her to come back to the city early. He was a nervous wreck and he suspected that Rosa was losing it. No one had seen Bruno since he stormed off and left his *mother* in an empty convertible in the middle of Market Street. The cameras just happened to get a close-up when she slid into the back seat. The thirty-second clip that ended with her legs in the air had gotten so many hits on YouTube that Rosa was now even more famous outside of the Bay Area. Or infamous. The live TV broadcast had cut to a commercial while one of the boys in black Speedos and a bow tie took Bruno's place behind the wheel so the parade could get moving again.

189

Ruth was torn between curiosity and dread about the coming weekend, knowing how temperamental Artie would be, not to mention Rosa's enormous and demanding ego. Ruth let Artie talk her into working Thursday and Friday nights behind the bar plus Saturday, for the *big day* and then that was it! She needed Sunday to recover and pack. The following week she and Sam were flying to Chicago for Adam and Alexandra's wedding, which was sure to be lovely and traditional and far less exciting.

Frank and Delia had already left for Chicago, so Ruth learned to find her way around the Hillsborough kitchen and discovered that she enjoyed making dinners for two. Having the place to themselves, she and Sam went skinny-dipping in the pool under the stars every night and Ruth felt free to sunbathe in the afternoons with her straps unfastened. Sometimes when she took a dip to cool off she didn't even bother to put her top back on. They'd spent most of Sam's spare time this week playing tennis and making love. Sam reminded her of a teenager in that regard and she wasn't complaining.

Ruth also got the chance to poke around and get a closer look at the house this week. She pondered what full-time life might be like in Hillsborough. She'd been happy to leave suburban Edina behind and pare back her belongings to fit a one-bedroom apartment in the Castro. Now the thought of expanding again it was a little frightening, but when she looked at Sam's sweet smile every day, the idea was growing on her.

The house hadn't seen a woman's touch in a long time… or had it? Delia was much more of a chef than a decorator and Sam's first wife—Jane's mother—had been dead for years. Had Sam been celibate all that time? Ruth wondered about so many things, like who had built this house and when and for what purpose? It was a lot older than Sam. She'd been here so many times that she felt contentment among the smells of the paneled wood walls and the scent from years of crackling fires in the hearths, but she'd never asked the most obvious questions. Her focus was always on the wonderful man who lived here.

The more Ruth thought about becoming the second—and last—Mrs. Sam Connor, the more curious she became. But she had plenty of time. There would be years of breakfasts in bed, long summer evenings on the patio or rainy winter nights beside the fire when she could listen to Sam's stories and tell him all the things he wanted to know about her past as well.

It was different here when they were alone... all alone and in love. It wasn't the giddy foolishness of a teenage crush. It wasn't like her first wedding night when she stood at the threshold of her life. She was past all that, past her prime, in fact, and so was Sam. She wondered how things might have been if she'd met Sam when they were young. Would she be more confident when she was a little thinner? Could she have loved Sam any more when he was a little more buffed and had more hair? Oh, plenty of guys half Sam's age had less hair than he did. Ruth decided that being past their prime was a delicious place for them both to be.

She was lounging beside the pool on Thursday morning feeling wonderfully relaxed. She rolled over on her back, lifted her arms above her head and stretched out in the sun like a cat. Where *was* the Bartholomew? "Ba—art!" Ruth sat up and looked around. "Bartholomew! Where are you, kitty-cat?"

The cat was adapting well to life here. He seemed to love exploring the grounds and chasing field mice behind the potting shed. Bartholomew had already picked out his favorite spots to nap as the sun moved from the windows near the breakfast nook to the master bedroom in the afternoon to the dining room windows in the early evening. From there it was only a few steps to see if someone in the kitchen had a treat for him.

"Meow," he padded up and gave Ruth's hand a lick.

"There you are, sweetie." She petted him until he rewarded her with a loud purr. "Are you enjoying yourself, Bart? This sure beats living half our lives in the snow, doesn't it?"

"What's that, dear?" Sam was standing at the kitchen doorway.

Ruth turned toward the sound of his voice as the cat yawned and ambled toward the house. "I was talking to Bartholomew."

"He seems happy here."

"I'll say." Ruth watched the cat step between Sam's feet, arch his back and demand some attention. "He's never had it so good. I remember the first time he got outside when he was a kitten. There must have been three feet of snow on the ground. He dashed back inside the house so fast! This must feel like heaven compared to being cooped up in my little apartment on Collingwood… or Teresa's."

"Yes, you mentioned Teresa was taking care of him for a while."

"It was Birdie most of the time, actually."

"Birdie?"

"The policewoman," Ruth reminded him, "Artie's old friend from his North Beach days… Birdie Fuller… she was house sitting for Teresa and taking care of Bart."

"Where was Teresa?"

Ruth was sure they'd had this conversation before, but it was just like him to forget a little thing like that. "Teresa went to a class reunion in Seattle with her ex-husband and his current husband. I was sure I told you all about it." Fortunately, Sam was good at remembering the things that really mattered.

"Maybe you did."

"And then Teresa spent some time at her mother's. I've hardly seen her since she got back, but she mentioned that her mother was doing better. When I asked about the class reunion, she seemed… I don't know… reserved, I guess, which is unusual for Teresa, if you know what I mean."

Sam laughed. "Jane used to tell me stories when she and Ben and the kids lived above Tim and below her."

"Well, it's true, she can be a bit loud, but she has a heart of gold. I'd trust her with my life, you know. It's just that lately she seems like a person who is either madly in love or in some kind of trouble."

"Those two situations can be similar, depending on the circumstances," Sam said with a chuckle.

"Is that how you feel about me, Sam? Does loving me trouble you deeply?"

"Never! I've never known anyone to trouble me less, while at the same time being exciting, provocative and downright sexy."

"You always know how to say just the right things, Sam. Do go on…"

"You're getting a healthy glow, dear. It becomes you, but don't get sunburned."

"Don't worry. I've got a gallon of sunblock on my face. How are you doing? How is your work coming alone? Shall I fix us some lunch?"

"I was getting myself another cup of coffee before I go back to it, but if you're hungry, darling, I can take a break any time."

After lunch the sun was hot. Ruth sat with her feet in the pool and finally finished the Stephen King paperback she'd been reading for weeks. She looked at her watch and realized she needed to get ready to leave. Bartholomew was asleep in the sun and surprisingly easy to get back into his carrying case. Sam was making progress at his desk, he told her, "…but I'd better keep working. I can finish this paperwork tomorrow and drive up to the city by the time you're done at the restaurant. Artie invited me to the big show on Saturday, too."

"Are the kids coming?"

"Jane said she would. I just talked to her a few minutes ago. She told me Artie roped her into helping with the applications and she wants to see who wins. The kids are too little to sit through all that. Ben said he'd stay home with them and maybe watch it on television."

"You and Jane can sit at the bar and keep me company, then. Scott is working the end near the kitchen, so we'll have you near the front door. You can slip out if it gets to be too much for you. It's sure to be quite a production and I'll need the moral support."

"Alright, darling Ruth," Sam stood and kissed her goodbye. "Drive carefully and I'll see you tomorrow night. No matter what happens, once Saturday is over we'll be together."

All in all, Ruth felt pretty satisfied with herself all the way back to the city. She turned the corner from 19th Street up the steep incline of Collingwood, hoping to luck out and find a parking place. There was one near the top of the hill and she grabbed it. Cars without a blue "S" parking sticker in the Castro neighborhood had to move every two hours. Her car insurance might be cheaper in Hillsborough, but Ruth intended to keep her registration at her Collingwood address forever, just for the sake of parking. She could leave her car in this spot for a couple of days until street cleaning time.

She set her purse on the kitchen table, let Bart out of his carrying case and flipped through the mail on her way to the front of the apartment. Ruth flicked on her computer to warm up and get her email. Then she looked at the calendar above her desk and gasped out loud. "Oh no! What an idiot I am!" Her voice was so loud that Bart came running. "Your mother is insane, Bart. She's a madwoman. How could I have been so thoughtless? I can't be in two places at once. Oh, what was I thinking?"

Ruth realized for the first time that she and Sam would be in Chicago for Adam and Alexandra's wedding at the same time Betty was getting released from the Redwood Valley Ranch. She grabbed a pen and notepad and reached for the phone. "Well, Bart, if anyone can solve this mess, it'll have to be me. I guess it's time to put the rest of my plan into place and find out who my real friends are."

Chapter 23

Tim dreaded Saturday at Arts as much as his Aunt Ruth did. He had more than enough drama in his life these days already. His kitchen was still a mess, work on the new deck had begun and worse yet, he lived in fear that his mother would pop up at any moment and shatter the comfortable patterns of his day-to-day existence.

All these crazy dreams about his childhood didn't help matters, either. Early Saturday morning his dreams had to do with work, what he called *waiter nightmares*. The kitchen was backed up and lines were out the door. Customers were irate and Tim was dropping things on the wrong people. Why couldn't he ever spill hot coffee on the jerks in his dreams?

"You okay, Snowman?" Nick wrapped an arm around his shoulder. "Bad dreams again? What time is it? What time do you have to be at work, babe?"

"Aw, I don't know." Tim opened one eye to read the alarm clock. "It's not even six. We don't have to be there 'til noon. We're not serving food because of the TV show… sorry I woke you."

"It's okay. Were you dreaming about your mom again?"

"Yeah. No. I don't know." Tim usually remembered important dreams, but these had already slipped away into darkness. "I haven't thought about my mother in years until the last few weeks. There's no way I want to see her! Do you think she'll really try to find me when she gets out of that place?" Tim asked, but Nick had already fallen back to sleep.

Tim stood at the toilet and blinked into the bathroom mirror. It was going to be a long day. He went to the kitchen, slid a filter into the coffee maker, measured four scoops and poured cold water into the well. He didn't bother to set the timer. All he'd have to do later was flip the switch.

Nick was right; the remodeling *would* be worth the hassle. The hardwood floor glistened in the early sunlight. White tape marked X's across new sliding glass doors onto the deck. The workmen had promised to finish the railing this week. Tim stood naked in his dusty kitchen and admired the view of Victorian rooftops sloping down the hillsides and the shadowy shapes of the tallest buildings through the misty morning fog downtown.

Back in the bedroom, Nick was lying on his side with his long blond hair tousled around his handsome face. Even though he was asleep, his arm was outstretched, empty palm still open, reaching out, waiting for Tim to return. Tim watched Nick's steady breathing from the doorway and realized how lucky he was. With Nick in his life, there was nothing he couldn't handle. Right now there was plenty of time to crawl back into bed and sleep for a few more hours.

Tim arrived at the restaurant at a quarter to twelve to find the TV crew snaking cables through the room and fastening them to the floor with gaffing tape. Artie was behind the bar cutting limes and taking an occasional bite of an omelet. He was in full-face make-up, but still in men's clothes. "Thank goodness, Timmy… at least *you're* on time. You're the only one I can always count on around here. Everyone else is late."

Tim wouldn't say so, but he thought Artie looked ridiculous without hair, in false eyelashes and broad daylight. "It's not even noon yet. Relax. This thing doesn't even start until four, does it? What time is Aunt Ruth coming in?"

"She worked last night until Sam got here around eleven. I sent her home and told her to be back by two. The live broadcast starts at four. Scott should be here by now to set up the bar for the both of them, but I've almost got their fruit done already. Arturo's been here with these television people since 9 o'clock this morning. The entrants are due at 2:30. Jake should be here by now. Phil should be here. Patrick should be here. James should be here."

"Are you gonna finish those potatoes?" Tim picked at Artie's home fries with his fingers. "Anybody heard from Bruno yet?"

"Not that I know of. Rosa's called twice this morning, but she didn't mention him and I didn't have the heart to ask. If you're hungry, get Arturo to fix you something. He's in the kitchen making hors d'oeuvres for later."

"No thanks, I'm not hungry." Tim stabbed a forkful of omelet and pushed it into a small triangle of whole wheat toast. "Nick and I had blueberry pancakes at my place."

"Before or after you had sex?"

"What makes you think—?"

"You sure did something to work up an appetite."

Before Tim could respond, the other waiters started arriving, plus Jane with both kids in tow. She plopped a stack of papers on the bar. "Here, Artie. Here's the final list for your doorman. I did it exactly the way you asked. Ben helped me, in fact. He pulled out applications at random and I checked to confirm that they were all complete, that everyone was over 21 and that everyone lives in local area codes. We confirmed twenty couples. I've called and e-mailed every one of them and they'll all be here by 2:30.

"Thanks, Jane. I'm glad I thought to ask you. I mean… you're the only person around here who doesn't work. I knew I could count on you to do a good job."

"Why does Uncle Artie look like a clown, Mommy?" Jane's little daughter Sarah asked.

"Because he *is* a clown, sweetheart." Jane turned to Artie and lowered her voice. "I'll give you an hour alone with these two kids and then I dare you to tell me I don't work."

Artie ignored her and asked, "Is there anyone we know among the contestants?"

"Yes, as a matter of fact—"

"No. Don't tell me! I want to look surprised if I happen to be on camera when the names are called."

"Who wants this list, then?" Jane asked.

"Bruno is supposed to be on the door, but nobody's heard from him yet. It wouldn't hurt to have one of our people there, too. James, would you mind doing it?"

"Sure." James took the sheet of paper. "Hey, my name's on this list and I'm not even dating anybody."

"That's not just the entrants, it's the entire door list," Jane explained. "That includes all the staff, Artie's and Rosa's guests, the TV crew, press people, Gavin Newsom and his entourage *and* all the contestants. Everyone is in alphabetical order."

"Oh, okay," James said. "I sure didn't want to get married."

"Where the hell have you been?" Artie snarled as Phil walked in the door. "You're late!"

"I told you I had a doctor's appointment, Artie," Phil picked up a slice of orange that was garnishing Artie's omelet."

"On a Saturday morning?" Artie slapped at Phil's hand and missed. "If you boys are hungry, go eat now. I don't want growling stomachs on the audio track and Arturo won't have time for you to be pestering him to cook something later.

"Is that what you're calling them now, Phil... doctor's appointments?" Jake asked. "We all recognize the sound of the snap of a rubber glove."

"Shut up, Jake," Phil tossed the orange rind back on the plate. "I told you about it last night, Artie, and besides, there was no reason for me to be here so early."

"We need to run a sound check as soon as—" Artie started to argue, but the phone rang and he was the closest one to it. It hadn't stopped ringing all morning. Once the show started, he was turning it off.

Jake asked Phil, "Come on. Where were you, really?"

"I had a client… incredible place on the far side of Potrero Hill. You can see the whole Bay Bridge and all the lights across the water."

"Hmmm… a dungeon with a view, huh?" Tim asked.

"Yeah, kind of… this guy was really kinky! You've all seen my ad in the *B.A.R.*, right? I mean… I advertise as a top, but… I don't know. I have an open mind, but this guy was almost scary. He got me all the way over there and then he told me he was into breath control. You really ought to do that with someone who specializes. Every now and then I get some far-out calls, usually from 'straight' guys—even *married* men—in town on business."

"Like what?" Jake asked. "Is everybody still doing crystal these days?"

"Yeah, some, but that's their business. A lot of the guys are into stuff they could do alone. For bondage you need a partner, I'll grant you that, but why pay me by the hour to watch them pumping or doing sounds? I could be sitting across the room reading a Danielle Steel novel."

"I'll see you later then," Artie hung up the phone and turned back toward his employees. "Phil, I was hoping you and I could run through my number one more time before Rosa gets here. Oh-oh! We're too late!"

Rosa Rivera swept in with her face made up almost as much as Artie's, but her head was covered in a scarf and she was wearing jogging clothes. Tim was surprised at how short she was until he realized he'd never seen her before without high heels. Bruno was following close behind, schlepping her dress over one shoulder with a wig box under his arm. He dropped everything on the bar and yelled, "How dare you speak to me like that, after all the times I've saved your ass?"

"Me? Speak to you… *figlio di buona donna*… like what? Why you little son of a bitch!"

"Hah! That's pretty funny! My own mother calling me a son of a bitch. Did you hear that, guys? Last week it was 'bastard'—*also* true!"

"I don't need you. *Siete inutili!* I've already hired your replacement."

"Fine! I didn't want to stick around here anyway. I can go home and watch you implode on live television in just a little while."

"Rosa!" Artie interrupted their argument. "Why don't you go in my office and relax? Jake, carry her things in there, will you? There's a nice full-length mirror and a make-up table. You can finish putting yourself together. Would you like a cup of coffee? How about a cocktail? Campari?"

Rosa didn't answer, but stormed off toward the back room. Then Artie caught Bruno before he could leave. "Listen, Bruno, I don't know what's going on between you two, but I'm not having it ruin my chance at appearing in front of a live television audience. You're the only one who's not afraid of her. Whatever happens, I'd feel better if you stuck around here, just in case…"

"I have no other plans," Bruno offered with a thick smirk.

"Good. How about working the door like we planned? James will help you."

Tim headed for the kitchen where things were quieter and Arturo put him to work right away. They arranged hors d'oeuvres onto silver trays, covered them with plastic wrap and placed them onto the top shelves of the stainless steel refrigerators for later. Tim tasted a dab of olive spread that was spilled on the counter. His mother would call these "finger sandwiches" back in Minnesota. The thought of his mother passed so quickly it was gone before the salty taste left his tongue. He was getting better at blocking unpleasant thoughts from his mind, but he still hadn't quite perfected the trick. Sometimes lately he could see the same images in his waking life that he did in his dreams.

Arturo asked him to go get a couple of lemons from behind the bar. Tim was curious to see what was going on out there anyway. The dining room was getting crowded, mostly with young men in tuxedos and boutonnières, a few drag queens and the occasional parent. Tim wondered whether Artie or Rosa would be more nervous.

Scott said, "Here's your lemons, Tim. Hey, you should grab a tray and start serving cocktails with Jake. The tables are filling up now."

"I guess you're right. If I was getting married I'd sure need a drink about now, whether it was televised or not." Tim brought Arturo the lemons and came right back out.

Artie was in full drag now. He was no longer the bartender, landlord and boss, but Artie Glamóur, a vision in red and silver sequins with a white hat perched so far back on the curls of his peach-colored wig it seemed a miracle that it stayed there.

Tim's Aunt Ruth waved to him from the front end of the bar. She was far too busy to come to where he was. Tim noticed that she had Sam safely tucked into the corner bar stool against the wall, with his daughter Jane beside him. She was not only enjoying a respite from her two kids, but no doubt curious to find out which of the twenty finalist couples she had so carefully screened would be the winners. Next to Jane was Nick, who must have just arrived. He grinned and waved too. Then there were Teresa, Marcia, Tony and Jeff, rounding out the rest of the gang from Collingwood Street.

Someone had posted copies of the schedule everywhere. Artie's song would be followed by a two-minute commercial, after which Rosa would introduce the former mayor Gavin Newsom, now California's Lieutenant Governor. Tim was taken aback at how handsome he was in person. Too bad he was straight and everyone knew it, since he had a wife and two kids and a house in the Haight/ Ashbury district. Still, he would always be a hero to gay-rights, ever since he opened City Hall to gay marriage during his first term as mayor.

Bruno was back in charge again, gesturing to Artie and Phil to stretch while Rosa scrambled between chairs and bar stools toward the stage. They all had explicit instructions to stay out of the way and not to serve cocktails while the live show was on the air, so Tim darted back into the kitchen.

Whatever he missed from the porthole window he could see on TV later. Artie would no doubt tape it and probably run his part on a continuous loop at the bar forever.

Ben and the kids were watching at home on Hancock Street. Little Sarah, whom Tim always called the magic child, was overcome with excitement. "Look, Daddy, look! Uncle Artie is all dressed up in a shiny dress! Can't we go to Arts and be on TV too? Please, Daddy? Please?"

Her little brother Samuel Timothy was too young to understand what all the fuss was about, but Ben started putting his baby son's shoes on him. He figured they might as well join the fun. "We'll go as soon as they announce the winners, okay? Get your shoes on too, Sarah."

They watched Gavin Newsom step up to the microphone. "Ladies and Gentlemen, it is my great honor as a long-time advocate of enabling each citizen to marry the person he or she loves, regardless of race, religion or sexual identity, to be here at Arts today on San Francisco's historic Castro Street. It is my sincere hope that one day soon these commitment ceremonies will be more than merely symbolic, but carry the full weight of law with all the rights and freedoms that my wife and I enjoy. Now that Don't Ask, Don't Tell has been repealed, it's only a matter of time."

There was a round of applause while the camera panned to Rosa, beaming, though she'd been glaring a moment ago and glancing at her watch. The camera panned the crowd and then landed on Artie, blushing at the kitchen doorway with Arturo beside him in an apron and chef's hat. "There's Uncle Tim!" Sarah shouted. "He's looking through the window behind Artie's shoulder."

"I want to especially thank Rosa Rivera for inviting me to take part in this momentous occasion, the first gay wedding on live television. Are we ready?"

There was a bit of off-camera fumbling as Bruno lifted a crystal bowl full of slips of paper toward the stage. "Please come forward when I call your names." Lieutenant Governor

Newsom drew one of the slips of paper to read the names, "Ladies and Gentlemen, we are gathered here today to witness the festive union of two loving souls… oh, this is interesting! I know one of the winners! Let's have a warm round of applause for… one of San Francisco's finest… Officer Birdie Fuller… and Teresa Shaw!"

"Oh, my God, Ruthie," Teresa turned white as she yelled across the bar. "I never intended for this to happen! Give me a shot of something. Make it a double and make it quick!"

Chapter 24

"Women?" Rosa screamed. *"Lesbians?"* Her eyes grew wider than even Bruno had ever seen them.

Folks watching at home would later remark that whoever called the shots from the white panel truck parked on Castro Street had done a brilliant job. They switched from the close-up of Rosa's face just in time so that the TV audience barely caught her fury.

"Artie, you big fat fool!" she screamed at him. *"Brutto ciccione!* How could you let this happen? I didn't want dykes in my beautiful wedding series! And what about my gorgeous coffee table book? I wanted two of the handsomest men you could find. Any of those couples in the front rows would do." At least four pairs of men gazed into each others' eyes and held hands a little tighter, sure that she was referring to them.

One of the cameras panned the room and caught Teresa belting down a shot while Nick and Marcia helped her stand up. The other camera caught Birdie as she bounded in the doorway from the sidewalk and worked her way toward Teresa. Birdie gave her a great big smooch and pulled her along the rest of the way to the stage.

Tim stepped out of the way just in time as Artie dashed into the kitchen with Rosa hot on his tail. Artie's white hat slipped backward just as Rosa caught up to him and pulled off his wig. "Artie, *voi idiot stupido!* I'm going to kill you!" The sound technician in the truck had switched off her body mike, but everyone in the restaurant could hear her through the still swinging double doors into the kitchen. Phil pounded out the Wedding March as loudly as he could.

What those inside the restaurant couldn't see was that Rosa's spiky heel slid on a blob of chicken liver pate that must have dropped on the tile floor. Her arms flew up as she stumbled backward and landed flat on her back with the wind knocked out of her. Artie replaced the hat and wig on his head, stepped over Rosa's supine body and triumphantly returned to the dining room just as Birdie and Teresa reached the stage.

Jane gave her father a peck on the cheek. "Maybe I'll watch from outside, where I can catch some fresh air, Dad. Rosa looks furious. What if she comes after me next? I didn't know. Artie never told me not to include women."

"Don't worry," Ruth said. "No one will let her hurt you. We'll hold your seat at the bar, though. Do you want to join her, Sam?"

"Are you kidding? I wouldn't miss this for the world. Sit down, Jane. You'll be fine."

Teresa was wearing her new purple pants suit. She wouldn't have dressed up at all if the boys who lived downstairs hadn't talked her into it. She thought Tony and Jeff must have entered, but they insisted that they hadn't. When they all walked over from Collingwood earlier, Marcia speculated that Tim and Nick would be the winners, so Teresa wanted to be there for them. Now here *she* was, standing up in front of a room full of people—strangers, mostly—with the former mayor of San Francisco asking her whether she *did* and whether she *would*... Her head was spinning so fast she could hardly understand what she was promising. Darn that Tim! Where was he now?

The last time Teresa had stood up like this was when she married Lenny right out of high school. Now Leonardo was a gay bear married to Theodore, who was called Teddy when Teresa first met him. And Teresa was standing up here with Birdie. She never imagined that Birdie would pull such a stunt. She'd dropped enough hints about it though, and Teresa had to admit they'd been having an awfully good time together. Birdie was a heck of a gal alright... *but the first time I got married it was to a gay man and it was all legal and legit and where did that end up? This time I'm marrying a woman and it only means whatever we say it means... but what does it mean? What does that make me?*

Tim was the only person she'd told that she was seeing someone special, but she hadn't told him who. Even when her mother in Seattle had suspected something was going on, Teresa hadn't admitted it, but wasn't it funny how a mother knows things? She might have invited her mother if she'd known they were getting married.

Hell, the first time she and Birdie did anything together, Teresa was out cold. She thought it was Bartholomew flicking a tongue in her ear and nuzzling her neck. Now here she was with Birdie standing beside her in her SFPD uniform, looking just as butch as she could be, even though Teresa was nearly a head taller in her new shoes that matched her purple pants suit and who knew how many pounds heavier than Birdie?

"Teresa?" Gavin Newsom repeated. "Miss Shaw?" Teresa looked down at Birdie with the brim of her cap sticking out from under her arm on the other side and Birdie's sweet face smiling up at her. What else could she say but, "Sure, what the heck? You bet I do, Birdie. I mean... yes, sir, Mister Newsom. I do!"

"By the powers vested in me..."

Tim made a half-hearted attempt to revive Rosa Rivera by splashing cold water in her face, but he aimed most of it at her wig, trying to get the curl out. Her eyes fluttered open and she started shouting again, *"Mazzo maledetto di faggots inutili!"* Tim could hear Artie on the microphone belting out *Fly me to the Moon*. It should have been loud enough to drown out Rosa's swearing, but Tim dumped another pitcher of water in her face, just to be on the safe side. When she staggered to her feet, swinging, Tim and Arturo wrestled her out the back door and locked her outside with the dumpster. That would fix her for a while, anyway.

Bruno told the technicians to insert another commercial while he had a few words with the Lt. Gov. When the live camera came back on, Newsom announced, "Ladies and Gentlemen, it seems that Ms. Rivera is indisposed at the moment, but we'd all like to congratulate Birdie and Teresa on the start of their new life together and I guess, since I have a few moments to fill…"

He looked at Bruno, who nodded and make the okay sign with his thumb and forefinger. "As all of you know, today's commitment ceremony is not legally recognized by the state of California or by our Federal government, but it is my fervent hope that one day soon it will be." Everyone burst into applause again, which led to a standing ovation. "I guess we only have a few seconds left on the air, but what the heck… As long as we're here, why don't I just marry all of you? You won't be on the television show and you'll still need to go down to City Hall to fill out paperwork for domestic partnerships, but if you'd like to line up over here two at a time… what's that?"

Bruno stepped up to the stage again and whispered something in his ear. "Wonderful! The photographer from Rosa's show, *Let's Make it Happen*, will take pictures of each couple as you say your vows and maybe they'll be included in the souvenir book about San Francisco weddings, too."

Tim helped Arturo get the trays of food onto the buffet table behind the piano. Then they wheeled the enormous six-tiered wedding cake into view. Teresa and Birdie got to cut it for photographs, since they were the actual winners, then everyone had some. The first thing Teresa did was take the tiny plastic grooms off the top of the cake. "Couldn't you have found some little plastic brides, Artie?" Teresa complained. She was already getting into the spirit of being a dyke.

"Teresa, Birdie… Arturo and I had nothing to do with the cake," Artie said. "That was Rosa's doing. Complain to her."

Arturo had gathered Scott, James, Tim and Jake together to open the back door very slowly. They figured Rosa would have had time to either cool down or she'd be even worse, but it turned out she was nowhere in sight. Tim went to join Nick at the bar and saw that Ben and the kids had arrived from Hancock Street.

Now they all heard a loud commotion at the front door. Rosa must have found her way down the driveway to Hartford and walked all the way around the block. Her dress was dirty; she'd broken a heel and she was still fuming. Bruno got to the door at the same time she did and he held her back by pointing to the cameras. "Do you want to be on camera looking like a drowned rat?"

"I'll get even with all of you!" She yelled and scowled and shook her fists while she ducked inside the white van, which eventually made its way through the busy Saturday traffic on Castro Street and back to the studio.

Artie got behind the bar long enough to help Scott pop open several bottles of champagne and pour glasses for everyone. Gavin Newsom joined them and made a toast to all the happy couples in the house while Artie took the stage again.

"On behalf of Arturo and myself and the entire staff of Arts, I'd like to thank Lieutenant Governor Newsom and all the television crew and… well, I guess Rosa's not here, so… thanks to Bruno and his staff and all the contestants, especially Teresa and Birdie. Now, maestro, I feel a song coming on."

"On a wonderful day like today,
I defy any cloud to appear in the sky…

Sam cornered Tim at the bar and told him that he and Ruth wanted him to come along as their guest to Chicago next weekend for Adam's wedding to Alexandra. "Sam, are you sure you want me along? I won't know anyone and I'll be the only gay person."

"You'll know us, not to mention the bride and groom. No excuses. You sound just like your Aunt Ruth. I know she'd feel more comfortable if you were there too. And I'm sure they've invited some of their gay friends. We'll all be family soon, Adam and Alexandra, Ruth and you and me. How about Nick? Can he come too? It'll be my treat… everything."

"I'll ask him." Tim turned back toward the stage to hear Artie singing.

"Let me say furthermore, I'd adore everybody
To come and dine — the pleasure's mine —
And SAM will play the bill!"

Sam laughed, waved to Artie with a "thumbs-up" gesture, kissed Ruth and raised his champagne glass high in the air. "And we'll have another wedding when we all get back from Chicago!"

Birdie and Teresa were sharing a slice of wedding cake at the window table. Nick and Tim faced each other on bar stools and held hands with their knees locked together. Nearly all of the couples were pleased with the way things turned out. Even though they may not be on television, they got to say their vows with the former mayor of San Francisco presiding. Leah Garchik was over by the buffet table, notepad in hand, asking Lieutenant Governor Newsom whether he missed being mayor, especially on a day like this. She would have plenty of observations for her *Chronicle* column from this event. Even Rosa Rivera, back at the studio, was relieved that her *Wedding Season* series was finally finished, at least the television part. There was still the coffee table book to edit and she was appeased that she could at least include photographs of all those handsome men in their tuxedos.

Tim was even excited about taking a little trip with his Aunt Ruth and Sam. He wished Nick could come with them, but Nick said he couldn't get away next weekend. He told Tim he had to work, but what he had to do was more important than anything at the nursery. He was one of the first people

Ruth had called on the phone the other night. She counted on Nick to be a key player in her big plan, once she and Sam got Tim safely out of town.

And Nick and Tim would make up for being apart next weekend by having another honeymoon tonight, just like they did whenever they were together.

Chapter 25

Tim had never flown first class before, but Sam insisted, and he was paying the bills. Aunt Ruth was seated behind Tim and Sam was on the aisle. The aisle seat next to Tim was empty except for a pretzel bag and a couple of magazines. He didn't realize he'd dozed off until the pilot's voice announced that they were over the Rocky Mountains. They would adjust their flight pattern to the north in order to avoid a big thunderstorm over Nebraska, but should still land in Chicago close to their scheduled arrival time.

Tim knew it was silly, but he felt a pang of dread about the possibility of flying over Minnesota. Then he remembered that his mother wasn't there right now. She was still in California, many miles behind them. Then he tried again to put thoughts of his mother out of his mind.

The last time he'd been to Chicago was with Jason, more than a year before his murder. Jason had dragged Tim along to the International Mister Leather contest over Memorial Day weekend. Tim's credit card got a good workout at Mr S Leather in San Francisco beforehand. That was also at Jason's insistence. Tim spent most of that weekend alone in their hotel room while Jason was off somewhere else doing whatever else with whomever else. It wasn't that Tim didn't have a few offers. It was just that he was so *in love* at the time

that Jason was the only man he wanted. And he still had all
that leather at home, collecting dust in the closet.

The cute blond flight attendant looked down at Tim.
"Can I get you another drink?" His voice was warm and
seductive and Tim's Gaydar worked just fine, even at thirty-
five thousand feet.

"Maybe just a glass of water and another pillow?" He'd
forgotten to take his HIV meds and he *was* thirsty for some
water. Tim felt foolish not to take advantage of the free drinks
in first class, but he didn't want to be drunkenly slurring
his words by the time they landed. He gazed at fleecy white
clouds over rolling hills that were starting to turn into squares
of Midwestern farmland. Those checkerboard miles would be
dotted with farmers in bib overalls on John Deere tractors this
time of year. And their horny teenage sons. Tim remembered
being that age, watching them with envy from car windows
while his life remained stuck in the city.

Now he was headed for Chicago. Tim tried to remember
the name of the serial killer who'd struck there... the one
who shot Versace. He'd passed through San Francisco and
Minneapolis first, then Chicago and finally Miami, where
his killing spree ended in suicide. Tim wanted to say Jeffrey
Dahmer, but that was the cannibal, the one in Milwaukee.
Wisconsin *was* smack dab in between, wasn't it?

"Penny for your thoughts!" Aunt Ruth picked up the
magazines and slipped into the empty seat beside him.

"My thoughts, huh? I was thinking about that gay serial
killer. What was his name?"

"What would make you think of a serial killer on such a
pretty day?"

"I don't know. What was his name?"

"John Wayne Gacy? Albert DeSalvo? That was the Boston
Strangler..."

"No, the gay one... Versace's killer."

"Canon... Cumin... Arthur something?"

"Andrew," Tim said. "Andrew Cunanan."

"I still don't know what on earth would remind you of him, but at least you weren't thinking about your mother."

Tim straightened up in his seat and turned to face her as best he could with the seatbelt fastened. "Aunt Ruth, I can go for days, months… even years… without thinking about my mother and I really like it that way. And then someone like you, for instance, insists on mentioning her and I have to be reminded. Why do you…?"

"I'm sorry, sweetheart." Ruth touched his hand. "I didn't mean to—"

"I'm sorry too. I didn't mean to snap at you… I was thinking of her just a minute ago, so it's not your fault. Oh… I'm still half asleep."

"No one could ask you to forgive her for what she did to you, whether she was drunk or sober. I didn't know anything about her coming to San Francisco, either. I hope you know that. I just hoped that shedding some light on those things you blocked from your childhood, you might be able to better understand—"

"Aunt Ruth." Tim gave her a pleading look and threw up his hands.

"Sorry, I'll stop, but there's just one more thing I have to tell you. By the time you get back to San Francisco, your mother will be far away from there and I'm pretty sure she'll never try to bother you again."

"Good."

The flight attendant returned. "Here's your water. Something for you, ma'am?"

"Nothing at the moment, thanks." Ruth strummed her fingers across her nephew's armrest, fondled her engagement ring and turned the diamonds toward the light from Tim's window. "Isn't that beautiful, honey?"

"Yes, it's so nice that you and Sam get to have a legal wedding, while we remain second-class citizens with the help of so-called Christians like Maggie Gallagher and the tea-party Republicans take over the country and the chicken-shit Democrats claim to be on our side, but don't do anything about it while the teenaged gay kids keep hearing how worthless they are until they kill themselves and—"

"Tim." She put her fingertips to his lips. "You know I agree with you 100%. And so does Sam. And so does nearly everyone we know. Someday we'll all have the same rights, but until then we just have to keep fighting for them. Maybe Sam and I will wait to get married. He won't mind living in sin with me until everyone has the same rights. There's no reason we can't just enjoy a very long engagement, is there? Let's do the best we can with the times we live in. And let's all try to have some fun in Chicago."

"At another legal, heterosexual wedding."

"Oh, I know… I know…"

While Tim was flying eastward, Nick was driving north to the Redwood Valley Ranch. He'd been having dreams lately too and he wasn't one bit psychic. In Nick's dreams, Tim's mother was holding up her Bible, a thick black book with gold letters and trim. She thrust the cross on its cover into Nick's face like she was fending off a vampire. "Is the Lord preparing a special place for you in heaven?"

Nick could still hear that voice as the dream replayed in his head. He wanted to scream back at her, "And is Satan preparing eternal damnation for you? I know what you did. I know everything, you hateful witch!"

"What are you talking about?"

"I know what you did to your son when he was an innocent little boy who looked to his mother for love and nurturing, but you turned his life into a living hell."

"How can you know anything, you heathen?"

"I know how you abused him, make him sick, hurt him, burned him, tortured him…"

"This is none of your business. Who do you think you are? Where is he? Where is my son?"

"You don't deserve to know anything about him. All you need to know is that you'll never see him again. And you'll never be able to hurt him again, not as long as I have anything to say about it."

Nick imagined her cringe, as if he'd slapped her with his words, as if he could return a fraction of the pain she'd caused Tim. But then the sickening glow crept back to her face and her eyes were flames as she sat up straight, defying him. "Where is Ruth? *Where is my sister*?"

"She doesn't want to see you either!"

Nick shuddered and tried to shake off the images from his dream. It was warm when he left the San Francisco this morning, but it was sweltering hot the farther he drove inland from the coast. The uniform—stiff black slacks, starched white shirt and black tie were scratchy and miserable. Nick braked the limousine and waited for a truck to cross the narrow intersection ahead. He had to get a hold of himself before he dealt with Tim's mother for real. If he could tell her off, he might feel better, but he'd made a promise to Ruth and had to trust that her plan was better than his instincts.

Nick pulled into the parking lot of the Redwood Valley Ranch as another car vacated a spot near the main doors. Nick took a deep breath and fixed his tie in the mirror. He stepped out of the air conditioning and into the miserable heat to put on the tailored wool jacket and visored cap. She had better be ready. He didn't want to stick around here in this get-up any longer than necessary. If she complained that it was too cold in the car, he could turn down the A/C, but he hoped she didn't complain about anything or it would be hard to hold his tongue.

Nick was glad he didn't see the receptionist, Miss Austin, or anyone else who might recognize him. He wore dark sunglasses, but he was still nervous about pulling off this plot. The Redwood Valley Ranch seemed accustomed to the comings and goings of chauffeured limousines. Considering the cost of the treatment, the clients could afford them. A young man Nick had never seen before led him across the grounds to the cabin and knocked. "Your driver is here for you, Mrs. Snow."

"Driver? I was expecting my sister to come."

"She sent me instead," Nick held out the old suitcase with the broken latch that had been sitting in Ruth's living room on Collingwood Street all this time. That was Ruth's idea, too. It still had her name tag on it and he offered it as proof to Mrs. Snow that Ruth had sent him.

"I don't need that. She bought me a new one. Where is my sister?"

"She said to tell you she'll check on you after you get settled in at home."

"Oh. I see. I'm ready to go now." Nick carried her luggage out to the parking lot and ushered her into the back seat. She didn't seem nearly as dangerous as in his dream. She appeared almost timid, broken like a once-wild horse.

She slept most of the way, so Nick calmed down. He took off his hat and loosened his tie and collar, watched the countryside glide by and almost forgot about his passenger until they crossed the Golden Gate Bridge. He jumped at the sound of her voice. "Where are we going? Where are you taking me?"

"To the airport," Nick answered dryly, professionally. "Those were my instructions."

The motels of Lombard Street flew past the windows. Nick had left the driver's window partway open after he paid the bridge toll. He loved the cool eucalyptus-scented fog streaming through the Presidio trees.

"But my sister… my son…"

"Your sister is out of town."

"But I might have left something at her apartment."

"I'm sure whatever you left behind would be in the old suitcase in the trunk."

"No, I've got to go there anyway."

Nick made a show of straightening his left arm and pulling back the sleeve to reveal his watch. "We have plenty of time to stop there. Do you have a key?"

Nick knew she didn't have a key even before she didn't answer him. He drove to Collingwood anyway and pressed all the buzzers at the front gate. There was no response from any of them and Nick wondered if Ruth had planned that too. "I'm sure your sister will ship you anything you left behind, Mrs. Snow," Nick said as she reassembled herself in the back.

Nick maneuvered the limousine up the narrow lane of Collingwood like a boat through a maze and managed a left turn onto 20th Street. When he reached Tim's house, the timing was perfect. One truck in the driveway belonged to the men who were finishing the upstairs deck. The bricklayers had pulled in behind the first truck to unload their supplies. Nick pulled in behind them and lowered the window as Ben came out the front door and approached the car. "May I help you?"

"The lady is looking for the owner of this building… Mr. Snow?"

"You won't find him here… nobody here today but the workmen. He's redoing the whole place, Mr. Snow is. He's got big plans for it, but we haven't seen him around here in quite a while."

"Thanks anyway," Nick closed the window and glanced back toward his passenger. "Ready to go to the airport now?"

"What about that restaurant? Maybe he's working. There might be someone there who knows where he is."

"What restaurant is that?"

"It's called Arts on Castro Street."

"Very well." Nick turned up Noe to 19th Street and took a right on Castro. Arturo was in his car, holding the parking space directly in front of Arts and there was a police car in front of him. They both pulled out to make room for the limousine. Ruth really *had* thought of everything. There were only a couple of actual customers at the bar. Nick recognized seeing them at Ruth's surprise birthday party. Scott was chatting with them near the waiters' station.

Artie was in a get-up Nick had never seen: yellow pants and a matching blouse, low-heeled shoes and a gray wig. He wore only a touch of powder, rouge and lipstick, a downright subtle look that must have taken amazing self-control. "Hello and welcome to Arts. We're not serving dinner yet, but the bar is open for cocktails…"

Tim's mother stiffened at *bar* and *cocktails* so soon out of rehab and stared at Artie, as if she could find a clue to Tim's whereabouts by analyzing this dowdy creature. "I'm not here for dinner. I'm looking for my son, Tim Snow."

"My Lord! You're Mrs. Snow? What a wonderful surprise! Come in. Come in and make yourself at home. How about a cocktail?"

"No, I couldn't."

"Suit yourself then, but come over here and sit down. I'd like you to meet my dear friend Amanda." Nick saw his grandmother at one of the large round tables, sipping an amber drink from a stemmed glass. "Terry, Chris… come and meet Mrs. Snow."

The two guys from the bar brought their drinks with them to the table. Now Nick remembered. They were the female to male transsexuals who ate at Arts often. Nick and his grandmother smiled and pretended not to know each other. When Ruth said she was calling on all her friends, she meant *all* of them.

"We're delighted to have you grace us with your presence," Artie continued. "Please sit down and let's get acquainted. I have been your… *son's*… employer and landlady for several years now, until he inherited that house on Hancock Street and your sister Ruth moved into the old apartment."

"I know," Mrs. Snow's voice sounded tired and faint. "I was just there looking for him… both places, but there was no sign of him…"

"No, of course there wouldn't be. He's remodeling that place of his on Hancock. What a wonderful thing, isn't it? He's helped so many people already, and now it will be modernized a bit. You've raised a very generous child, Mrs. Snow, always thinking of others in need… such a good Christian. You must be so proud."

Betty Snow tried to smile as she fondled her Bible and a small square purse she held in her lap. Artie looked toward the door as Nick opened it for the next arrival. "Oh, look who's here… Marcia! Come and meet Mrs. Snow."

Ruth's neighbor who used to be a boy named Malcolm, the only genuine transsexual that Nick knew personally, swept into the room. "Mrs. Snow? You're not *the* Mrs. Snow… what an honor! I can't tell you how grateful I will always be…" Nick was starting to grasp the full extent of Tim's aunt's invention now and he loved her it. He half expected to see Rosa Rivera come out of the kitchen, but it was probably too soon for her to reappear at Arts after the wedding debacle.

"Grateful? For what?"

"So many people, receiving a surprising inheritance, wouldn't have thought to turn right around and practically give it away. I'm so grateful for everything!

"Where is my son?" Mrs. Snow's voice grew stronger now. Her eyes widened as she ogled the liquids in each of their cocktail glasses.

"How long has it been since you've seen your child, Mrs. Snow?" Marcia asked.

"It's been since he was in high school. I don't remember… over ten years. Maybe closer to fifteen."

"He must have changed a great deal in all that time, don't you think?" Marcia smiled ever-so-sweetly. "Are you sure you want to see him? Maybe it would be better to leave the past in the past. That's what I did."

"Of course I want to see him! He's my son, my only child. Where is he?"

"In the hospital," Artie declared.

"Which hospital? Is he sick? I'll have that driver take me there right away."

"He's not sick," Marcia started to laugh. "Besides, the hospital isn't here in San Francisco. He's down at UCLA. They have some of the best doctors. I had my own surgery done there."

"Surgery? What surgery? My son is having surgery?"

"Isn't it wonderful?" Artie went on. "From what we've heard, he spent so much time in the hospital as a little boy that he's almost looking forward to this hospital stay, especially when you consider the eventual glorious outcome."

Nick's grandmother, Amanda Musgrove, said, "Mine was so long ago I had to go to Copenhagen, the same place Christine Jorgensen had hers done. Nowadays, people can stay right here in the States. Look, here come some more of the folks from Hancock Street. We have a little support group that meets once a week in the afternoons. With all the construction going on, we're using the restaurant this time."

"Your Tammy did such a marvelous thing," Marcia said, "providing so many people a place to live and to help each other out while going through all the preparations…"

"Tammy?"

"Look who else is here now," Artie shouted. "Mrs. Snow, I'd like you to meet Teresa. She used to be Terrence. Come on in, Teresa. Come over here and meet Mrs. Snow. This is Tammy's mother. Isn't she a dear?"

"You look kind of familiar," Betty Snow gave Teresa a suspicious glare.

"Do I? Well, I've been around." Teresa was curious to have another look at the homeless woman she'd found in the laundry room several weeks ago.

"We were just telling Mrs. Snow how she'll have a new daughter soon," Artie said. "Now that Ruth is practically married and moving out, Tammy can move back into Tim's old apartment and everything will work out just fine."

"My sister is married?"

"She will be any day now." Artie couldn't help but rub it in. "Didn't you know? What a shame…"

Tim's mother was turning white from holding her breath.

"Are you alright, Mrs. Snow?" Marcia asked. "How about a glass of water?"

"Scott," Artie shouted. "Would you bring Mrs. Snow a glass of water." He gave a little smile. "Unless you'd like something stronger. Scotch? Gin? We have a full bar."

"No… I can't…"

Mrs. Snow looked up toward the young man who carried her water glass and then she saw a tall black man behind him. Artie said, "And this is your sister's hairdresser, Rene."

"Hello." A frosty Mrs. Snow made no move to shake his hand.

Rene sat down next to Amanda. "How do you do, ma'am."

"But you're not a—"

"No ma'am," Rene laughed. "I may be just as nellie as pink ink, but I ain't about to mess with no operations when it comes to the family jewels. I just come by and help the girls with their hair and give them some make-up tips, you know."

"And here comes Burt," Artie announced. "Burt's a pre-op. We used to know her as Birdie, but he's still a cop. The female-to-male ones use the top floor on Hancock and the male-to-females are on the bottom. It's so sensible... not having to deal with all those stairs when you're learning to walk in heels."

"But the Bible says..." Mrs. Snow started in, holding her Bible in her fist.

"Not a word about high heels," Teresa was actually wearing a dress and so much make-up that she didn't look like a real woman. "I go to Bible study on Tuesday nights. I know the good book backward and forward."

The front door opened again and Gladys Bumps arrived. "Hello, everyone. Sorry I'm late. Is the bar open? Good!" Nobody but Artie recognized her at first. They'd never seen her in any kind of drag that wasn't outrageous, but today she was dressed down—*way* down, like a little old lady Sunday school teacher.

"Hiya, Gladys. Get a beer from Scott and come join us," Artie yelled across the room and then spoke to Mrs. Snow in confidence. "We're trying to get her to drink something more ladylike than beer, but at least she uses a glass now, instead of swilling them straight from the bottle."

Betty Snow eyed the beer and started to tremble. She clutched the Bible to her bosom and her whole body shook.

"My son must repent! You must all repent this wickedness and be saved! Homosexuality is a sin! The Bible says so!"

"Did you used to work for the DMV?" Marcia asked.

"Yes, it's a sin, I'll grant you that, Mrs. Snow," Birdie—Burt—Fuller piped up. "The Bible says homosexuality's an abomination, alright. But don't you see? That's the beauty of it. Tammy won't be homosexual anymore. She'll be a woman and a heterosexual woman at that. Once I get my operation, Teresa and I will be just like any other regular old straight couple, just as righteous as you and Mr. Snow. 'Course, the Bible says their men back then had several wives, but one like Teresa's about all I can handle!"

Birdie let out a laugh as Teresa beamed at her and then pointed at Mrs. Snow's Bible. "It also says in there that you can sell your children into slavery and that people live to be hundreds of years old and Noah rounded up two of every animal on earth in a wooden boat."

"They're replicating Noah's ark in Kentucky now," Amanda Musgrove said. "It's as long as two football fields and they're gathering up a heterosexual pair of every animal on earth. There are millions of kinds of insects, you know, and the fundamentalists don't believe in evolution."

Gladys set down her beer glass. "So that means Noah must have rounded up a pair of every kind of bug in the world. I wish he would have let the mosquitoes die out. And why would he want to save the termites... on a wooden boat?"

Everyone laughed except Tim's mother. Amanda shook her head. "You'd think people had never heard of allegory."

Betty Snow turned toward Amanda and eyed the amber liquid in her glass. Teresa leaned forward and spoke under her breath, "I'm not sure what the Bible says about a mother who poisons her own poor little boy and burns his feet and then takes him to the hospital so she can shack up with the doctor... and all behind her husband's back."

Betty Snow cringed as if Teresa must be talking about someone else.

"It's amazing how well Tammy turned out," Artie said, "considering what a fucked-up childhood he had… pardon my French."

"Where is that driver?" Mrs. Snow whispered. She would have screamed, but she couldn't catch her breath. "Help me! Driver? I have to get to the airport."

Nick rushed to the table, pulled out her chair and offered his uniformed arm.

"Goodbye, Mrs. Snow!" Artie called after her.

"It was wonderful meeting you," Marcia said. "We'll tell Tammy you came looking for her. She could send you pictures of the way she looks now! Does she have your address?"

Teresa walked to the limousine with Nick and Tim's mother, who grew frailer by the minute. "What a shame you're going to miss Ruth's wedding and you have to rush off before the butterfly emerges from her chrysalis. Well, you have a safe flight back to Minneapolis, y'hear? And keep in touch!"

Nick drove the rest of the way to the airport in silence. They were just in time to check in Betty Snow and her new suitcase at the curb. Nick ripped off his tie, his jacket and chauffer's cap and rolled up his sleeves before he got back inside the limousine. It was hot at the airport, but a cool bank of fog was pouring in over the city. It welcomed him back like a blanket of peace. Betty Snow would never see San Francisco again and best of all, no one in San Francisco would ever see her again, either.

Chapter 26

"We did it, Ruthie, we did it! Everyone was marvelous. You should have seen us. Everyone played their parts and did exactly like you said." Artie was so excited to finally reach Ruth on the phone that he barely let her get a word in."

"I knew you could pull it off, Artie…" Ruth was grateful to her friends for following through with her plan and still she felt guilty at the same time. Betty Snow was her only sister and she hated to lie, but after all she'd done to Tim, she deserved it. Gender reassignment surgery was no big deal in San Francisco in 2011, but Ruth knew it would be shocking to someone like Betty and if that's what it took to get his mother out of Tim's life, it was worth the deception. Still… Ruth never liked to deceive anybody… or give up on them.

"Especially Nick's grandmother," Artie was still carrying on. "I mean *really*… Amanda Musgrove is already intimidating enough as a woman, but the thought of her having once been a man! It was too perfect! She kept her voice real deep the way she does, you know, and that darling Nick was such a handsome chauffeur with his hair slicked back and he looked so elegant in his uniform. Between him and Amanda and me, I was sure one of us would laugh, but nobody let on. We all stayed in character."

"Artie, that's just great." The most important thing to Ruth was that Betty got through it all without a drink. Maybe her stay at the Redwood Valley Ranch had been worthwhile. Maybe, just maybe—Ruth always hoped for a miracle—the day might come when she would be sorry for all she'd done and Tim could forgive his mother and they'd all be reunited as one big happy family… someday… in Ruth's dreams.

"Birdie was in her uniform and Teresa was so done up she looked like a drag queen," Artie giggled. "Marcia helped her out with her hair and make-up earlier at home, of course." Artie was delighted to relive every detail he could remember for Ruth's sake. As far as he was concerned, the whole afternoon had been great fun.

"Ruth, dear…" Sam's voice in the background was loud enough that Artie could hear him too. "Are you going to be tied up on the phone long?"

"I'm talking to Artie in San Francisco."

"Hello, Artie!" Sam called out. "I just noticed the time. Alexandra's parents want to take us to dinner. I'll go knock on Tim's room and see if he's ready."

"I've got to go, Artie. We'll talk soon." Ruth was stepping into her shoes. "Give everyone back in San Francisco all my love and thanks and tell them we'll be back in a couple of weeks. Call my cell if you need to reach me for any reason at all… b-bye."

Tim was across the hall finishing up a call with Nick. "The wedding was beautiful, if you like that sort of thing."

"How was the reception?"

"Grand. Alexandra's father must be as rich as Sam. She didn't marry Adam for his money, I guess. Oh, I almost forgot… I danced with her. She's really sweet. I asked Adam to dance, but he wouldn't… not as cool a guy as I thought he was."

"Aw, Snowman… it was his wedding reception. And it's Chicago, not San Francisco. Besides, I'm sure there were tons of straight guys there who would have flipped!"

"Still, it would have been fun if he had."

"You just come home and I'll dance with you anytime, babe."

"Sam's knocking. I gotta go to dinner. Love you. Bye."

By Monday, Tim was more than ready to leave his Aunt Ruth and Sam and Chicago behind and fly home alone. He missed Nick more than he wanted to admit and he missed San Francisco too. The late afternoon sun was glaring, but Tim wouldn't pull down the shade. He wanted to see if the Golden Gate Bridge looked any different from a first class seat. But the fog was pouring in and covered the roadway of the bridge, leaving the tall orange towers jutting out like a dreamscape. Tim stared out the window and decided that if San Francisco didn't exist, someone would have to invent it.

On the cab ride in from the airport, the temperature dropped as the thick summer fog enveloped them. Tim thought he was coming home to an empty house, but two trucks were in his driveway on Hancock Street. One was Nick's, but he didn't recognize the larger one. Tim could hear stranger's voices, struggling on the new back deck. He was frightened at first until he heard Nick's voice yell down, "Snowman! Come up the back way. I have a couple of surprises for you." Tim could only see the corner of something that looked like an enormous sculpture. Nick said to someone, "Thank you, guys. That's the perfect spot."

Tim waited for two burly movers to descend the back stairs before he could climb up them. "What's going on?"

"Welcome back, babe." Nick kissed him and gave him a bear hug. That was all that really mattered to Tim right now. "I'm so glad you're home. Did you miss me?"

"Of course I missed you. What surprises?"

Nick stepped back out of the way, "Ta-da!"

"What the...?"

"It's a bench. I had it carved from your old redwood tree. There was one big healthy section about eight feet long in the middle. Do you like it?"

"It's amazing!" Tim sat down and rubbed the palm of his hand against the smooth grain of the armrest. Its seat was curved and wide enough to lie down. "It's not a bench; it's a sculpture. It's beautiful."

"I got the idea a long time ago," Nick said. "I was on my way to bid on a landscaping job in Napa County and I noticed this place along the road, so I stopped and looked around at the guy's work. He's quite an artist with a chain saw. His wife does most of the finishing. They were really nice people."

"How old do you think that tree was?" Tim gazed down at the stump in his backyard.

"I don't know… a hundred years or so."

"So it was just a baby, by redwood standards. They live for thousands of years in Northern California, don't they?"

"It was sick, man. It wasn't gonna get any better."

"I know. I wasn't complaining. All I'm saying is now I have a bench instead. It's carved from one solid piece of wood and even though the tree died, the bench will last forever, won't it?"

"I'm not sure if I know what forever even means, Snowman, but it'll last a lot longer than either of us will, that's for sure."

"You said surprises… plural?"

"Yeah… at that same place where the guy does the wood sculptures, the first time I stopped by, they had this little dog and she was so sweet, but she was very pregnant. Come on inside and I'll show you. You said you wanted a dog, right?" Nick slid open the door from the deck onto the kitchen and gave a whistle. "Here boy…"

A furry brown streak tore around the corner, skidded across the kitchen floor and lunged into Tim's arms. "Hey there, Buckaroo! It's so cute. It is a he, isn't it? What kind of dog is he?"

"It's a he, but we're not exactly sure. The mother is a Jack Russell terrier, but he's a half-breed."

"Oh, good… a Cher fan from birth."

"She got loose when she was in heat and they figure from the coloring that the father might be the Doberman up the road."

"He's adorable!" Tim was on his hands and knees, playing tug of war with an old sock the puppy had found somewhere. "But a Jack Russell is so little and a Doberman is…"

"Pretty big," Nick finished his sentence for him.

Tim looked up over his shoulder at Nick with a grin. "Ooh, I know just how that poor bitch must have felt."

Nick laughed and stepped closer to straddle Tim's head in his crotch. "You weren't exactly shortchanged in the endowment department yourself, Snowman. I'll bet nobody's ever called you 'Tiny Tim.'"

"Not that I can remember."

"What do you want to name him?"

"I don't know… what do *you* think, Buckaroo?" The puppy wagged its tail and jumped up into Nick's arms as he crouched down to join them on the floor. "How about Buck? That's a butch name for you, little guy, but you might grow into it."

"I don't think he'll get as big as a Doberman," Nick said. "His paws aren't very big, but he'll grow some."

"He's beautiful. Thanks… for everything."

"Well, he's not just yours, you know. I figured we could raise him together. He's a country dog at heart, so he should probably get used to the city in small doses. I figure he'll get the best of both worlds that way. So… how does it feel to be a parent, Snowman?"

"Great. Any more surprises for me?"

"Only that I scheduled your new skylight for this week. They're coming on Wednesday to put it in, so I thought you might want to spend a few days with me up north while your kitchen is torn up again."

"We sure did this remodeling job backward, didn't we? We should have started with the skylight and then done the deck and left the kitchen floor for last."

"Don't worry. I already hired a cleaning service to come in on Thursday. So, how about it? Do you and Buck want to spend a few days at the river this week? I have to drive back first thing tomorrow morning."

"You bet." Tim couldn't stop smiling. "I have some things I promised to do for Aunt Ruth tomorrow, but I could drive up tomorrow night."

"That'll work out great, Snowman—" Nick tried to speak but he had a face full of puppy kisses.

Tuesday morning Tim went by his Aunt Ruth's apartment on Collingwood Street. He'd promised to water the plants on the deck and bring in the mail. Tim thought it was about time she changed her address at the post office and moved the plants to Sam's place if she wasn't going to live here anymore. He set the mail on her desk in the living room window and noticed something missing from his last visit. His mother's old suitcase was gone. It was just as well.

Then it crossed his mind that maybe Aunt Ruth was testing him. If he remembered the plants and the mail, maybe he was responsible enough to take care of the cat next time she left town. Then he remembered that Bartholomew was moving to Hillsborough too. Now that Frank and Delia were gone, Sam would probably line up another couple to cook and do the gardening and keep an eye on the place and feed Bart when Sam and Aunt Ruth went away.

Tim made a dozen trips from the kitchen sink with the watering can. Then he sat down among the smells of jasmine and damp earth in the little garden off the kitchen, *his* old kitchen and now his Aunt Ruth's former kitchen. Even though Ruth and Sam didn't get legally married, they might as well have. She'd spent most of her time in Hillsborough all summer. Sam had paid Arturo and Artie a year's rent in advance on this place, but even so, things had changed and Tim hated it. As much as Tim knew that change could be good, he always had a hard time adjusting.

Tim had fond memories of his own here on Collingwood Street. This was his first apartment in San Francisco. His dreams only came at night in those days. He worried lately that they were turning into frightening visions during his waking life. He hated to admit it and he tried not to think about it, but his clairvoyance was growing stronger every year. These days, it seemed to happen at any old time.

And now he was sitting here being angry at himself for feeling melancholy... and over what? His Aunt Ruth's happiness? His old apartment? A cat? He'd rather have a dog, anyway. And now he and Nick had one, not a prissy little gay thing that cost a fortune, but a good old butch country dog. He never really wanted a cat. Cats were too damned independent.

Tim stopped at Arts on his way back to Hancock Street. The restaurant would be different with Ruth gone. While Tim knew she'd be back in his life as soon as she and Sam returned from Chicago, no one was sure if she'd come back to work at Arts again. She didn't need the money, but it had never been a matter of need. She enjoyed it, or so she always said. Maybe part of her reason for working there had always been to keep an eye on her nephew.

Artie was breaking in a new bartender named Steve. He seemed friendly and capable enough, but Tim knew the customers would ask for Ruth so often that he almost felt sorry for the new guy. Artie introduced them and asked, "How was the big wedding in Chicago?"

"It was nice, I guess... pretty fancy but not nearly as much fun as the big day here at Arts. How are Teresa and Birdie doing?"

"They're packing for their cruise already. That was part of the prize they won."

"How's business?"

"Better than ever. That kind of advertising is priceless. We were even on Fox News!"

"Oh, that's all we need, to have the restaurant taken over by right-wing conservatives. Gay republicans will flood the place. GOProud and the Log Cabin group will be fighting to make Arts their headquarters! How the hell did we get on Fox News?"

"One of their blowhards did a story on Gavin Newsom, how he's still pushing gay marriage against the will of the people of California, especially now that he's moved from the Mayor's office to a bigger stage in Sacramento. They had some nice shots of the restaurant though, from what I hear, and a close-up of *moi*. It was just a still shot. I wasn't singing, but everyone who saw it says I looked fabulous."

"Are the offers flooding in for you to perform, now that they've heard you sing on Rosa's live TV show?"

"Not exactly," Artie frowned. "They never showed me doing an entire song on TV, just a few bars and then they cut away to some pre-taped video of Rosa giving instructions for ordering her damned coffee table book. I've got the DVD of the show right here if you want to borrow it."

"Speaking of Rosa, has anybody heard from her?"

"Not directly," Artie said. "I read about her in the *Chronicle*, though. Leah Garchik says Rosa got an offer to do a new TV show in L.A. That day of the parade, one of the guys in PFLAG marching with his gay son was totally enamored with her. It turned out he's a big TV producer. Bruno is moving down there with her. I guess mother and son have patched things up again, at least for the time being."

"Bruno seems more the L.A. type," Tim said. "They both do. I'm sure they'll be happier there than in San Francisco. We're a little too provincial for them, don't you think?"

"Speak for yourself." Artie was dying to talk to Tim about the charade they'd pulled off in order to get his mother to leave him alone. But Tim had insisted for so long that he didn't want to talk about his mother. Artie didn't dare to bring it up first. Besides, it wasn't his place to do it. Ruth should be the one to tell him. Or maybe Nick. Sooner or later it was bound to come up and then the whole story would come out. "Do you want to borrow this video of Rosa's wedding show here or not?"

"Maybe I should. Nick and I are going to spend a few days up at his place while they install my new skylight. We can watch it there. His cable is iffy sometimes up there. Did you hear we got a new puppy named Buck? Maybe we'll all watch it together one of these nights, if your singing doesn't make him howl too much."

"You brat!" Artie stuck his tongue out at Tim. "Keep it as long as you want. I have more copies."

Ruth and Sam flew back from O'Hare to SFO the next week. She was perfectly willing to go by way of Minneapolis if Betty needed her, or so she told Sam, while trying to convince herself that she meant it. But she called first, from their hotel in Chicago, and Tim's father answered with a grunt.

"Hello? Is that you, Bud?"

"Yeah… whoosis?"

"Hello, Bud, it's Ruth Taylor, calling to see how my sister is doing."

"She's asleep."

Ruth was glad to hear that Betty had made it back alright and that she and Bud were still living under the same roof. Ruth never expected Bud to be warm and conversational. She was relieved that he was polysyllabic. "Well, there's no need to wake her. I just wanted to make sure she made it back in one piece after her trip to California."

"Yep."

"Say, Bud… did she happen to mention Tim?"

"We don't say that name in this house. I'll tell her you called."

Ruth heard the click when he hung up the phone, but she went ahead and said good-bye afterward, anyway. She wanted to put a final period on the end of that sentence, as if instead of saying "good-bye" she was saying "Amen."

Thursday night in Monte Rio, Tim thought he might never need to have sex again… at least not that night. He would drive back to the city in the morning after three perfect days and nights at the Russian River. They were lying in Nick's bed, exhausted and satisfied. Tim ran his fingers across Nick's chest, looked up and asked, "Do you still want to get married?"

"What?" Nick jumped a bit while Tim outlined the features of his face with his fingertips.

"You heard me. Do you still want to get married?"

"To you?"

Tim playfully tweaked Nick's nose. "No, to Rosie O'Donnell, you schmuck!"

"After all this time I've been trying to talk you into it, after all my bugging you, after Teresa and Birdie and all those handsome guys at Arts in their tuxes… now you want to get married?"

Tim rolled on to his back. "Not right this minute, but… sure I do, if you still want to."

"You mean get 'married' married? Like fly to some state where it's legal, married, or 'domestic partner' married, or just have a commitment ceremony and a party?"

"Fly away and get 'married' married, I guess…"

"What made you change your mind, Snowman?"

"All those things you just mentioned, I guess, plus the fact that you're the best thing that ever happened to me."

"No."

"Yes, you are…" Tim stroked Nick's chest for emphasis.

"I didn't mean that… I meant yes, I probably *am* the best thing that ever happened to you… if you say so… but…"

"Absolutely… so what are you saying *no* about?"

"No, I don't want to get married."

"*What*?"

"I've thought long and hard about it, but you were right. You talked me out of it a long time ago."

Tim looked down at Buck, as if the pup could give him a different answer. "Why not?"

"I don't think we should mess up a good thing, that's why not. We have the perfect arrangement as it is. You can live in the city. I can live in the country. We can still see each other as much as we want."

"It's never as much as I want."

"It would be, Snowman. I'm afraid you'd get tired of me if I was around all the time."

"Never!"

"Let's save it for when we're old."

"I don't believe this!" Tim wasn't sure if he was more shocked or disappointed.

"Let's wait until it's legal, anyway. Everywhere. None of this nonsense where we're husbands in Iowa, but we set one foot over the Minnesota border and we're divorced."

"I don't want to get married in Iowa and I have no plans to go back to Minnesota… not in the near future, anyway."

As he mentioned Minnesota, Nick remembered that Tim's mother was back there now. This might be a good time to tell him about Ruth's elaborate scheme, but as long as Tim didn't broach the subject, neither would he. "Hey, we can do a domestic partnership deal if you want, but we're not exactly domestic partners since we each have a place of our own."

"What about hospital visitation rights, Nick?"

"I hope you won't be in the hospital again any time soon, but even that time after you wrapped my old truck around the tree at the bottom of the driveway, I didn't have any problem visiting you … and that hospital was in Sebastopol, not in San Francisco, where you'd expect…"

"I have no memory of that time."

"Even if we got a so-called legal marriage in one state, it wouldn't give us any of the federal rights, like Social Security, tax benefits. I'm willing to go to a lawyer, sign medical power of attorney, redo my will and all of that. We should straighten those things out, anyway. Neither of us has any siblings or anyone younger to leave it to… besides Buck, I guess." The dog opened one eye. "Yeah, boy, I'm talking about you, you little canine heiress… but marriage? Nah… let's enjoy our honeymoon years first, Snowman."

Tim had such a strange look on his face that Nick felt compelled to lean forward and kiss him. "I couldn't love you any more than I do now, married or not, okay? Trust me."

Tim squeezed him tighter. "I do, Nick, I do…"

"You sound like you're talking to the preacher man already."

"I meant that I do trust you… *and* I love you."

"And I love you, Snowman. We can still love each other to death, forever and ever, but you need your freedom, Tim."

"No I don't, Nick, I don't—" Tim couldn't help laughing and Nick joined him.

"You know what? I was watching one of those shows on TV the other night where they were debating gay marriage. They had a minister from a gay church back east somewhere and this homophobic priest who was spouting the usual Catholic line. The priest was saying that gays need to choose to turn away from their sinful lifestyle. Then the gay minister insisted that homosexuality is not a choice. I've always believed that too, haven't you?"

"I sure didn't make any choice," Tim said. "The only choice I ever had was whether to be honest with myself or try to suppress it and go crazy."

"Exactly," Nick held him tighter. "But that gay minister on TV kept saying, 'Nobody *chooses* to be gay. Who would willingly *choose* to be a homosexual and subject themselves to all the hate and prejudice and scorn of society? No one *ever* would,' he said."

"So?"

"Well, I got to thinking… it wasn't that way for me at all. I mean… I know I've been luckier than a lot of guys, growing up with the parents I did and my grandparents were really cool, too…"

Tim had closed his eyes and was listening in silence, but when Nick stopped talking, Tim opened them again. "And…?"

"And I said to myself, '*I would! That's who!*' I'd choose to be gay. When I see all those miserable-looking housewives at the mall with their screaming kids and their husbands who look so unhappy… then I think of how good it feels to be with you like the past couple of days. Maybe that's why people are afraid of us. We're happy. They're afraid to be honest enough with themselves to be this happy. If I'd known I was going to meet you, I would have chosen to be gay a hundred times over. Wouldn't you, Snowman?"

But Tim couldn't answer, not in words. He wished he could be as sure as Nick was about everything. Tim didn't know what he would have chosen if he'd had a choice. Nobody had to remind Tim how different his background was from Nick's. He'd spent all his first years in San Francisco going through men like they were dancers auditioning at an open cattle call or actors he was screen testing for the juicy leading role of his lifelong lover. Had he finally cast the role now with Nick? Would there still be time to audition another man now and then for a walk-on part while Nick remained the star?

As if Nick could read Tim's mind, he said, "And besides, Snowman, what if Anderson Cooper decides to come all the way out of the closet and dumps his hot husband and wants a roll in the hay with me? I couldn't lie. I'd have to tell him I was married… to you."

"You think he'd pick you over me?" Tim gave Nick a playful slug in his hard stomach, ran his fingertips up and down the dark blond treasure trail of fur and flicked his tongue into Nick's navel. He lifted his head long enough to say, "If Anderson can't decide, he could take us both on at once, huh?"

"Who knows what might happen?" Nick's long strong fingers massaged the back of Tim's scalp through the soft brown locks of hair while Buck spun around and readjusted himself at the foot of the bed.

All Tim knew anymore that night was that life had led him to this moment in time and it felt just right. The last thing he remembered was the sound of the Russian River trickling far below them, bubbling over and under the logs and rocks that got in its way on its journey to the sea. Within a few moments they had fallen into a deep dreamless sleep, all three of them.

A sneak peek at
Chapter 1

from

Mark Abramson's

California Dreamers

Book 6 of the Beach Reading series

Chapter ONE

d on Craigslist:

Psychic Jobs in San Francisco
Reply to: see below
8:50 AM PDT

Are you psychic? Do you have what it takes for our psychic phone line? Work from home and make up to $1000 per week. We value the unique talent each Psychic makes in the lives of our clients. Are you a skilled Tarot Reader, Clairvoyant or Astrologer? Would you like to work from home, keep flexible hours and earn great pay? Look no more. We pledge respect and integrity. You must have a genuine gift and love helping people. We prefer psychics with telephone experience, but will consider all. Get in on the ground floor and become a star.

Blessings and love…

• Principals only. Recruiters, please don't contact this job poster.
• Please, no phone calls about this job!
• Please do not contact job poster about other services, products or commercial interests.

Tim Snow smiled, switched off the computer and went to bed. He sometimes wondered when he was younger whether he would grow up to become one of those people who told fortunes for a living. He knew he'd inherited "the gift" from his grandmother on his mother's side, but he thought of it like a propensity for brown hair or big feet and he barely remembered his grandmother anyway. Besides his so-called "gift," all he had of her was the photograph of the two of them that he kept in a frame on his bedside table. His parents seemed embarrassed to talk about her when he was growing up and Tim knew better than to ask many questions.

Ever since Dr. Hamamoto prescribed the new HIV drugs, Tim's dreams had grown stronger. He'd been spared any frightening visions lately; at least while he was awake. One night he dreamed that Congress passed a law prohibiting gays from adopting pets. The authorities were already taking dogs away from lesbian couples to euthanize them—the dogs, not the lesbians—rather than let them grow up without proper male role models. Tim wasn't sure how this affected the rest of the country, but the dog owners he saw every week in Dolores Park were up in arms.

The *Bay Times* ran an interview with a woman prisoner, convicted of sleeping with her German shepherd. She denied having "improper" relations, though they would have been heterosexual by definition *and* consensual, she insisted. The headline in the *B.A.R.* that week read: *Playing it straight to walk the dog*. The *Chronicle* interviewed a widowed grandmother in Daly City whose late husband had rented the apartment over their garage to a gay student. Authorities took away her fifteen-year-old cat. She admitted that she missed Puddles, but she'd always voted Republican because it was the party of God. Now she was leaning more toward the Tea Party. She was quoted, "If Congress says the cat has to go; then the cat has to go. I'm no terrorist!"

Tim woke up laughing. This dream was during an afternoon nap and he couldn't believe it foreshadowed anything real, the way his nighttime dreams sometimes did.

He took his HIV drugs at bedtime. He even had nightmares lately where his phoned was tapped; he heard footsteps on the sidewalk behind him and felt someone's eyes follow him down Castro Street. He was sure that his mail, even the PG&E bill, had been steamed open and sealed shut again.

Tim and Nick's new puppy named Buck, like a child of divorced parents, was adapting well to life with two homes and two fathers. His parents may not have the right to marry, but they loved each other very much. Nick Musgrove took Buck for long runs on the beach near Jenner where he got to sniff the rotting fish, kelp, and other culinary treats of the Pacific. Weekends at Tim's house on Hancock Street in San Francisco meant learning to socialize with other dogs in Dolores Park. Nick came down to the city on Thursday afternoons or Friday if he was busy at the nursery. Tim usually drove his old Thunderbird convertible up to the Russian River after the Sunday brunch shift at Arts restaurant on Castro Street.

Buck drew a lot of attention wherever he went. Now Tim understood why he saw so many dogs in the Castro; they provided the perfect opening if you wanted to talk to someone. Tim was sure that some of the other single dog owners trained their pets to run up and sniff at the crotches of the cutest guys. Tim felt more and more that he and Nick were "married," whether or not they had a ceremony or any legal documents. Even so, there were tempting times when the handsome dog walkers on the neighborhood sidewalks offered much more than talk of breeding and training.

On Saturday morning, Tim and Nick took Buck to meet Tim's Aunt Ruth. She had been living in Tim's old apartment on Collingwood Street and working part-time at the restaurant, but she finally married her wealthy lover Sam Connor and moved to his estate in Hillsborough. This was the first time Tim and Nick had been down the peninsula since Ruth and Sam returned from their honeymoon. Tim barely turned off the engine when Buck jumped from Nick's lap and bounded out of the car. "Buck, get back here!" Nick scolded and said to Tim, "It was my own fault for not holding onto him tighter, but I hate to see him get in the habit of running off like that. You might have the top down sometime when you're stuck in traffic and he'd think it was okay to jump out of the car!"

"Hello, boys!" Sam came toward them from the direction of the tennis courts. He crouched as Buck ran toward him and Sam's face became the object of a generous coating of canine saliva. "What have we here?"

"Hi, Sam!" Tim shouted. "That's Buck."

"He's a friendly little guy, I'll say that for him."

Nick postponed his intended scolding when Ruth appeared and she got more kisses from Buck. "What an adorable little fellow you are! Yes, you are!" She scooped up the puppy and handed him back to Sam so that she could give hugs to the boys and take the bundle of paper from under Tim's arm, "Thanks for picking up my mail. I put in a change of address, but I guess they're not going to forward the weekly specials from the supermarket or these catalogues. Look, Sam, there's a big sale on children's clothes at Macy's. She and Sam smiled at some private joke between the two of them before she turned back to *the boys*. "I'm glad we're past the age of having to worry about having children," she went on, "and I'm delighted both of you could come down for lunch today. It won't be nearly as tasty as when Delia was here, but we'll make do."

"As I remember, you're a very good cook, Aunt Ruth," Tim said. "You were always trying out new recipes and pushing them on Uncle Dan and me when I lived with you in Edina. I think you were trying to fatten us up."

"It worked on Dan," she said, "but that was a long time ago. Sam has been after me to hire a new cook ever since we got back from our honeymoon, but I'm having fun doing the cooking myself. I've never lost my curiosity about trying new things." Ruth put one hand around Sam's neck and nuzzled his ear with her lips.

"I'm not complaining, dear." Sam smiled and hugged her. Tim tried not to look.

They walked through the formal front entrance of the Tudor-style house and through a cavernous hallway toward the kitchen. Tim accepted that they were newlyweds, but this was his Aunt Ruth, after all! She was an attractive middle-aged woman, but he didn't want to picture her *doing* it. Tim had to admit that he and Nick were visitors to Sam's estate, now Ruth's home too, but if he and Nick could be discreet about their sex lives, why couldn't straight people?

"I'm sure whatever you make will be great," Nick said. He didn't notice Tim's discomfort. "We're not fussy and I'm starved."

"Good," Sam said. "It's going to be simple. I was waiting for you to arrive before I put these burgers on the grill." He set a pitcher of iced tea on the poolside table as Tim and Nick sat down in padded wrought-iron chairs. "What time is it? I must have left my watch in the bedroom."

"Twelve-oh-five on the dot," Ruth called from the kitchen.

"Would you boys like something stronger than tea?" Sam asked, filling tall glasses with ice from the poolside bar. "How about a beer or a Bloody Mary… Nick?"

"Not for me, thanks. Iced tea is fine."

"I have to work tonight," Tim said.

Ruth carried out a large tray loaded with buns, condiments, chips and a bowl of potato salad. "How are things going at the restaurant without me?" she asked Tim.

"Okay, I guess," her nephew replied. "Everyone misses you, especially Artie and me… and the customers always ask if you're ever going to set foot in there again."

"We'll have to stop in one of these days, Sam," she said. "No, Buck, that's not for you. What should I fix for this little guy? Is it okay if he has a corn chip? They're organic."

"Maybe just some water," Nick said. "I'll get his bowl out of the car."

"How about tomorrow?" Ruth asked. "Sam, you're overdue for a visit with your grandkids and I could stop in

MARK ABRAMSON

246

and surprise Artie and Arturo. We're coming into the city tonight for dinner anyway."

Buck stood on his hind legs and waited for her to drop the chip in his mouth. Ruth turned to Tim and said, "Sam wants to show me off to some old friends of his and make sure they approve."

Sam put his arm around her waist and nuzzled her neck. "It's too late now if they don't. If we're spending the night in town, I should call the Fairmont and see if our favorite room is available."

"I have an even better idea, Sam. Let's spend the night in my old apartment on Collingwood and take the whole family to brunch tomorrow?"

"Whatever you say, darling…"

"I'll call Ben and Jane this afternoon and see if it's good for them," Ruth said. "Don't tell anyone, Tim. I want it to be a surprise."

"My lips are sealed," Tim promised and in spite of being leery of the honeymoon subject, he asked, "How was your trip? The card from Spain was postmarked three weeks ago, but it arrived yesterday. How is it being back in California and living as a respectable married woman?"

"It feels wonderful," she answered.

"It was great," Sam added. "It was so nice to be in Europe and not have to think about work for a change. To be honest with you, I was afraid my new bride would be bored when we got back. You can only have so many games of tennis and laps in the pool and horseback rides in the hills. I hope you boys brought your swimsuits."

"I'm never bored. You know me," Ruth assured him. "I feel a little guilty, though. How many women my age fall into a life with a man they adore and such a lovely home? One of these days, I'm going to take up a hobby or maybe find some volunteer work and give something back to the world."

"Do you have anything in mind?" Nick asked. He was squeezing ketchup onto his hamburger and relieved that

Buck was chasing squirrels up a tree beyond the gardener's shed instead of begging at the table.

"When I lived in the city and was tending bar at Arts, I used to walk by that little shop, *Under One Roof*, all the time." Ruth poked at her salad. "That's the place where the proceeds go to AIDS causes. I've often stopped in to buy gifts and thought about volunteering a few hours of my time, but never got around to it and I was right there across the street! Now I'm all the way down here and I just don't know... I should see if there's anything I'm qualified to do at the local humane society. I've always loved animals."

"That's a fine idea, dear," Sam said. "There's always something we can do to help the less fortunate, whether they're two-legged or four. All I seem to find time for is writing the occasional check at Christmas."

"Nick donates merchandise from the nursery and he helps out with *Face to Face*, the Sonoma County AIDS organization," Tim said. "I'm the one who should do more."

"There's no reason not to, is there?" Ruth asked. "Take some time to think about what you'd be good at, Tim. Then have a look around. Something will fall right into your lap and I'll bet you could set aside a few hours a week you won't even miss. That's what I intend to do."

"I'll have to think about it." Tim leaned over to pet the dog.

"You don't have to change the world, you know. You'd be surprised how much a smile or a kind word can do to make someone's day. Maybe one small action can put a whole chain of events into motion that will make a huge difference. You must remember that old woman in Minneapolis, don't you, Tim?"

"Huh?" Tim was thinking about whether he would have time for a nap before work tonight.

"She left a fortune in her will to the neighbor boy just because he was thoughtful enough to put her newspaper through the mail slot on rainy days instead of throwing it from his bicycle to the front door. I don't mean that you

should do good works for any monetary reason, of course."
Ruth laughed and reached over to stroke Sam's chin with
her fingertips before she went on, "Sam could have been as
poor as a church mouse and I still would have married him...
just as long as he had this handsome face and so many other
wonderful attributes."

"I said I'd think about it!" Tim was afraid his Aunt Ruth
was going to start talking about their sex life again, but she
poured some more iced tea and changed the subject.

Back in the city that night, Tim had dreams about sweating
over a steam table in a soup kitchen. He looked terrible in
a hair net and couldn't imagine that this dream had any
meaning except that he'd fallen asleep during a documentary
on the History Channel about the Great Depression. He was an
adequate cook, but only because he picked up a few pointers
when he lived with his Aunt Ruth and later from working
in a restaurant. He couldn't envision helping humanity with
his culinary talents. What *was* he good at? He rolled over and
nuzzled up to Nick's naked body. There had to be something
besides that, too. He fell back to sleep.

When he thought about his dream later, it seemed so real.
Nick had to head back to Sonoma County early because there
were a couple of stops to make on his way to the nursery, but
it was still before sunrise. Tim could let him sleep another half
hour. Tim and Buck would drive up in the Thunderbird after
the brunch shift at Arts.

*Tim slipped into a pair of running shorts, put coffee on to brew,
opened the sliding glass doors onto his deck and sat down on the
redwood bench. Buck scampered after him, made three counter-
clockwise circles and settled between Tim's bare feet. It was one
of those rare quiet moments in the city. The only sound was a fly
buzzing past Tim's ear and then the distant engine of a small plane.
Then a shower nozzle hissed in the house next door and a tenor voice
singing an aria emerged with the steam out the bathroom window.
Someone's trash clattered down a garbage chute, the J-Church
streetcar whooshed up the hill beside Dolores Park and a siren*

filled the air. For some reason it reminded Tim of bagpipes and he wondered if deaf people would be happy to know they were missing out on the annoyance of ambulances and fire trucks. All in all, Tim was glad to be alive. The coffee was done and it was time to wake Nick, so he went back inside.

Tim should have known he was dreaming when the clock jumped ahead to 4 p.m. He was dead tired after brunch, but he'd promised Nick he would drive up to Monte Rio tonight. Buck had seemed fine about being left alone for a few hours while Nick was at work, but the further they went in the car, the more agitated he became. By the time they approached the Golden Gate Bridge the dog had scrambled up from the floor onto the passenger's seat and started barking.

"What is it, boy?" Tim asked and tried to pet him. "Do you need to stop already? I thought you did your business before we left home." The puppy kept spinning around, jumping down under the dashboard and back up onto the seat and he kept on barking. Tim had never seen him like this.

"Settle down, Buck!" Tim was getting riled now. Traffic on the bridge was heavy. Only two northbound lanes were open with so many weekenders returning to the city. Tim was angry at himself for not putting the top up, rather than risk Buck jumping out again. Nick had warned him about that just the other day, but he couldn't stop now in the middle of the bridge. It was sure to be hot on the other side of the rainbow tunnel, anyway. "I'll pull over in a minute, boy. Hold on!"

Tim was in the slower right lane in bumper-to-bumper traffic. A beat-up camper jerked and sputtered and burned oil in Tim's face. There was no place to stop before the scenic overlook at the north end of the bridge. Before he could grab Buck, the puppy leapt out and started running. "Buck! Get back here! Stop, dammit! Where do you think you're going?"

Tim was furious! He had to wait for a parking space to open up. By the time he grabbed the leash and leapt from the car himself, Buck was out of sight. Tim ran back toward the bridge as fast as he could until he could finally see a speeding ball of brown fur barreling down the pedestrian walkway. He tried whistling, but the sound flew away on the wind. Buck seemed to be chasing someone he knew, *but he was only a puppy. Who else could he know? Nick was already miles from here. "Buck! What is the matter with you? Come back here!"*

Now Tim saw the stranger in a charcoal gray suit. The man kept running with Buck at his heels. They were halfway to the north tower when the man set something down on the walkway. Then he climbed onto the rail and jumped, as gracefully as an Olympic high diver. Tim yelled, "Buck! Come back here!"

A bridge employee arrived from the opposite direction at the same time as Tim. He stepped off his motorized cart and asked, "Did you know the jumper?"

"I didn't even see his face," Tim shook his head and clipped the leash to Buck's collar, "but this is my dog." Tim peered over the railing at a white sailboat gliding through blue water toward the St. Francis Yacht Club and a Norwegian tanker headed out to sea, but there was no sign of a human being. Then Tim realized that Buck was still standing guard over a briefcase the man had left behind. Gold lettering was embossed on the side: C. B. Harriman.

Tim came around because Nick was shaking him. "Tim. Wake up! Come on… wake up! You're having another bad dream. It's okay, Snowman. You're safe."

"Where's Buck?" Tim asked as he opened his eyes. They were in Tim's bed. The clock on the dresser said four fifteen. It was still the middle of the night. Nick didn't need to leave for Sonoma County anywhere near this early and Tim didn't have to get up to work the brunch shift at Arts for several hours. Foghorns howled in the distance and Buck was asleep between their bare feet.

Charles Bradford Harriman pulled his silver BMW into a private ramp off Fourth and Berry Streets. It was hard to believe he'd fallen into such a comfortable life after so many years of hard times. He tried not to dwell on the past. This career was all about the future…

To be continued…

About the Author

Born and raised a Minnesota farm-boy, Mark Abramson has lived in San Francisco so long that he feels like a native. He is thrilled that the *Beach Reading* series, his first foray into fiction, has been so successful and he is deeply grateful for all the supportive emails from fans of Tim and Nick, Aunt Ruth, Artie and the rest of the cast of characters. He would also like to make clear that his mother, aside from being a Christian, is nothing like Betty Snow. She is smart and kind with a great sense of humor and she doesn't even drink.

9 781590 211434